THE HERO REBELLION 3
REGAN

BELINDA CRAWFORD

HENDRIX & FAUST
PUBLISHERS

SECOND EDITION

Published by Hendrix & Faust, Publishers in 2026

Text copyright © Belinda Crawford 2018

ISBN: 978-0-6488745-7-7 (ebook)

ISBN: 978-0-6488745-8-4 (paperback)

This is a work of fiction. Names, characters, businesses, places, events, locales, and incidents are either the products of the author's imagination or used in a fictitious manner. Any resemblance to actual persons, living or dead, or actual events is purely coincidental.

PRINTED AND BOUND BY INGRAMSPARK.

Australia: Ingram Content Group AU Pty Ltd, Melbourne, Victoria. US: Lightning Source LLC, La Vergne, Tennessee / Allentown, Pennsylvania / Jackson, Tennessee, United States. UK: Lightning Source UK Ltd, Milton Keynes, United Kingdom. Europe: Lightning Source UK Ltd, with facilities in Germany, France, and Spain.

The authorized representative in the European Economic Area is Lightning Source France, 1 Av. Johannes Gutenberg, 78310 Maurepas, France. compliance@lightningsource.fr

For you,
dear reader.

IN THE BEGINNING

Humans colonised Jørn; they travelled across the galaxy intent on a better way of life, away from the influence of Earth. But the drones they sent ahead, the ones that told them that Jørn was their new paradise, missed something; a native spore toxic to all Terran life.

Genetic engineering, blending DNA from Earth and Jørn species, saved their crops and livestock, but the colonists refused to use the same technology on themselves. Instead, they took to the skies, turning their five great colony ships into cities that floated above the spore's reach.

But one colonist, Dr Augusta Woolsey, had a different vision of humanity's future, one where humans could walk Jørn's surface without the protection of suits or re-breathers. A vision of a humanity genetically altered to live in harmony with the planet they called home. She put into motion a plan that would take centuries to come to fruition and set two artificial intelligences to oversee it, Ayumon and the Librarian.

Hero destroyed Ayumon and thought Woolsey's plan done, but the Librarian would not be stopped. It used Hero to access the resources it required and betrayed her, leaving her stranded on Jørn's surface.

CHAPTER 1

The giant fleshy stalks of tree-grass pressed against Hero from all sides. Moisture beaded and ran down the spear-shaped leaves, catching between leaf and stalk before spilling over to run down her collar.

Long slender grubs left slimy, luminescent trails over the back of her gloves and across her shoulders. Other things hopped and slithered and croaked, but Hero didn't take her eyes from the canopy.

Insects swarmed over flowers the size of her chest, their fat, thumb-length bodies bisected by a violent green stripe. They filled the air with a buzz that settled in her ears heavier than the wet air on her skin.

Her palm sweated against the jwak's soft gel-filled grip. The short, fat stun-stick was a comforting weight in her hand, a reminder of nights spent bent over her workbench as she pieced the stick together, her room lit with holoscreens and the heady rush as the jwak boosted her telepathy. It was a reminder of other things too, of the voices in the back of her head, of rage and violence and escape.

Hero tightened her grip on the jwak. Its power sunk into her bones and shot up her forearm, chasing away memories that a year of living on Jørn's surface couldn't dim.

A new hum vibrated over her skin, deeper than the buzz of the insects – *scarpa*. The thought intruded: a soft, smooth green that had once belonged to a man named Guy, until he'd pulled her off her intended target and she'd popped his mind like a bubble.

The jwak thrummed again and the pimple-like sensors amongst her hair tingled as her visor snapped into place, seeking the drone she could hear but not see.

Lines and diagrams tracked in front of her eyes, zooming through the gaps in the canopy and the swarms of scarpa.

The hum grew louder and her visor tracked it, before locking on to an oval-shaped shimmer in the sky. Hero's heart sped up, but she didn't move. The drone flew into sight, sunlight gleaming off its casing.

She stopped breathing.

Guy's soft green voice told her the scarpa would confuse the drone's sensors. It tried to shove the knowledge of the swarm's heat signature and intense electrical field at her, but she pushed it back, focusing on the jwak's warm, smooth grip.

The tech flew onward, the hum fading as it passed overhead, leaving the buzz of the scarpa to fill her ears. But still Hero didn't move, save to tear her gaze from the sky and back to the marsh's gloom.

Where there was a drone, there might be a hunter. For a split second she was blind as her visor readjusted to the dark. Nothing moved but the thickets of tree-grass. Even her visor was still, its lines and diagrams quiet.

She waited for a minute, then two. The nerves faded from her bones, her breath coming easier the longer nothing moved.

Power lashed the air. The heat of a stun bolt grazed her lips before it splattered beside her face. Energy wrapped the stem behind her in crackling ribs of white.

Hero's visor tracked the source, pinpointing the spike in energy as the weapon powered another shot.

She ran. Mud sucked at her boots, roots snagged her feet and turned her first two strides into a stumble. She caught herself before she could face-plant in the mud, sinking the jwak into the muck. She yanked it out and kept running.

Hero ducked and wove through the marsh, the jwak's power pumping through her legs and expanding her lungs. The hunter crashed behind her, their steps hard but steady, like they knew the twists and turns of the marsh almost as well as she did.

A thicket loomed ahead, its leaves and stalks packed so close together that not even a scarpa could buzz between them.

Unless it knew where to look.

Hero zigzagged, diving out of the hunter's sight, searching for the half-bent stalk. She plunged into the tiny pocket of air behind it, the gap almost too tight even for her short, flat-chested frame, forcing her to twist and scrunch her shoulders.

She slipped behind the tree-grass and into darkness. The thicket pushed against her and squeezed her shoulders, trying to force her out; the thick scent of rotting leaves filled her nose.

Hero ignored everything but the hunter splashing closer. Her hand tightened on the jwak, its power fizzing under her skin and shivering up the inside of her forearm to fill her with a heady buzz that made the leaves greener, the shadows darker, and the *slosh-splash* of the hunter a crystalline bell.

He came into view. His envirosuit encased him from top to toe; not a single scrap of skin or twist of hair was exposed. His pistol pointed at the mud, the barrel glowing with another charge. He halted, poised like a 'pard on the stalk. Hero imagined him listening to the sounds of the marsh – the buzz of the scarpa, the sigh of the thickets – then his mouth moved. His words were muted by his helmet, but there was an AI reflected on the inside of his faceplate. A thrill ran through Hero's chest.

The hunter had an uplink to the planetary nets, which meant somewhere in the bracer wrapped around his wrist were the codes she needed to activate her own.

Hero didn't waste a second. The jwak's power swirled in her bones as she stretched her telepathy toward the man. There was a moment of resistance, a thin shield of lavender at odds with the man's blue-coloured thoughts, before she was gliding past images and half-formed words to seek the sweet spot between his sleeping and waking minds.

The hunter collapsed, asleep before he hit the mud. His pistol fell from nerveless fingers, a glowing weight sinking into the sludge.

Hero wriggled out of her hiding spot. Excitement made her stomach jump and haste made her clumsy. The jwak tangled in the thicket, the knot of old foliage almost yanking it from her hand before she remembered to slide it back into the sheath on her thigh.

The fine buzz drained from her bones, making the world dull – the green no longer as vibrant or the shadows as rich – and steelcrete seemed to slip into her boots, the added weight making her stumble. Hero shook it off and crouched beside the unconscious hunter.

He was sprawled in a narrow channel, his back propped against the base of a thicket of tree-grass, a tall bulky obstacle she had to pick her way around. Hero plunged a hand into the mud, searching for the pistol, fingers closing around hard plasform. She shook clumps of muck off the barrel, wiping it clean on the man's envirosuit, and placed it into the small pack she swung off her back before digging out a dataslide and a thin, battered tendril of biogel.

Hero peeled open a section of her bracer, pressing the slide into the input and one end of the tendril next to it. The other end went into a port on the hunter's bracer.

The program she'd grown went to work cloning the hunter's comp, a progress bar on the inside of her visor inching toward completion. Tension crawled up and down her spine with every molasses-like increase of the progress bar.

Nervous, she searched the dark marsh, stretching the visor's sensors and her telepathy as far as they would go. Did the hunter have a partner? How long before they came looking?

The marsh was quiet and the sky clear, with only the buzz of the scarpa reaching her ears. That didn't stop her knee from jiggling or the prickles running up and down her neck as the cloner crawled toward completion. It ticked over ninety-seven per cent and Hero's hand hovered over the tendril, ready to snatch it out of the hunter's bracer. Ninety-eight and her heart beat harder, the prickles pooling at her nape. Ninety-nine and she had the bag half slung over her shoulder. One hundred.

The loud *squish-shhhluck* of a boot pulling out of mud froze her hands. Hero's gaze snapped up, scanning the marsh with brain and visor.

The thickets swayed, the bugs glowed in the snatches between shifting leaves.

The *squish-shhhluck* came again. Hero wasted no more time searching for the source; she snatched the tendril from the man's bracer, slapped the telltale port closed, and ran, shoving the biogel back into her backpack as she went.

A bolt of light fizzed through the air, and then another. Hero threw herself down one branching channel after another, leaving the stun bolts to smack into the tree-grass. Their buzz had almost faded from her ears before she heard the new hunter's pursuit. They didn't crash through the marsh like the first, they didn't splash or misstep.

Hero reached back mentally. The familiar sharp black of the woman's thoughts made Hero stumble.

Her knee kissed the mud before she found her balance. The sound of the woman's pursuit grew closer. Hero lurched onward, clipping her shoulder against the tree-grass. She turned – just once, just for a second – eyes picking out the human-shaped shadow behind her, visor closing on the woman's face, illuminating dark eyes and darker skin.

Hero swallowed and pushed more power into her legs.

This particular Klaude hunter hadn't been part of the plan. Before she'd run away, Hero had only seen the woman she knew as Smit once, as a snatched glimpse from a fleeing shuttle, but since then Smit had dogged her steps like the woman could *smell* her. And now. .. now Smit should have been somewhere far, far away, chasing the ghost of a rumour she'd had spent a whole month planning and programming before slipping it into the Klaude's network during her last raid.

It should have worked. She scrambled to find the answer while panic bloomed. Leaves lashed her chest and slapped at her helmet. Blue coalesced on the edge of her awareness and teased her vision as Demona's remnant rose in her veins, filling her head with outcomes and strategies. Roses crept their way up her nose as Demona ate the panic rising in her gut and replaced it with something hard and hot and joyful.

She could do this. Her grip tightened on the jwak. She *would* do this.

Ahead, a few thin shards of sunlight pierced the marsh's gloom while the channels between thickets grew wider and the mud shallower until her boots pounded on stone.

Tree-grass gave way to boulders and Hero leaped over a waist-high rock.

A screen popped up on her visor, showing the marsh behind as Smit burst out of the gloom, moving fast for a woman whose hair was thick with grey.

Hero ran faster, the breath burning in her lungs, gaze locked on the haphazard tumble of 'pard-sized boulders ahead. She slipped, her feet going out from under her and her hands sliding out in front. Pain and cold, slimy mud and moss skinned her palms. She scrambled upright as Smit pelted closer, close enough for Hero to make out the creases around the hunter's eyes.

The boulders were just there, their misshapen, jagged edges softened by rain and the pervasive grey-green moss that covered everything. Not far now, not far.

Her visor screamed a warning. Smit's breath was hot on her neck, the woman's hand reaching for her shoulder.

Hero threw herself the last metre and into the shelter of the boulders.

A 'pard leaped from the shadows before Hero hit the rock. For a second, with the sun in her eyes, she thought it was Fink leaping over her, sweeping Smit up in his forelegs and tumbling her to the ground. Then the sun emerged and she could see it was Red looming over the hunter. A cinnamon-coloured mountain of teeth and claws, his six muscular legs were tense, his claws unsheathed, and his long hairless black tail jerked from side to side. His ruff was a blood-red halo, his ears flattened as his snarl filled the air. The rich sound matched the promise of violence in his eyes, but it couldn't cover the high-pitched whine of a pistol being charged.

Hero clutched the jwak and—

'Stop.' Smit's voice was soft, steady, and filled with plasteel. Hero froze. Demona crawled through her bones even as the jwak filled her with power.

Red's snarl reverberated between the boulders. Another, deeper growl answered him as a wall of mud-splattered fur and muscle appeared atop the boulder behind the 'pard.

Orth loomed over them, the sternard's blocky head and chest covered in thick scales, his cloud-white fur turned grey-brown with marsh mud. He crouched, gaze locked on Red's vulnerable nape, his inch-long teeth on display.

'It doesn't have to go this way, Regan,' Smit said, never taking her eyes from Red's snarling muzzle. 'A year's long enough for you to have been running, long enough for us to have found a way around the kill warrant on Fink. Put the stun stick down and I'll call off Orth.'

Hero got to her feet, her gaze darting between Orth and the pistol pointed at Red's chest. 'I don't believe you, and even if I did, I won't help the Klaude start a war.'

'That's not our plan.'

'But that's what you've been doing.'

'The rucnarts and the qwans—'

'—aren't the ones you should be worried about.' Hero stabbed at the woman's thoughts. For a second she held Smit, freezing her hand around the pistol, locking her muscles in place. Hero tried to slip deeper, to send the woman to sleep just like the other hunter, but no matter how she twisted, the faintest touch of lavender was in her way, a static shield like the one in the other hunter except stronger.

It smelled of Norah but had none of her restless energy and none of her presence, as if she'd placed it there days ago.

Orth slammed into Red, and Hero's hold on Smit snapped. The sternard's scaled chest knocked the ruc-pard out of the tiny clearing before the giant beast launched himself into the marsh after his prey.

Smit rolled, her pistol swinging toward Hero.

Roses bloomed in Hero's nose and exploded on her tongue. She embraced Demona, the remnant's memories filling her muscles as she ducked, twisted, and leaped. Her foot lashed out, and the pistol went flying. It clattered against the rock, and for three tense heartbeats Hero and Smit stared at each other.

Hero had been aiming for the woman's face, or her shoulder, anything to end this before it began, but the pistol had been a lucky shot and the part of her that was blue and roses – the part that had once been a woman named Demona – knew she wouldn't get another.

Hero tightened her grip on the jwak, her thumb finding the dimple in the biogel. It hissed and the cylinder, once the length of her forearm, suddenly matched her for height.

Smit didn't even alter her breathing. She just moved, hands snapping at Hero's face, and all Hero could do was get out of the way.

Demona streamed through Hero, taking control of her muscles to jerk the elongated jwak up and down and sideways. She slapped at the woman's hands and elbows, her feet and her knees, but Smit moved faster and faster until one strike was coming before the other was leaving, each piling atop the other in an endless rain of bone and skin. And all the while the woman pinned Hero with her midnight gaze, hard and implacable.

Air burned in Hero's throat and down into her lungs, struggling to get around the pounding in her chest. Each of Smit's blows shuddered through the staff, making her hands hurt, a feeling that spread up her arms to her shoulders. She pushed the woman back, aimed a kick at her belly—

Quicker than a linch-adder, Smit grabbed Hero's foot and twisted.

There was no hopping, no desperate bid to keep her balance, Hero just lurched sideways, her torso following the twist of her foot, and slammed into the rock. Pain radiated through her forearms and from her face where she hadn't quite caught herself in time to stop her nose meeting the ground.

'I can see Demona in your moves girl, but she was bigger than you. Taller. Stronger. Meaner.' Smit crouched beside Hero, the armoured knees of her envirosuit in line with her nose. 'What worked for her won't work for you, girl. You need to find your own way.'

'Like this?' Hero rolled, colliding with the woman's knees, throwing her backward. At the same time Hero swung the jwak around, its ends collapsing into themselves.

The woman caught the jwak, the shortened end thunking into her gloved hand before it could hit her faceplate. 'Next time, girl, don't warn your—'

Smit jerked, lips pulled back in a teeth-baring grimace and her eyes wide as the jwak pumped her nervous system with enough energy to make a 'pard numb for a week.

Hero shifted her fingers on the grip. The fizz and crackle of the stun field ceased, and the woman collapsed.

Ribs aching in time to the throbbing in her cheek, Hero got to her knees. She crawled to Smit's side. The hunter's bracer was dark, its power cells overloaded, but Hero sought the indentation inside the woman's wrist and when she brought the hunter's vitals up, they were green.

The weight on Hero's lungs lifted, and she dropped the woman's arm to riffle through her pockets. She stripped the scant rations and med supplies before hunting down the pistol she'd kicked from the woman's grip. It had landed on the other side of the clearing, wedged under a rock.

A shadow fell over her as she bent down to pick it up. Her fingers curled around the grip, seeking the trigger even as she reached out mentally.

Hero glared up at Red. 'I hate it when you creep up on me.'

Then listen better or bring the kitten. Derision and the sharp sting of resentment coloured the last word, accompanied by an image of Fink. Red's nose lifted to the air. His half-moon ears swivelled back and forth, not resting for a moment. *Were they done? He heard the buzzy things.* A memory of drones filled the words.

'Yes.' She slipped the pistol into her backpack and vaulted onto the 'pard's back. There were new scratches in the saddle – ragged tears too deep to have come from anything but claws – and there was blood in his ruff.

'What did you do with Orth?' She projected an image of the white sternard.

Red bounded up the rocky slope, leaving the clearing and the marsh behind. An image pressed against her thoughts; Orth stretched out in the mud, his eyes closed and his massive chest rising and falling with every slow, steady breath.

Hero cast a last look over her shoulder. Orth was out of sight, hidden somewhere beyond the boulders, but not the drones zooming toward them, skimming the top of the marsh. They were close, so close she didn't need her visor to see the shimmering blue light of a stun charge forming on their noses.

Red wound around the last boulder and together they disappeared into the tunnels carved into the mountainside beyond.

CHAPTER 2

The drones didn't follow them in the tunnels. Her visor picked up their hum as the drones sat in the mouth of the cave, echoing off the dark stone walls way past the point she couldn't see them.

Those first few months, when her brain had still hurt from the new power pounding through it, the Klaude had pursued her almost as hard as Tybalt, and their drones had followed her everywhere, including the tunnels. They'd whipped around corners and under vines with a dexterity that had put Fink to shame, and had almost caught them once, shooting Hero with a stun that sent fire through her veins and trapped her in the cocoon of her body, slumped over the saddle while Fink charged ahead.

The scarpa had hit a second later, the cold earthy sense of a qwan riding the swarm. Hero hadn't seen them hit, but she'd heard the sharp fizz and snap, and smelled the horrid stench of tiny bodies frying on the drone's shielding before its powerpaks overloaded and a boom shook the air.

Tybalt had had other methods, subtler than drones but more dangerous. He'd caught up to them mere weeks after she'd run away. There hadn't been any scarpa then, just a big open plain and nowhere to hide. She'd leaned low over Fink's neck and urged him faster, until a comm and Tybalt's familiar, serious face had her drawing him to a halt.

He'd invoked the magic words – *Mum* and *med bots* – and guilt had her boarding the old transport shuttle. The guilt had weighed her telepathy down enough that she didn't sense Julia Zass creeping up behind her with a stunner until it was too late.

When she woke Fink had still been out, bundled up in the back of the shuttle behind a sheet of plasteel, and the familiar sound of a hypostick had been fading from her ears. She'd laid Zass out cold before she even knew the doctor was there and a heartbeat before the familiar menthol taste of the meds could block her telepathy.

Taking Tybalt out had been harder. He'd used those magic words again, told her how her mum had asked for her even as the med bots were slowly putting her face back together. He had told her how worried they all were about her being alone on the surface, how hard everyone was working to bring her back safely, when Hero shot him in the chest.

The stun bolt dropped him like a rock. Zass might have pumped her full of meds, but she'd forgotten to take the jwak. Hero had left them there, the shuttle plonked in the same patch of plains where they'd found her, and stuck to the tunnels ever since.

It was safer in the tunnels, even if it was Red watching her back, not Fink. She tried not to let the thought hurt, shoving away the memory of Fink's preoccupation with the pack and the ever-growing distance between the two of them. Instead, Hero closed her eyes and folded over the front of the saddle, willing her limbs to become jelly as she sunk into the last thick fluff of Red's winter coat. Ignoring the hairs that snuck under her visor, Hero escaped the feeling that she was fraying, thread by thread, by losing herself in someone else's memories.

She cracked open one of the doors at the back of her psyche and Guy slipped out, a gentle green as soft as rain-filled clouds, so unlike Demona's hard blue. The remnant's memories played inside her eyelids. In them she was taller, broader and older. There was a dark line framing her vision where the respirator clamped over her nose and mouth. The air that filled her lungs carried the metallic taste of the oxygen filter strapped to her back, while the visuals from a trio of drones played across her visor. Only practice let her monitor the three drones as they catalogued plants and insects, while the rest of her scanned for threats and kept her feet straight on the uneven ground.

'How are we doing, Thy?' The words rumbled out of her chest, too deep and too solid for her own short, skinny frame, but just right for the barrel chest and thick jaw of the remnant's memory.

Demona's hard, sharp voice sounded in Hero's ear, even though the woman was five metres ahead, the lower half of her face covered in the same respirator that covered Hero's. 'This bloody place goes on forever.'

'That it does. I ain't seeing much here except a few new specimens for the exobiologists to go crazy over. Want to call it a day?'

'No. We still have the last present to leave behind.' The green-haired woman caressed a fist-sized cube attached to the sling across her chest.

Hero grunted, the sour taste of disgust creeping up the back of her throat. She was too old and not angry enough to appreciate the relish with which Demona planted the explosives. 'So, leave it already.' She was due for a few days' leave after this assignment, and she at least had a life outside of this crap.

'Engineering says the next junction will give us optimum coverage.' Demona gestured to a claw-shaped outcropping of translucent golden stone. *Tartz*, the geologists called it.

Engineering had a little too much to say in her opinion. The Klaude would have learned more if they'd studied the strange organic architecture instead of sending in a team like theirs to wipe it out. Not for the first time she wondered what it was they were so afraid of and whether those rumours about the wildlife were true.

Something large moved on one of the feeds on her visor. Reflex had her reaching for the stun pistol nestled in the holster under her arm. 'I don't think we'll make it that far. I have a rucnart incoming, closing on drone three.'

Not just closing, Hero thought as the massive, six-legged animal stalked out of what she'd thought was a shadow but was another damn branch in the endless system of tunnels. The animal pinned her with a violent orange gaze, seeming to look through the drone to scrape its gaze across her consciousness. Then the damn thing was rushing the drone. The tech's stun field went up a heartbeat later, but it didn't slow the giant beast. Its upper set of eyes popped open and then scarpa were swarming the drone and all Hero could see was the fizz and snap of the stun field.

'Shit. Thy,' she yelled, even as she rerouted the other two drones. 'Set that charge *now*, I've just lost drone three—'

Something darted across one of her other screens before blinking text replaced drone one's vision. *Critical damage. Unit offline.*

Drone two shorted a second later. Broken glimpses of fangs and a close-up of the pebbles that lined the tunnel floor filled its screen.

Hero's heart pounded hard, the muscles in her neck and across her back tightening with the clench of her jaw.

'Demona.' She didn't yell, not this time, just holstered her pistol and swung the rifle from her back, eyes glued to the shadows. 'Get your gun.'

A rumble jogged Hero out of the remnant's memory. It lingered for a heartbeat, the vision of vine-draped tunnels overlapping the pale stone and petrified roots beneath Red's paws.

She blinked, trying to dislodge the ghostly walls covered in leaves instead of the twisted, skeletal sticks that clung there now. The rumble that roused her turned to a snarl. Red's chest vibrated between her knees, his ruff prickling under her cheek.

Hero tore her gaze from the claw-shaped knub of tartz.

They stood at the edge of the tunnels where the rock spilled into a manicured forest. Trees stretched overhead. Slim trunks reached upward until they split into a nest of limbs, tangling with their neighbours to create a vaulted ceiling. The brilliant light of scarpa buzzed through the undergrowth, while the soft glow of smaller insects trailed though the canopy, outlining branches like the power veins in her bracer.

Red slinked out, the gentle clink of pebbles under his paws

turning to the crunch of fallen leaves. Tension played in the muscles along his spine and in the way his ears swivelled. It seeped into Hero's knees and through her bones, settling in the knot between her shoulders and creeping up the back of her neck as the close confines of the tunnels fell further and further behind. She was aware of Red stretching his senses, straining his ears and nose, alert for the slightest sound of a rucnart or a qwan.

Hero did the same, pushing her awareness outward like a tripwire, leaving a thin mental skin in their wake. Around them, the only movement came from the insects tending the canopy and the rustle of an ersia, the feathered rodent only half-seen in the thick line of silver-blue hedges lining the pathway.

The tension eased from Hero's shoulders and Red's ears.

The ersia's pair of tufted ears, feathered tips blending with the foliage, caught Hero's attention. She teased the ersia's awareness. The little creature popped its head above the leaves, its big black nose twitching in the middle of its flat, round face. Hero tickled its mind again, flitting along the edges with delicate little pokes and prods.

The creature flared its nostrils and opened its second set of eyes. The ersia chirped, both sets of eyes on Hero. It tip-toed around Hero's psyche, a warm pitter-patter as if it were slinking from stepping stone to stepping stone. It brushed against her here and pulled away there, leaving a bright burst of citrus and curiosity in its wake.

Hero tangled her awareness in the ersia's while Red padded along the path. She skimmed the scent of the leaf-loving grubs it hunted and the faint rustle and twitch of its pack mates scattered throughout the carefully tended forest. She kept going, finding the strange little fissure in the hard shell that protected the rodent's intellect. It was too perfect to be natural but without the raw edges of a wound, as if someone had stuck a pin in it before the rodent was conceived.

Hero hadn't realised she'd slipped through the fissure until she was on the other side, already cloaked in the delicate tingle she'd learned from the swatai. And there she was, in the control centre of the ersia's mind. She saw herself through the rodent's eyes – folded over Red's shoulders, arms and legs limp, her face half-buried in his ruff.

She wound deeper inside the critter, urging it forward, wanting to see if it was dirt that was making her cheeks look hollow and her eyes sunken, or if it was just the way her skin sucked at her bones.

The cold, iridescent tingle of a third intelligence crept up on Hero, nipping at her mental heels and wrapping itself around her. It was slow at first, gentle – like a breeze raising goose-flesh along her arms. It wasn't until the ersia stopped, halting hard enough to dislodge Hero's hold on it, that the other's knife-edged touch stabbed at her.

Fear ripped through her, a puke-yellow shaft of panic making her heart stop and her breath catch, before anger flushed it out. Demona rose, her essence twisting through Hero's, a boost of rage and power. Blue lightning pooled in mental hands. She shattered the cold, iridescent grip with a thought before sending another – dark chocolate crawling with blue – along the chilly pathway that led to the other. She wrapped her claws around it and yanked.

Hero barely heard the pop or the ersia's horrid little squeal when its mind burst; all she saw was the void inside her head and n'Tao, the rucnart, snarling at her from the other side of the mental battle-ground.

The huge Jøran stalked forward through the void, his sleek triangular snout lowered, long pointed ears held close to his skull. All four eyes were fastened on Hero, the top ones – the orange of a dying sun – boring into hers, trying to weaken her knees. She summoned the lightning back to her hands.

N'Tao paused, a sleek slice of darkness in the void. The fine green and black pattern of his coat appeared to twist and bend with each breath, while night stained the ground at his claws, spreading outward until the Jøran was lost in shadows. There was something in the shadow, a sense of danger and secrets, that crawled up Hero's spine and settled like a stone in her gut.

'What do you want?' she said.

The rucnart snarled, ears flat, anger and pain swirling around his paws. Even in the void, the Jørans didn't like it when she used her voice; they liked it even less when she let her emotions colour the air around her.

She took a breath, drew the bright red of anger and the yellow of fear back inside her, burying it under her shields. *What do you want?* she said again.

She had the puzzle? A snapshot of memory flashed between them. Despite the awkward angle and the distorted image – like a wraparound holo flattened onto a screen – Hero recognised the scarpa buzzing around huge white flowers, and herself crouched in the marsh, stealing the code from the hunter's bracer. It sent a jolt down her spine and fear swirled through the anger in her gut. The Jørans had been spying on her again.

You know I do, she said.

Then they were ready. A different memory fragment flashed between them: a cluster of rucnarts with qwans riding their shoulders, their number impossible to tell in the dark. It carried with it the restless stomps of paws and rustle of wings.

No, Hero said.

One moment n'Tao was on the other side of the mental void and the next he was in her face, crossing the distance between them with the physics-defying impossibility of the mental plane. His head was the length of her torso and each of his four eyes was the size of her fist. He wound himself around Hero, towering over her, and pinned her with a fierce orange eye. *Why?*

The question filled the air, turned it as orange as the Jøran's eyes, and squeezed her chest.

You set fire to the last one.

The memory of riding through the night, Fink an unhappy grey shadow in the moonlight while a qwan flew overhead and rucnarts glided through the tall grasses. It flowed into another of Hero prying open an access panel while a swarm of scarpa – directed by the cold earthiness of a qwan – buzzed overhead. A fuzz of ersia swept past as the airlock cycled open.

And? The word vibrated, long and slow, the hint of a growl making it ripple.

You weren't meant to do that.

Says who? You?

You—

I said nothing.

The cities needed those crops, Hero said.

Then they shouldn't have taken land that wasn't theirs.

How were they supposed to know?

They know. A brief flash of memory: humans swaddled in enviro-suits faced qwans and rucnarts. It was gone almost as soon as it appeared, but not before Hero recognised the thin-faced man standing at the front. Dorich, the man who led the Klaude. *We told them. They did not listen and now we shall teach them respect.*

Humans have guns. Hero flung her own image into the air, of blood and pain and sharp pulses of light ripping holes in stone.

So did the ones before. The void transformed into the empty hallways of an alien outpost, the strange curving walls covered in intricate carvings that threw twisting shadows. She'd been in one of the subterranean complexes only once, when the fear of being caught before she could cancel Fink's kill warrant had muted her wonder at the membrane-like doors and the mountain-sized generator that pulsed and squeezed with metallic muscles.

Anger and pain laced the rucnart's memory, the emotions blended to form a new emotion – a word – dipped in the distinct, multi-hued focus of a memory passed from generation to generation. It slithered down Hero's spine and lodged behind her heart, bringing with it the copper tang of blood and the taste of alien flesh on her tongue, echoing the blood and betrayal that stained her own memories of the outpost.

For a heartbeat they flickered in the void, Trainer Ella pointing a gun at Fink, Timon bleeding on the ground, Norah turning her back on them and over it all, the Librarian betraying Hero for its own ends.

The memories shattered as n'Tao pushed his face close to Hero's, so close she could feel the swish of the rucnart's eyelashes against her cheek. *She had three moonrises. If she was not there, they would come for her.*

A cold, earthy ball appeared in the air, its surface writhing with images, the surrounding space vibrating with hard pulses of determination. A thought packet, a dense ball of information. She didn't want to touch it; the skin along her back crawled at the thought and her fingers trembled, but even so, Hero plunged her hands in.

The emotions and images swarmed over her skin in a thick, sticky film that swallowed her arms, neck, and face. It crept into her eyes and over her ears and nose. She saw a canyon squashed between the fold of two mountains, its sides the bright raw grey of newly cut stone. White cubes of buildings were scattered across the canyon floor, and the great sprawling disc of Cumulus City darkened the sky.

The memories receded, their sticky residue clinging to her skin, leaving the rucnart's instructions to sink into her brain. When her vision cleared the rucnart was gone and Red, his thoughts a sweet orange-red, was brushing the edges of the white void.

Hero blinked, the sweep of her eyelids slow and heavy, and returned to the world.

Red's purr rumbled in her ear while a question hovered between their minds.

Hero pushed herself upright. 'It was nothing,' she lied. 'Just an ersia.'

CHAPTER 3

The brush of the unseen 'pard's mind was the only indication they were almost there.

The carefully manicured cathedral of trees and tended pathways had long since given way to wild forest. Densely packed trees surrounded them now. Among them, a trio of 'pards shadowed Red as he picked his way down the centre of a stream.

There was no thinning of trees to warn them of the precipice, just a growing roar.

Red pushed through an overhanging wall of leaves and stopped.

The sun assaulted Hero's eyes. She squinted, raising a hand to escape the glare.

Under Red's paws the stream rushed over a rocky ledge and down to the cool, clear river below. Other streams flowed over the same ledge, some in trickles, others in great jets that arched through the air and crashed in the water.

Above the river, the afternoon sky sat atop a carpet of forest, vivid greens mixed with darker hues, punctured in places by the mottled brown trunks and spreading branches of the forest behemoths. Here and there, bursts of purple-red and orange crawled over the canopy, while brilliant blue ribbons of water wound through the forest, seeking the darker blue of the ocean on the horizon.

A fine mist cooled her cheeks and clung to her visor, beading on the plasglas and running down to drip off her chin. Hero wiped the moisture away, the weariness in her bones forgotten.

Golden fur flashed in the corner of her vision, one of their escorts stepping up to the ledge beside them. A thought pulsed between Red and the golden 'pard, a brief flash of images and emotions.

She grabbed his ruff, legs gripping his sides, even as she spread her awareness, searching for a threat. 'What?' she said.

Red didn't answer, just backed away from the ledge, tension shivering under his skin.

Hero caught an image of the river, the water deep, the bottom sandy. Nowhere did she sense a threat, just the echo of the other 'pard mirroring his actions and a creeping sense of mischief. Still, it wasn't until Red stopped backing up, his gaze intent on where the stream met the horizon, that Hero understood.

Her breath stopped and her hands clenched in Red's ruff. 'Oh, no you—'

Red shot forward, the horizon getting bigger and bigger, the ledge closer and closer. They burst out of the forest and into thin air, the ground replaced by the deep blue of the river, far, far below.

For a second they hung in the air. The golden 'pard there with them, and on the edges of her perception was the unmistakable hum of the pack below.

The sharp splash filled her ears before the river sucked them under. Water rushed over her, filled her nose and tried to suck her helmet off. The sky glimmered overhead, getting further and further away as Red sank, taking her with him.

Panic exploded in Hero's chest, hot and jangly, swarming up her throat. She kicked away from Red, only half-conscious of his mental yowl when her boot met his muzzle, and swam for the sky. She pushed and clawed, the surface always just out of reach. Her lungs burned and that sick feeling was clogging her throat, filling her mouth—

Air. Hero burst out of the water and gasped, the sound long and ragged. The water exploded as first Red and then the golden 'pard erupted beside her, swamping her under another wave. She swallowed some of it, even as she tried to push herself back up. Red and Gold thrashed and tumbled around her, their joy filling her even as the panic rushed back.

Mawberries wrapped around her, the sweet fizz filling Hero from the inside out before black paws gripped her ribs. Grabbing onto Fink's ruff was a reflex, just like clamping her legs tight to his sides as he propelled them out of the water. Her heart didn't stop pounding until they were on the shore, the pale sand mixing with grey stones and emerald moss.

Hero loosened her hold and slipped off.

Fink nudged her shoulder, breath warm on her neck. Water turned his coat blood-red.

'I'm fine,' she said, resting her forehead against his side. She hadn't expected it, hadn't thought her lungs would burn like that or that the water would swallow her. Hero gulped and shivered, burrowing against Fink's side, which was warm despite his soaking coat.

Fink coughed and nuzzled her back. His touch was gentle, but Hero could feel the hard, sour note of rage behind it.

She pushed away. 'Don't get angry with me. It's not my fault. Red's the one who decided to leap off a cliff.'

He growled. *She shouldn't have left the den.*

'Why? Because you wouldn't come with me?'

The pack needed him to—

'*I'm* your pack.' Hero thumped her chest. 'Me.'

Yes, but the Matriarch—

'No.' She sought the centre of herself, peeling back the layers of her mind and thrust it at Fink. For a heartbeat, it was like it was supposed to be – seeing through Fink's eyes, feeling the water trickle down his forelegs to pool between his toes and sensing Fink doing the same. They fit inside each other's skulls, filling in the dips and hollows in a perfect, seamless whole. *Just you and me. Pack.*

Fink ripped himself away, the mental walls crashing down around him.

Pain exploded behind Hero's eyes, enough to make her gasp. Fink whined, and she saw the echo of her pain in the way his ears clamped tight and his whiskers quivered.

The thin, bitter edge of desperation rang in his words. *No*, he said. *Pack.* The warm musty scent of fur, a tangle of kittens, stalking an oversized ersia through the forest, the warm presence of other 'pards at his back. *Large. Warm. Many. There was room for her too.*

A splash and the purring cough of a laughing 'pard snapped Fink's gaze around as Red lumbered out of the river. The gold 'pard came out after him, water flying as she shook her coat, but it was Red who held Fink's attention.

The growl started in his chest, a quiet rumble that grew with the renewed swell of his anger.

Hero had time to feel him tense, to feel his confusion turn to anger.

Fink exploded.

Hero fell hard on her arse, the sand skinning her palms as Fink's roar filled her ears. She had to blink before the tangle of cinnamon and brown fur made sense.

Red and Fink rolled across the shore, all snarls, teeth and mawberry-scented rage. The golden 'pard remained in the river, the water lapping at her knees, eyes and ears fixed on the brawl.

Impatience curled the golden 'pard's lip and a quiet thread of disapproval emanated from her, speaking of too many fights like this. The battling 'pards rolled toward the water forcing Gold to leap out of the way, eliciting a snarl and a sharp snap of teeth from the female.

It should be done already. Gold's voice was warm and soft. *Darsun should have claimed his place moons ago.* Gold didn't put it to words, but the accusation rolled off her.

Hero glared at her. 'Fink,' she said. 'His name is Fink.'

The 'pard flicked her ears but said nothing.

A mental shadow brushed past Hero, drawing her gaze up and around to Orin. The massive black 'pard was perched atop the cliff, the waterfall rushing past his paws. *It was his name, if the cub wanted to be pack,* the 'pard said.

I'm his pack, Hero shot back.

Orin grunted, the sound echoing inside her, along with images of teeth, claws, and fur, the synchronised stalk of hunting 'pards. There was something else in the thought, a hint of older memories quickly squashed before he said, *She was not a 'pard.*

Panic welled in her chest, seeping from the million scratches left by months of growing distance between her and Fink. The threads being frayed just a little more, exposing the roiling ball at her core—

Hero cut the thought off, crossed her arms over her chest and pushed away the panic to concentrate on the sun warming her face, chasing the chill from her bones. The nanoskin she wore under her clothes took care of absorbing the water still soaking her breeches and shirt.

Red and Fink still rolled on the river bank, claws and teeth flashing and snarls filling the air. Gold flicked her tail in disgust while Orin lay on his rocky ledge, black eyes following the tumble of fury as they rolled back into the water.

Hero got up and left them to it.

CHAPTER 4

Morning came as slowly as the night had come fast, but Hero had to wait, for the thin glow of dawn didn't reach all the way down in her little cavern. It barely even grazed the top of her tent, just filtering past the thick vines that trailed through the giant crack in the roof of the cavern until morning passed to noon. But at least it meant that the tiny bugs that liked to crawl up the inside of her tent, drawn toward the light, had found another place to be.

Not for the first time, Hero wondered what it was about caves that 'pards found so attractive, especially the wet ones.

Hero rolled onto her side, dragging the sleeping bag tighter around her nose, letting her breath warm the air; the heat on her nanoskin cranked until it was like a layer of the sun. The tent was warm, the temperature sensors indicating so just an hour ago, same as they had for the past three months.

She should have been toasty, should have been pushing the sleeping bag off her legs before she boiled. Maybe if the cold had come from outside that would have been the case. Instead, she huddled inside her fabric cocoon, trying to keep her nose warm.

Her stomach churned with an empty grumble, as familiar as the nausea that crawled up her throat. Morning was the worst time – especially since she'd had to start rationing powerpaks and stealing them where she could, like the pistols she'd taken in the swamp. Limited power meant she had to wait for the sun to hit the tent and charge the batteries before she could drown out the chill in her bones by burying herself in code. No whiling away the long hours of the night fiddling with the tent's nanites or the sensors on her scalp.

Thoughts tickled at the edge of her awareness. She reached for them without thinking, slipping into a shared dream. 'Pards slinking through the forest, noses to the air, ears twitching as they stalked a pack of oversized ersia, the long-eared rodents three times as tall as their hedge-tending cousins.

Hero yanked herself out. She shivered, muscles locking up and teeth clenching. Just that little touch and her bones were back to being ice, her telepathy eating what little warmth the nanoskin and her shivers had provided.

It hadn't always been like this. Those first few months on the surface, her nose had dripped blood like a tap, and then the swatai had swallowed her for the first time and she'd had her first glimpse of the seething core. She could do things now – with her mind, with other minds – things that would have ripped her apart a year ago.

She was stronger, her telepathic reach further. Taking over another and controlling them like her own limbs was as easy as breathing. But she needed to feed the gaping core at her centre, and food wasn't cutting it. She needed raw power.

Hero wriggled until she could see the jwak resting in its cradle at the bottom of the sleep mat. Her palm tingled just looking at it. The powerpaks she'd stripped from the stolen pistols stuck out of its side, the light on their sides slowly draining to empty.

Light caught in the black grooves bracketing either end of the stun stick's gel-filled grip and winked off its stubby silver ends. It had taken her half a year to scrounge the parts for the telescoping ends and weeks to build them, weeks in which she'd been able to ignore the cold growing in her bones.

None of that was really what had her huddled up in the sleeping bag though. Her bracer weighed heavy on her arm, the stolen authorisation key burning a hole straight through to the memory of n'Tao's snarl.

There'd been something there, in the shadows that had pooled at n'Tao's paws, that raised the hair on the back of her neck. An image, a feeling, a memory?

She sat up, shucking the bag, snatched the jwak and clutched it to her chest. Warmth radiated from the sensors amid her hair and the stick glowed. A shudder gripped her hard, locking her fingers around the grip. Her knuckles turned white and the muscles in her neck ached from the force. For a second, she thought her jaw might crack and her teeth would turn to pulp, but then the jwak glowed.

Light peeked out from between her fingers, washing her chest in soft white. Her palms warmed first, the heat sinking through her skin to the tiny bones in her hand before it shot up her arm and exploded.

Hero gasped and closed her eyes. Warmth cascaded over her skin, its dancing ripples leaving faint lines of gold in their wake before sinking to her marrow.

Her fingers unclenched and she fell backward onto the sleeping bag, the jwak still pressed to her chest. The cold was still in her bones but the jwak was chasing it away, pumping power through her nervous system, filling her up like no high-density nutrient pack ever could.

Eventually the cold faded, leaving room for a hunger that had Hero rolling to her knees and peeling a hunk of fire-roasted ersia out of its vac-wrap despite the nausea still riding high in her throat. The edges of the meat were coated with a thick layer of char, and the middle was tough enough to make her jaw ache as she chewed. She let her memory wander back to n'Tao and the nameless thing around his feet.

It crawled up her spine like the nausea, but no matter how much crudely roasted ersia she forced down, the feeling wouldn't inch back toward her stomach.

Still in her hand, the jwak gave her a little thrill, a shot of power to chase away the cold in her bones. She cradled it against her chest, holding it in place with her knees while she pulled her boots on. Holster, helmet, and she was pushing out of the tent.

The first rays of the sun had lightened the cavern's gloom, but it didn't stop the damp and chill from settling on her skin.

The shallow depression where Fink used to sleep was cold, the nest of dried grass and shed fur damp from the morning dew. Her heart hitched a little at that but she no longer worried, no longer sent her awareness scurrying through the den in search of him. Instead she turned to the darkness at n'Tao's feet, to the secrets and anger she'd sensed in it, as she wandered out of the cavern.

The 'pard kittens butted into her thighs one after the other; three large furry heads – the tufts between their ears losing the downy fluff of kittenhood – rocking her from side to side with enough force to make Hero stumble into the tunnel wall.

The ever-present vines cushioned the impact, the purple-red creeper a dense mat between her shoulder and the rock. The sharp, spicy scent of crushed leaves filled the air, while ahead the three furballs turned back for another pass at Hero's hips, worming over and under each other, an intricate knot of black and tan fur.

She pushed away from the wall, planted her feet, and growled. The furballs growled back, their black-flecked muzzles wrinkled above incisors half the length of her pinkie – a stark white against their pale gold chins – and their half-moon ears pinned to fuzzy heads.

Hero stood her ground.

The furballs stalked forward, shoulder to shoulder. Everything, from their paws to their tails, moving in perfect unison.

From where she stood, Hero could sense the way their minds wound together, a wall of salt and popcorn with a hint of caramel. It stretched ahead of them, trying to crush her before they came within pouncing distance.

Hero widened her stance, the soles of her boots digging through the carcasses of old leaves to grip the stone beneath. Where the furballs' mental wall was a finely woven mesh, hers was a chocolate-coloured hover, dark and bitter. She sent it careening toward them.

The kittens didn't falter, not even as a bright yellow flare of panic flickered across their mental wall. Instead, they crouched a little lower and increased the volume of their growl, until the sound echoed in Hero's ears.

The jwak lay heavy against Hero's thigh. She imagined she could feel it tingling through the thick fabric of her breeches and the thinner line of the nanoskin beneath. Slowly, so the kittens could see, she reached for the stun stick, wriggling her gloved fingers over the grip.

The salt and caramel mesh wobbled, worry fraying the popcorn-flavoured strands. The lead kitten – Porta – who had golden eyes ringed in thick black markings, planted her forepaws and snarled, the sound thick and wet.

Hero grinned and lowered her hand.

Porta pounced.

Hero ducked and spun, the jwak in her hand, the end snapping blue-white with a stun charge, and—

Whomp. Another kitten was on her back, bearing her to the ground. Her hands slammed into the leaf litter, cool and damp under her palms. She didn't need to see Ath to know the kitten's jaws were open wide, angling for the back of her neck. The kitten was in her mind, unaware that she was twisting past his shields. A mental twist and then Hero was scooting out from under Ath's body as he flopped on the ground, a snore already rumbling in his chest.

A yowl filled Hero's ears. She spun around and there was Porta, all white fangs and pink gums, leaping for her throat. Hero threw herself to the ground, rolling as she shoved the jwak into the soft, pale fur of the kitten's belly.

Hero was still rolling when Porta landed atop her brother, the furball's paws still twitching with the stun. Hero came to her knees and—

Raa huffed, the miniature 'pard's breath filling Hero's nose with the scent of old fish, before her tongue left a line of slobber from Hero's chin to her cheekbone.

'Urgh, Raa.' Hero pushed the kitten's muzzle aside only to have it swing back and aim another fishy lick at her ear. Hero squirmed away, dropping the jwak in favour of protecting her face and neck from the kitten's rough tongue. 'No licking! You know I hate the licking.'

Raa pruckled, the 'pard's little chest bouncing with the rumbling cough that was part purr and part chuckle, and bowled Hero over. The next thing Hero knew, the kitten's forepaws were pinning her shoulders to the leaf-littered stone and the 'pard's nose – wet and warm – was under her chin, her tongue carving a long, rough line from jaw to ear.

'Raa!'

The furball pruckled again and continued her assault, the toasted corn flavour of her mind bright with victory.

A sharp cough and a cold black thought had Raa scrambling away, ears flat and foreshoulders hunched.

A shadow filled the cavern entrance, its broad chest covered in a rich layer of blue-black fur, while its pointed muzzle and yellow eyes swallowed what light pierced the gloom.

Orin swatted the kitten with a giant forepaw, sending the little 'pard tumbling into the same pile as her litter mates. His disapproval filled the space. Hero only caught the edge of the rebuke, but the black miasma threatened to crush her too, the emotion rich with the image of 'pards working together – running through trees and stalking through tall grasses – not leaving their pack mates to fall while they waited to claim the prize.

He wrinkled his muzzle. *No victory*, he said.

Raa whined, the sound crawling into Hero's ears.

Orin snarled.

The kitten shut up.

Hero picked herself up, brushing dead leaves from her pants.

She didn't see Orin's paw. It threw her against the wall and drove the air from her chest.

She gasped, sucking in oxygen as fast as her lungs could take it. There were stars in her eyes, little supernovas blotting out her vision, but she had no trouble hearing Orin huff or understanding the black-edged collection of images, scents, and sounds that flooded from him to her. They all added up to one thought. *Too slow*, he said.

Hero pushed off the wall. 'I beat two of your kids, didn't I?'

The big black 'pard huffed. *Just kittens.* The thought was carried on memories of the three balls of fluff rolling in the sun and playing with his tail.

A blue-grey 'pard, muzzle liberally salted with white, melted out of the gloom behind Orin. There was a molasses-like quality to Apani's movements, a halting slowness that spoke of age and joints that clicked and popped. Still Orin – bigger and without a thread of grey in his space-black coat – dipped his shoulders and moved out of her way.

The pack's matriarch hummed and brushed up against his side but didn't pause in her slow-moving stalk.

The water-kin came last night. Apani's mental voice was a smooth silver hum, calm and even, save for the unease rippling under the surface. It bubbled up in snatches of memory, of tiny monsters under the water. *She must go to them.* An image of Hero standing in a small cave, an ink-black shape gliding through the water lapping at her toes. A sense of urgency, a hint of recrimination that she hadn't done so already and unease sliding through her gut.

They'd brought her to the water-kin to heal, Apani said, the unease in her tone turning sharp with rebuke. *She was healed; now the rest endangered the pack.*

Hero scowled, the bracer once more weighing on her arm, her stomach roiling with the emotion in Apani's voice, threatening to bring up her barely digested breakfast. 'I'm going,' she said, nausea and a different sort of unease making her tone short.

Orin lifted his lip at Hero's grumpy tone, a snarl and a sharp nip rumbling on the edge of his regard, but Apani did nothing. She glided past, the only sign of her displeasure the sharp flick of her tail as the full, ancient weight of her attention landed on Hero.

Ruc-pards had an almost human-length lifespan – over one

hundred years – she had known this since she was a kid and had been given a suitcase-sized ball of tawny fluff with a big red bow around his neck for her birthday. But Apani felt older than that, the great sparkling dome of her mind heavy with secrets, glimpses of memory that teased Hero with the scent of soil in her nose and the weight of a rider on her back. The pack spread out around Apani, gently vibrating threads that formed a fine network of half-seen knowledge.

It wasn't like facing n'Tao in the void; there was no menace from Apani, no shadows pooling around her paws, and it wasn't fear that made Hero's knees tremble. It was awe.

'I'm going,' she said, softer this time.

Apani chuffed, her thick silken coat brushing against Hero's arm as the matriarch slinked out of the cavern.

CHAPTER 5

Leaves brushed Hero's face, blue-green velvety stars the size of her cupped hands, thick veins pulsing with a pale light. She pushed them aside and ducked under the overhang of rock that resembled smoky plasglas. Tartz, Guy's soft green memories reminded her: a resin left by scarpa and shaped into sharp, angular patterns by their tiny claws and teeth. There was a memory of the patterns too, but no name, only a sense of wonder as she ran fingers over similar shapes, her hands older and blunter, skin protected from the outside world by the thin black gloves of an envirosuit.

Hero shook the memory away, but the image lingered as she entered the cavern beyond.

It was small, barely the size of a hover but large enough for a 'pard to roll in the shadowed pond. The water filled all but a sliver of pebbled shore, its surface sparkling under the light of the vines that crawled up the walls, reaching for the jagged tear in the dirt and stone above. Fist-sized flowers, closed tight in teardrop shaped buds, waited for the moon. Scarpa – smaller than the thumb-sized giants of the swamp and with pale violet bands around their midsections – buzzed among the closed blooms, the sound filling the cavern with a gentle hum.

Pebbles cascaded down the short slope and into the water. Her uncle reclined on the surface, an apparition with perfectly parted blonde hair and a half smile. The crystal-clear water sparkled just like the mischief in his eyes, the same deep brown as Hero's.

He looked the same as the first time she'd seen him, standing atop the underground lake the 'pards had pushed her into in an effort to heal her overstretched mind. She'd become stronger since then, had embraced that part of her heritage that made Norah fear her, and had discovered new things that made her fear herself.

So, did you get it? Paris's words were a chorus of colours and scents that glimmered with the pale gold and sweet vanilla of her uncle's voice.

'Yes,' she said, sitting on a large, flat stone at the pond's edge. A spongy blanket of dark purple leaves softened the rock. She plucked some leaves and squeezed them between her finger and thumb, releasing the sweet, tangy fragrance that reminded her of Chef 's scrapple-cherry tarts.

Well? Paris spread his hands.

'Well what?'

Did the code work?

'I haven't connected yet.'

Paris sat upright, crossing his legs beneath him and resting his hands on his knees. The twinkle disappeared from his eyes and a frown marred his brow. *Why not?*

Hero's hands slapped her knees, and she stood. 'I just haven't, okay?'

Between one breath and the next, Paris was standing too, the toes of his thick-soled boots hovering a hairsbreadth above the water's edge. *You risked much, little fish. Too much, and against our caution, to squander your prize now.*

She glared at the apparition above the pond. Even if Paris's voice hadn't changed from pale gold to a deep shimmering blue-black, she'd have known d'Ojon was talking through him; the collection of minds that governed the tribe were the only ones who called her little fish. The elders' thoughts blended one into the other, until the individuals made a shifting whole.

'Go away, d'Ojon. I was talking to my uncle.'

A ripple broke the pond's surface and just as suddenly as he had stood, Paris was back sitting cross-legged on the water. *The elders have a point, Hero.* His voice rang pale gold.

'I don't want to hear it.'

But you shall, and better from us than the tree or air-kin.

Images of rucnarts and qwans accompanied the thought as a small triangular head broke the surface. Water beaded off dark red mottled down to run over a slim, angular snout. The swatai stood upright on long slim feet, webbed toes spread wide. It used its thick tail for balance and tucked both sets of flippered, wing-like arms behind its back. Even standing, the top of the elder's tattoo-covered crown barely reached Hero's knee.

Raised copper swirls marked its chest, the intricate loops following the lines of its ribs and winding around its arms. The patterns meant something. Paris had tried to explain it to her: how the loops and whorls told of a swatai's family and which tribe they belonged to, and how the lines and angular shapes curling up their necks and over the back of their skulls described their position within it. It might have made more sense if she'd ever seen more than a handful of the aquatic Jøran natives.

We cannot protect you if you will not listen. There was something funny in the way d'Ojon projected the word 'protect', as if the individuals that made up the collective didn't agree on what it meant. Their projection was a pair of discordant images; a parent guarding its young, and a farmer directing the minds of its silver-fish shoal, tweaking behaviours here and there, instilling new ones until the massive fish were as obedient as a cleaning bot.

A shiver ran down Hero's spine. There had been something cold in that last image, a sense of calculation that reminded her of the shadows at n'Tao's feet and knotted her stomach. 'I don't need you to protect me.'

Do you not? The elder waddled out of the water. It had been more than a year since the 'pards brought Hero to the swatai and she still didn't know the little male's name. To her, they were all d'Ojon, their minds so meshed that where there was one, so were the others. *It has *been a tide-cycle since you were one with the tribe. How do you feel?*

One with the tribe. Hero hugged her arms to her chest and stepped back from the water. The memory haunted her nights, the sensation of all those minds weighing on hers, of sliding between them and then under, feeling like she'd never ever breathe or think for herself again. More than that though, was the chilling relentless core of herself that the collective had exposed but couldn't see. She shivered.

'I'm fine,' she said.

We do not believe you.

'That's not my problem.'

But it will be. D'Ojon shifted his flippers, smacking them against each other in annoyance. *The tribe is home, why do you fear it? We only want what is best for you.*

What was best for her? Her mother had used that excuse too and if the cold, hard emotion d'Ojon had accused her of wasn't holding her guts prisoner, Hero would have sneered. Instead, she swallowed. Hard.

'Who says I fear it?' she said.

You do, little fish. It was only one elder standing in the water. She could have picked him up and served him to the 'pards, but as he regarded Hero with all four eyes, she became aware of the fragments of a dozen intelligences sharing his gaze.

The elder waddled closer, his thick, sleek tail leaving a furrow in the pond's pebbled bottom. D'Ojon unfurled one of his mid-arms – shorter and daintier than the uppers, the fin tapering into three slim digits that looked almost like fingers – and reached for Hero's knee.

She scrambled backward, pebbles crunching under her soles, and stumbled, landing hard on her arse.

Even Paris winced.

D'Ojon pinned Hero to the ground with his gaze, his upper eyes, red as fresh blood, glowing with the weight of collective minds. He waddled closer and tension filled Hero's limbs, made her muscles tremble and her stomach churn, but the collective wrapped mental tendrils around her brain, drowning her in their endless sparkling blue-black, the colours shifting with the attention of a dozen minds.

Your fear is a sour thing, little fish, a stain clouding your mind.

D'Ojon came level with Hero's foot, and then her knee. The blue-green glow of the leaves turned his red coat a deep, bloody purple.

Hero's gaze locked with the swatai's glowing red one and she forgot how to breathe.

The elder's fingers trailed over Hero's cheek, the delicate digits leaving shards of ice in their wake. But it wasn't the physical touch that had a scream rising in the back of her throat.

The collective power of the elders swamped her. It lasted just a moment, but that moment was eternal. She was no longer Hero. The deep sparkling blue consumed her, not like Demona had – boiling up, feeding on her anger and the promise of violence. The elders pulled her under and split her apart, scattering her across a continent, a thought here, another there, until she was looking out of a dozen pairs of eyes, listening with a dozen ears, feeling the rush of the tide against her tail, the slide of stone under her belly, and the warmth of a human cheek under her flipper.

She was Hero, and she was more. She was elder, one and yet many. She felt herself stretching, felt the others winding through her like she wound through them, the weight of their eyes behind her gaze. The fabric of her mind expanded, thinning more and more until the chocolate threads that were Hero were almost too thin to see, leaving the bright, swirling core of herself exposed.

The elders didn't sense it, or feel the heavy frightening thump that shook every strand of her scattered being. The further she stretched, the deeper it became, reaching forth with a relentless hunger, searching for what was missing, a piece of itself to fill the hole at its core. And when it didn't find it, wrapping a bright sticky tendril around an elder and—

Golden light slipped under the tendril and tugged, loosening its hold.

The elders let her go and Hero wrenched back into herself, her body scrambling backward, hands and feet sending pebbles flying.

Fear made her skin clammy and heightened the sick feeling in her stomach, pushing it up her throat until all she wanted to do was to throw up.

D'Ojon didn't move, save to close his upper eyes, leaving the bottom blue ones locked on Hero. When he spoke, it was without the weight of the other elders behind him, the blue-black of his touch lightening to the azure of deep ocean. *Fear, little fish, holds you back.*

He's right, Hero. Paris stood on the pond's edge, his pale gold words a balm against the panic pounding her chest. *You're part swatai, like I was.* A snapshot of the swirling core came with the thought.

Hero scooted further backward until the smooth rock of the cavern's entrance was beneath her palms. 'No,' she said. 'I'm not like you, I don't need them.'

Your egg-kin was stubborn too, little fish, but even he saw the sense of communion when the lack almost killed him.

'I am not my uncle.'

No, you are much more troublesome.

Paris laughed, the sound ringing in Hero's mind instead of her ears. *If you had known me when I was younger, d'Ojon, you may take that back.*

The swatai cocked its head. *But we do, tar-et.* The image of a sleek, golden fish accompanied the elder's use of Paris's tribe name, the animal sliding through brilliant blue water, the delicate web of its unfurled feeding fin glistening in the water-rippled sun. *However strange you may be, you are still just a remnant, alive only within the tribe, just as are the human minds that live in the little fish.*

Paris stopped smiling, the twinkle vanishing from his gaze.

So you keep reminding me.

D'Ojon slowly nodded before he turned to Hero. He opened his upper eyes and the rest of the elders were there, pressing on Hero's brain. *I will go, little fish, but not far. You will need us soon. In the meantime, open your prize. We wish to know what you regard more than our wisdom.*

With more grace than he had pursued Hero, d'Ojon waddled back to the pond and slipped under the water. The swatai's fins unfurled and with a single graceful flick of his tail, the elder's mottled red body was gone, sliding into the dark depths of the cavern and the network of underwater tunnels beyond.

'Why did you have to die?' The words were past Hero's lips before she had a chance to think.

Paris sighed and sat back on the water. *Because I'm like you, and because I found the swatai too late. Even among the other hybrids, we are special.*

The image of the restlessness at her core hovered between them, and the memory of the gentle golden tug that had prevented it from destroying an elder.

'I don't want to be special,' she said.

He smiled, but his eyes were sad and his lips twisted. *It's too late, you already are.*

CHAPTER 6

There were holes in the tent's outer shell, four jagged rents the length of Hero's forearm. The dome, an otherwise hard layer of nanofibres, rippled and flapped around the marks of yet another fight between Red and Fink.

Hero's visor scanned the holes. She frowned. After three days, the torn edges were still trying to knit themselves together. She would need to steal a repair kit from somewhere, more than one if she could get her hands on them. Plus a nanite booster for her clothes and another for her saddle's nanoleather.

She plopped down beside the tent, stirring up a small puff of dust, and rubbed the stain that hadn't quite faded from the fabric stretched across her knees.

The nanofibres were wearing out – too much mud, too many tears, scrapes, and rips were burning through the fabric's reserves before the nanites could replicate themselves. Soon, there would be holes in her pants just like there were in her tent.

She'd learned pretty quick in those first few months that her mum had been right. Living on the surface wasn't anything like the Zebra Fry vids she'd liked to watch. For one, they hadn't mentioned a thing about the tiny, hair-like bugs that lined the inside of her tent at night, finding their way through the double layer of nanofabric no matter what she did.

If it hadn't been for Guy's memories, twisting through her own like wisps of fog, she'd have stepped in a methi nest and had her leg chewed off by the thumb-length ants in her second week, or eaten the purple tubers that the 'pards scoffed like candy, or gone for a swim in the creek full of carnivorous fish, or a million and one other things that could have got her killed.

A big chilly drop of water shattered against her skull, the trail of cold weaving through her hair and past the sensors to wend around her ear. Another followed, and another before she looked up. Rain hit her in the face, the sudden downpour freezing her skin before rolling off her jacket and breeches.

If only the cold could freeze the relentless, hungry pulse in her core. It no longer shook the fibre of her being, but had settled behind her heart in a relentless, hungry hum. Hero rubbed her chest, trying to ease the sensation.

She'd known exactly what it was the first time the elders had swallowed her, recognised the sensation when the tendril began to squeeze. And just like this time, a sweet golden warmth had pulled her away before the swatai's psyche popped.

Hero shivered. Paris had saved her twice now. She wondered what the elders would do if she swallowed one of them up like they'd swallowed Paris. Would she even be able to do it? The hum at her core, cold beyond anything, said yes.

How had her uncle known when it seemed even the swatai were blind to the danger within her?

How? How? How?

The question plagued Hero, but so did a few others. How to control the hunger? How to cancel Fink's kill warrant? How to get the supplies she needed?

The last two, at least, she had an answer for.

Hero kept her face to the rain, watching the drops as they fell through the cracks in the rocky ceiling. They clung to the roots piercing the rock and ran down the spears of milky tartz hanging above. The rain was cold, but she enjoyed the feel of it washing the dust from her face, and trickling around the sensors stuck in her hair.

There would be a fine mist clinging to the inside of the tent that night and the enviro controls – already compromised by the damage to the outer shell – would strain to keep the moisture at bay, but she was used to that. Just like she was used to the grit that collected behind the crease of her ears, and the buzz of the tephi – crawling bugs, smaller than the tip of her finger – that swarmed her tent at night; a creeping film of phosphorescent dust that slipped through microscopic cracks to crawl up the tent walls and climb in her nose.

After sixteen months, one week and eighty-six hours, she was even used to the silence. Sort of.

It wasn't the lack of sound because, Old Terra, there was enough of that – purrs and growls, warbles and howls, crashes and snaps – to drown her thoughts and chase away sleep. It was words she missed, the hum of syllables that vibrated through the air instead of her psyche, flowing together in a logical, comprehensible music.

She missed Tybalt's slow deep voice, the babble of her class-mates, and even her mum yelling at her.

Hero's heart squeezed. The thought of her mum brought up the last memory she had of her, one that wasn't even hers. She'd thought that fact would have dulled the scream of sirens, blurred the emergency lights strobing the wreckage, making the shadows deeper and the flames brighter.

It didn't. The stolen memory was embedded inside her: the way the hover had crumpled, the smell of burning plasteel, the yells, the screams. But it was her mother's charred and blackened face that stayed with Hero, the way her ear had melted and the stench of burnt hair. Not even the fine, alien shimmer of the person she'd taken the memory from could lessen the sick feeling in her gut or the lump that clung to the back of her throat.

If she hadn't run away, her mum wouldn't have been out when Cumulus City's generators failed and her hover wouldn't have crashed.

She squeezed her eyes shut and dashed the rain from her face, pushing the guilt back into its box. Lights came on inside the tent as she pushed past the flap, a soft glow that spread outward from the dome's spine. Hero shed her jacket and boots in the tiny vestibule before stepping into the main, wedge-shaped compartment.

Saddlebags clustered around the sleep mat, nutritionally balanced contents long since eaten, the vac-wrap the food had come in refilled time and again with meat cooked over a fire. The white and brown lumps of tubers and berries poked out of another, stuffed in among ratty pants and the skeletons of pilfered tech.

A shiny white dome sat atop one saddlebag. Hero scooped it up and dropped it onto the sleep mat in a single, smooth motion. The sphere flicked on, a bright green-white glow rising from its surface, a familiar command prompt appearing above.

Connection initiated. Input authorisation code.

If this didn't work... Hero took a deep breath and stuck her bracer through the text. The dome pulsed and a column of light swallowed her forearm. The bracer came to life, power running in golden veins through the biogel, and then it was gone. The column of light, the dome, and her bracer all turned dark.

She held her breath for one heartbeat, then two, eyes glued to the shiny white dome.

It remained dark.

Disappointment burst through her chest. The breath she'd been holding rushed out and she let her arm fall to her side. She'd been so sure this time—

Light blazed in the tent, shooting up from the dome's surface before spreading outward in a thin fan of white.

Connection to planetary network stabilised. Ready for query.

Hero stared at the thunderhead grey words floating before her, success holding her vocal cords still, just for a second. A second she didn't have. Who knew how long it would be before the Klaude noticed the connection. Maybe they were already getting ready to cut her off or track her location, maybe all the time she had to find what she needed were these few moments. Even if the Klaude were deaf and dumb, there was always the Librarian, omnipresent and patient as only an AI could be.

She still didn't know why it had betrayed her all those months ago, why it had wanted access to the Farm's network so desperately that it had lured her to a secret facility built under a mountain.

A frown scrunched her brow. Even if that had been the question she needed answers to, they wouldn't come to her if she just stared at the screen. It was time to focus, to get what she needed and get out before the wrath of everyone came crashing down on her. Except when she spoke, it wasn't to hook into the forgotten little subnet hidden in the backup archives of Cumulus City's transport system.

'Patricia Regan.' Her voice shook, and she had to clear her throat. 'Medical status.' Her bracer tingled and there was a sharp pinch on the inside of her wrist as it took a DNA sample.

Identity confirmed. Releasing records.

Screens flooded the tent, words and numbers and recordings filling the space until it was like swimming in light and noise. On one screen there was a holo of her mum in a regen tank, half of her face covered in a delicate blue-green web. Another had her lying motionless on a bed, her skin no longer cracked and bleeding but shiny and clumped with scars, not just on her face but spilling over her neck and down her shoulder, not stopping until they reached her hand where two of her fingers had melted together.

Reports played in Hero's ears, phrases like 'regen unit failure' and 'nerve damage' weaving through the images until vomit boiled in her gut and threatened to score the back of her throat. She gagged, but before she could heave, the screens winked out and a face filled the space in front of her. Black hair and black eyes inhabited the screen as Tybalt stared out at her, his dark bushy brows pulled tight in a familiar look of concern.

'Hero.' Worry weighed Tybalt's voice like it did the corners of his mouth. 'I had Doctor Zass embed this recording for when you accessed your mother's records. Your mother's fine but...' His mouth twisted. 'There were complications... equipment failures.'

There was something in his hesitation that made her wish Tybalt was right there in front of her so she could read him. Something other than the rebuke she saw gathering between his brows.

'You need to come home, Hero,' he said. 'I know you think you're doing the right thing – the only thing you can to save Fink – but you're not. Come home and we can work something out. But breaking into outposts...' Tybalt's mouth flatlined while the crease between his brows turned black, their points dipping with anger. 'I've seen the security holos. I don't know how you're doing it, but using wildlife to help you break in is...' He paused, jaw tight. 'You contaminated an envirodome. Entire crops had to be destroyed—'

Delicate fingers tipped with soft pink nails clasped his shoulder, halting the flow of words. Doctor Julia Zass leaned into view, her round face serene and her long brown curls falling carelessly over her shoulder.

'He's worried about you Hero. We all are, but right now there are things bigger than you at stake and it would be helpful if you came home.' She paused before adding, 'Voluntarily, since the last time—'

Hero slammed her palm into the recording. *The last time.* Anger blazed through Hero's veins. Waking up to find herself trussed up inside the shuttle still rankled. It wasn't being shot that made her angry, but the betrayal and the fact that she should have seen it coming.

She'd waited for them to wake up, well out of sight but not out of hearing. Tybalt had yelled at her then too, his words different but his meaning and his disappointment just as clear and just as able to bring tears to her eyes.

She wiped them away, squashing the raw slice that Tybalt's words had opened in her chest. She had a mission, a purpose, and it didn't matter what Tybalt or anyone else thought. She didn't need them.

Patricia's shiny, scar-knotted face stared out at Hero. She shoved it away too. It was only a matter of time before the Klaude - or even worse, the Librarian - noticed her connection to the nets and she still had to retrieve what she'd risked capture and the d'Ojon's wrath for.

Hero cleared her throat. 'Access transport archive, taxi maintenance. Search for "glowy roach magnet".'

There was pause, a split second that stretched into ten and made Hero's heart leap and her palms dampen. Eleven seconds, twelve, thirteen.

She should have gone for the archives first, shouldn't have wasted time—

The file popped up and relief flooded her chest. She opened it, fingers shaking. Building plans, laying out the long lines and circles of an outpost, filled the tent. She grabbed one, spinning it in place before expanding it, sucking the other plans and diagrams into the one she held. When she was done, the outpost spun before her, a collection of boxes connected by a web of passages, all of it squashed between the walls of a canyon and the mountain that loomed above.

A flick of her wrist and the model found a new home in her bracer's memory, leaving two small screens to hover above her knees. Hero reached for one. Codes sprang to life, complex strings of numbers and letters, next to swirling strands of DNA, everything she needed to bypass the outpost's security.

The screen fuzzed and spat.

Remote authorisation being queried.

The message had her fingers flying, saving the codes to her bracer and reaching for the second screen. There wasn't much time now.

The second screen played before she touched it. Timon stared out at her, his shoulders hunched and his expression almost lost in darkness, like he'd crammed his tall, thin frame into a closet.

Hero frowned, peering at the fabric draped over his shoulder. It looked like a pant leg.

'Okay, so...' Timon cleared his throat but didn't raise his voice above a deep whisper. 'There's not much time here. I got those plans you wanted. I don't know what was in that virus you gave me, but I'm real glad you told me to use a public terminal. The thing shat itself like three seconds after I got the goods.

'I hope it wiped the security holos like you said it would, because there were cops all over the arcade like five minutes later. I reckon I saw your old minder, you know, the one with the hair.' Timon held his hands out from his head, his long dark fingers lost among the clothes, but Hero had no trouble picturing Imogen Lambert's tight, white-blonde curls or the agent's light-sucking black uniform.

'Hero.' Timon paused and his expression, half-hidden in the gloom of his closet, turned grave. 'I know you're not getting much news down there, none of the feeds or bulletins, but things are bad up here. One of those biodomes I got you the plans for... it was infested by wildlife and they had to burn all the crops. There were others too, and not just here but near the other cities. They're talking about food shortages, and with the problems with the outer 'burbs...'

He leaned forward. 'It's getting scary up here. Whatever you're doing, do it quick and come home.' The screen flickered and died.

CHAPTER 7

There wasn't any tiptoeing around 'pards, not when they denned in a cave where everything from the rustle of her jacket to the creak of her boots echoed. And not when Fink stood in the cavern mouth, the moonlight rimming his ears in silver.

There was a rumble in his chest, the sound low enough that Hero wasn't sure whether she heard it or if the vibration was in her bones.

No, he said, packing the thought with so many images and impressions that Hero stumbled.

The first and strongest was of herself as she was just then, standing with her feet planted and her hands wrapped around the straps of her backpack. The other images came in flashes, memories and emotions hitting her one after the other until it made her dizzy trying to figure them all out. There was the both of them running from drones, stalking the Klaude, breaking into outposts, stealing supplies, hiding under bushes and overhangs. Under it all, pounding behind her eyeballs, was anxiety, fear, and a bone-deep weariness that dragged at her soul.

Fink was tired of running and hiding.

She blinked. 'You don't even know where I'm going.'

She was going to another Klaude den. She was going to try again. 'Again' was an image of holograms spinning in the air, the blues, pinks, and greens highlighting the concentration lining Hero's brow and the quick, almost feverish jerks and flicks of her hands as she manipulated the code. *He didn't care about the end hunt.*

Hero gritted her teeth, shoving aside another bombardment of memories. 'The kill warrant. It's a kill warrant, and we can't go home until it's gone, or the Farm will send people to... to...' The word stuck in her mouth, or maybe it was the panic trying to crawl up her throat at the thought.

To end him, Fink said. There was just one image this time, a fuzzy multihued pack memory drenched in sadness. A packmate lay still and silent on the ground, eyes glazed and body cold.

A tear prickled the back of Hero's eye.

Fink stepped close and nuzzled her side, surrounding her in the warmth and the sweet, dusty scent of his coat. *It did not matter, they were already home.* Impressions of the pack flooded her: the flash and pounce of the kittens, the silky touch of fur against his cheek, purrs and snarls and grumbles echoing off cavern walls, the now-familiar buzz of pack mates sharing his awareness as they hunted. Fink was threading them all together with peace, contentment, belonging—

Hero ripped herself out of his embrace. 'The pack. Isn't. Home.'

Outrage threw Fink's muzzle high. *It is. Food, shelter, family—*

'Raw ersia, freezing caves, the fights...' Hero stalked sideways, moving around Fink toward the river beyond the cavern's mouth. 'I'm not a 'pard Fink, I don't belong here.'

He sat and the confusion that swamped him hit Hero in the chest, the sharp sting of surprise, the growing ache of sadness and the sour taste of conflict. His ears twitched with every new emotion, dancing like some kind of fit.

He belonged here. The thought was soft, a forlorn little whisper that tried to wriggle its way into Hero's heart.

She slapped it aside. 'No,' she said, standing at the cavern's entrance, the moon at her back. 'You belong with *me*.'

Her words reverberated against the stone, the last one echoing again and again, growing smaller until it faded to nothing. She waited for Fink to say something, to twitch his ear, to flick his tail or snarl, but all he did was sit there, a dark silver shadow in the moonlight. He looked like a kitten who'd been punched in the nose.

Hero spun away, fighting down the lump growing in her chest, but not before her eyes caught a flicker of movement dipping into the cavern. The unmistakable silver hum of Apani's presence caught her attention.

Hunching her shoulders, Hero strode into the night, boots crunching over the lagoon's pebbled shore with nothing but the moon to light her way.

CHAPTER 8

The sun had risen hours ago, trickling through the treetops and lighting the forest floor from pitch black to a deep gloom.

Hero clambered over a root the size of a small mountain, pausing at the top. Weariness sank into her bones and weighed down her eyelids. Somehow the ache in her legs was throbbing in time with her heart and she wanted to slide down the root until she could rest her back against its moss-covered skin and close her eyes the rest of the way.

She'd been walking for hours, stumbling over sticks the size of her forearm and crashing through hollows filled with leaves. Her knees and her toes ached, while her cheeks stung with the same pinpricks of ice that made her nose numb.

The map on the visor teased her, the yellow dot of her location a steady pulse on the route through untamed forest. She was barely halfway to the rendezvous with the rucnarts, just over a quarter if she was being honest.

If only Fink could see she was doing this for his own good and come with her, they'd be there by now. Hero swayed and her hands slipped.

A puff of moist, hot air bathed her face.

Hero opened heavy eyes.

Teeth and the fine, chiselled muzzle of a rucnart met her gaze.

Tiredness vanished and a sharp spurt of panic fuelled her mad scramble back over the tree root. A sqwark from her helmet and

Hero swung about, jwak in hand and a mental fist lashing out before she recognised the second rucnart creeping up behind her.

N'Tao snarled even as he staggered from the mental blow. The other rucnart behind her growled in response, its breath vibrating the hairs on the back of her neck.

Hero stumbled away from both. The jwak's power fizzed in her blood, making the surrounding forest greener, the shadows darker, and the angry orange glow of n'Tao's upper eyes hotter. Her feet tangled in the undergrowth and she fell.

She swallowed, her heart a wild thump in her chest. Lightning pooled in mental hands, but Hero held it back even as the rucnart stalked closer. *It was an accident,* she thought at him, the words steady despite her heart pounding in her veins.

I know. N'Tao stalked closer. *If I didn't, h'Ran would have eaten you.*

Above them, the other rucnart snapped her jaws. H'Ran was younger, with shades of yellow in her coat and a raw, swirling anger rolling off her in waves.

You are late, n'Tao said, drawing her attention back to him.

Hero got to her feet, the jwak still tight in her grip. *The moon's not up yet,* she said.

Above, h'Ran snorted, the derision evident in the wrinkle of her muzzle.

You are slow and the moon will rise and set before you reach us, n'Tao said.

'How would you know?' Hero said, forgetting herself long enough to speak instead of think the words.

H'Ran's snarl was deeper and bloodier than n'Tao's had been, her rage at the unintended insult saturating the air. The jwak was already spinning around, the end snapping with a stun charge while a similar bolt gathered in Hero's mental hands.

N'Tao interrupted them both. *We know how we always do, hybrid.* A scarpa buzzed overhead and somewhere close was the gentle touch of an ersia. *Get on, the moon comes swiftly.* An image of Hero clinging to h'Ran's back hit Hero between the eyes, while h'Ran's outraged yowl pierced her ears. There was no thunk or sound of violence, but in the second it took Hero's focus to return to the outside world, h'Ran was off the tree root, her belly touching the ground.

Anger, revulsion, fear. They quivered around h'Ran, saturating the air along with the deep bloodthirsty snarl rippling from her throat.

Hero backed up slowly. *No*, she mouthed, barely stopping the sound from passing her lips. She turned and faced n'Tao. *No*, she said again, firmer to cover the waver in her voice. *I can walk—*

N'Tao was in her face, giving Hero the opportunity to appreciate the fine point of his muzzle and the pearly white of his teeth.

On, he said.

Hero didn't argue. Gingerly, trying to touch h'Ran as little as possible, she climbed on to the rucnart's back. It wasn't easy; h'Ran was bigger than Fink, bigger even than Orin. With her belly on the ground, h'Ran's back was level with Hero's ribcage, and what should have been a smooth, graceful leap became an awkward belly-flop. The rucnart's snarl grew in volume with every new inch of human flesh to touch her hide.

H'Ran's revulsion rolled up Hero's arms, made her want to scamper back off and retch. She swallowed it down, tightened her mental shields until she imagined she might suffocate inside them, and gripped the rough hair at the base of h'Ran's neck.

Can we go now? The thought came out strangled and a little thin from the weight of Hero's shields, but clean of the fear that gripped her chest.

N'Tao didn't answer, just leaped atop the root and into the branches above. H'Ran followed a second later.

Hero wished she had a saddle and the familiar weight of a harness over her legs. H'Ran ran and leaped along the tree branches like they were wide and flat skybridges, instead of narrow and rounded, without the walls to stop them from plummeting to their deaths.

Thick, hand-sized leaves blocked her view of the drop but her helmet had no trouble calculating the metres.

H'Ran's back was broader than Fink's and the points of her shoulders more prominent, but it was the resentment and anger coursing under the rucnart's skin that made it difficult to hold on. Everywhere Hero touched, the emotions seeped through, boiling up her arms, prickling along her thighs, until the urge to throw up had taken up permanent residence in the back of Hero's throat.

Resentment wasn't the only thing to escape h'Ran. On the long ride through the treetops, in between gravity-defying leaps and mad climbs up and down trunks, when Hero felt herself sliding down h'Ran's back or over her shoulders, the memories slipped through.

Disjointed and rambling without the coherence of speech, they rose and fell with h'Ran's emotions. A boom that shook the trees. Dust and pulverised rock choking the air. Humans in envirosuits controlling drones big and small as they turned a rocky little canyon into something bigger and wider.

The memories flooded her, zapping past almost before she could process them, and then they slowed. Day became night, the boom of the drones falling silent, and the chill of a winter moon left the air clear of dust. H'Ran stood on the edge of the denuded canyon, a qwan riding her rump while the rest of the hunting party spread out in a semi-circle around n'Tao. The humans stood before them, the light from their drones shining off their faceplates. Their growls and spits grated on h'Ran's ears, the discordant sounds like claws in her skin, making her ruff stand on end.

And there, next to a short male – Dorich, Hero recognised his thin-face – was the human not-kin. Her face was open to the sky, long black fur tumbling around her shoulders, another disgusting human-breed poking its snout out from under the not-kin's fur.

'Norah.' Her former best friend's name slipped past Hero's lips, while regret and loss punched her in the chest.

Under her, h'Ran froze, fury and discomfort rippling through her hide.

Hero clamped her lips shut and did her best not to move.

Eventually, h'Ran resumed her stalk through the treetops.

The memories and emotions under h'Ran's skin didn't stop, but they changed, other sights and sounds intruding. Hero latched onto the brief glimpse of Norah, capturing the moment and drawing it behind her shields. Ignoring the swirls of emotion, Hero focused not on Norah, whose lips didn't move, but on the man standing next to her.

Even though she'd only met him twice, Hero recognised Dorich's sad eyes behind the faceplate and the slow deliberate march of his words through h'Ran's revulsion.

'We will be expanding our territory.'

Concentration lined Norah's brow. 'N'Tao says no and...' The lines on her forehead grew deeper, eyes squinting as if in pain. She gasped and fell to her knees.

Harish screeched, bursting out of Norah's hair to dive at n'Tao's face.

A half-dozen rifles snapped up to envirosuited shoulders.

Anger and bloodlust clouded the memory, obscuring it like a bad line of code. Eventually, the harsh chilli flavour of h'Ran's thoughts settled.

Norah wasn't kneeling anymore. Dorich, barely a hand taller, was supporting her against his side while Smit had stepped in front, her implacable midnight gaze fixed on n'Tao. Norah herself was pale under the usual gold of her skin, making the bright red of her nosebleed stand out all the more.

Fury and the mad desire to sink her fangs into human flesh was still riding h'Ran's veins, making it difficult to pick out Dorich's words as he bent over Norah. 'What did you see?'

Norah gasped, her gaze fixed on n'Tao before flicking over the tree-kin spread out behind him. H'Ran growled and bared her fangs, making sure to flex her claws when the not-kin's eyes landed on her.

'War,' the little not-kin said.

'How? They don't have the resources, or the weapons.'

H'Ran opened her upper eyes and the not-kin jerked her gaze away, but not before the rucnart saw the knowledge Norah had gleaned from her, and Hero recognised the same shadows that had clustered at n'Tao's feet.

'They have Hero.'

The memory ended.

CHAPTER 9

Hero crouched on a branch in the forest above the outpost and scanned the thin, flat-bottomed valley. She was high in the branches of a forest behemoth, half-in and half-out of the endless mental void.

The leaves partially obscured her vision, but even half a kilometre back from the edge of the clearing, her visor could see enough.

The outpost had changed in the year since she'd last seen it. Hero remembered Fink slipping and sliding through a narrow canyon choked with scrub, his exhaustion making him clumsy. Phara had clattered along behind, the long flight through the forest leaving the toa-mare just as weary. Timon had been slumped over her back, half-asleep while Orin led them and Red brought up the rear.

The sharp little outcropping, with the crooked spindly stump of an ancient tree perched on top – a natural marker above the human-made airlock and the alien compound behind – was gone. Instead, a shiny white tunnel ran into the mountain, a conduit between the new structures and the vast alienness of the underground complex, made by hands neither human nor Jøran.

Hero tried to push aside the memories of cold, echoing halls with walls covered in intricate carvings, a mountain-sized generator at the centre of it all.

She concentrated instead on the loose cluster of white boxes scattered between the mountains, seeing them through the pearlescent film of the void. Some of the boxes sat atop each other, others next to each other, making rectangles and cubes connected by half-buried tubes. The flat disc of the city floated above, and where the sun made it through the thin gap between the city and the mountain peaks, the sunset stained the outpost buildings in orange and pink, casting long shadows that grew longer as the sun fell. When dusk had fallen and the city's twinkling lights were obscured by cloud, the outpost lit up from within.

Standing still as a holo-statue within the void, she took it all in: the featureless white boxes easy to pick out by the rectangles of light pouring from their windows, the steady sweep of security bots and the electromagnetic shimmer of an invisible fence. She painstakingly translated the data, separating knowledge from emotion before feeding it into the colourless sphere of data between her mental hands.

Sweat trickled between her eyes and clung to the tip of her nose as the effort to maintain awareness of her physical self while she filtered information took its toll.

Constructing a thought packet wasn't like doing mental battle, or winding her way through another's mind. There was no need for the power coiled at her feet, or the bands of chocolate gathered around her hands. It would have been easier if there had, if she could have just blasted the packet into existence.

It was the need for control that had her hands trembling. The delicate threads of mental energy wanted to buck and rage in her grip, the force of the power at her feet surging up her legs.

It was only willpower that held it back, a level of concentration that let her sift through experiences past and present to assemble the knowledge that the Jørans would need to navigate the compound with its human technology.

Even after a year of training, with d'Ojon rapping her mental knuckles for every mistake, she still hadn't mastered the skill. She couldn't construct spheres so clear and precise that they dissolved at her touch, leaving nothing behind but knowledge. Hers always carried a smear of chocolate, small hints of emotion that made the rucnarts snarl and the qwans snap their beaks as whatever she'd been feeling seeped into their minds. She certainly couldn't construct a packet while she was fighting, or running, or doing anything other than standing like a holostatue, something they'd all learned the first time n'Tao had recruited her.

They'd raided a small outpost then, an abandoned building almost reclaimed by the forest. She'd clutched Fink's ruff tight enough for her hands to cramp, and sweat had dampened her brow despite the chill night as she wrangled her knowledge into a mental sphere. It had been hasty and rich with the nerves working up and down her spine.

She'd passed the packet to a qwan, somewhere in the branches above them. The bird's chilling screech had just about stripped the skin from her ears, as it crashed to the ground in an uncoordinated mess of wings, talons, and thoughts.

There'd been snarls and fangs and n'Tao was in Fink's face. They learned that human emotions, even half-human ones, could be dangerous.

Another screech, this one of a brightly plumed linch-adder, snapped her back to the present. Her concentration wavered and colourful memories slipped from her grasp to stain the sphere.

'Harish,' she whispered. Where Harish was, Norah wouldn't be far away.

As soon as the name passed her lips, Hero froze within the void. She gritted her teeth and reached into the mental sphere. Gently, she pulled out the image of Harish and the bright explosion of emotion and memory that had slipped in with it. As always, something remained behind.

She wished she didn't need the Jørans so much: their strength, their numbers, the way they had turned half the planet's wildlife into tools that made her bracer seem crude. But without them, the Klaude would have snapped her up in the first few months, and she never would have got this close to cancelling Fink's kill warrant. Now though, she needed to pull all traces of Norah from the sphere.

If the rucnarts knew her one-time friend was in the outpost, they might convince the qwans not to go ahead with the—

A sudden puff of hot breath on the back of her neck made Hero jump. The colourful smear of memory and emotion tied to Norah almost escaped her grip, but she managed to pull it out of the sphere before turning to face h'Ran.

The rucnart glared with all four eyes, her lips pulled back from her teeth and her muzzle wrinkled with menace.

What? Hero said.

H'Ran snorted, pressing her muzzle closer to Hero, as if she could sniff out a lie. The rucnart pushed at Hero, an implacable wall of distrust.

Hero strengthened her shields, shoved the memory of Harish away and inched her hand towards the jwak.

A sweet, piercing trill and a hard buffet of air interrupted the stare-off.

The qwan's four great wings moved in a steady rhythm, the upper pair beating downward while the bottom ones stroked upward. The waterfall of intricately curled and interlaced metalwork around its neck twinkled with every powerful beat.

The moon is rising. The qwan's voice was cold and clear. *We wait for you.*

I'm done. I have the scans, Hero said, her hand still hovering near the jwak even as relief flooded her system.

The qwan nodded, more mental than physical, and it stretched its awareness toward Hero.

Hero extended the painstakingly constructed sphere. The qwan hesitated a moment, wariness in its touch as it tasted the packet. A faint shudder worked its way through the Jøran's mental fingers, and Hero knew she hadn't completely erased all the emotion from the sphere. Before she could fix it, the qwan snatched it from her hands and was gone.

H'Ran disappeared with the qwan, leaping from branch to branch and vanishing into the darkness below.

A breath that Hero hadn't known she'd been holding escaped her lungs, and for a second relief made her knees weak and her heart light. She'd done it, constructed the sphere and hidden Norah's presence. Now all she had to do was infiltrate a base crawling with the very people who wanted to catch her, then hack the Farm's network and take down that kill warrant. But first, she had to get down from the tree.

Heights hadn't bothered her before she came to the surface, but then she'd descended through the branches of a forest behemoth with a dead hover belt. It hadn't been a long fall, but it had been long enough. The pain and sickening snap when her ankle broke still echoed in her memory.

She hadn't used the belt since.

She swallowed the tiny bubble of unease in her throat and checked the harness strapped around her hips. With an eye on the belt's power reserves, Hero stepped off the branch. She fell, not in a deadly plummet but a controlled glide, swift enough to rustle the ends of her jacket.

The belt's power light flashed an angry red, a heartbeat before her feet touched the ground.

Her visor switched to infrared in the gloom, and she could see the forest sloping downward away from her, dotted with rounded lumps of moss-covered tree roots and the longer shapes of fallen branches. Shadows moved among the green: the quivering of ersia among the undergrowth, and rock squirrels scurrying along branches looking just like the Old Terra rodents except for their armour-plated backs and curling horns. There was no name for them among Guy's memories, but Hero had seen the Jørans use them like miniature battering rams more than once.

A cluster of ersia gathered around Hero's feet, their noses and ears twitching. Some stood on their hind legs, their broad, flat feet bigger than their heads, dextrous forepaws fiddling with the fist-sized lumps attached to their packmates' backs. The surface of the packages seemed to writhe in the forest's soft gloom – the movement was mesmerising. She put a hand out to steady herself and blinked as her visor zoomed in on the bundles. Only then did she pick out the fluttering wings and striped bellies of hundreds of tiny scarpa wrapped around...

Hero blinked again, trying to identify the sphere, but the scarpa's electromagnetic field jammed her visor's sensors. The cold, glassy touch that permeated the ersias' minds brushed hers.

Hero whipped her gaze upward.

A qwan, its brilliant green feathers smooth and glossy, peered back at her with both sets of eyes. The weight of its telepathy pressed on Hero, a solid crystalline wall of nothingness – not a slither of anger, curiosity or disgust, just a cold, clear presence studying her.

Hero swallowed and broke away from the bird's gaze. The qwans scared her almost as much as the elders, sending chills down her spine and making her stomach cramp.

H'Ran may have snarled and snapped, but the qwans were silent, watching and studying her whenever she turned around. Their touch was everywhere, in the rock squirrels scampering over branches, the scarpa attached to the ersias' backs. Sometimes Hero felt them probing her mental shields with sharp little thrusts that were gone almost before she was aware of them.

Hero noticed one now, but when she turned to meet it, she found not a shadow of the qwan's presence but the Jøran itself. It caught and held her, its mental talons sinking past her shields only to meet the blue and green of Demona and Guy rising from the back of her consciousness to form a second, very human skin under her shields.

The qwan recoiled. The speed of its withdrawal made Hero's eyes cross and weakened her knees. Even as she staggered, she sensed the qwan's frustration and the whisper of an idea, something that teased the edges of her consciousness and had trepidation coiling in her gut.

A dark shape slinked through the branches above, and the qwan turned its attention upward to clack its beak. A rumble answered it and then the qwan was pinning her with that four-eyed gaze again, not to probe her awareness but to whisper in her ear.

Now, it said.

The ersia took off, bounding down the mountain unhindered by the undergrowth that reached her waist. Hero jogged behind them, careful not to stumble in the ferns, sliding over rocks and fallen branches as gracelessly as she'd climbed onto h'Ran's back.

The boundary between forest and canyon came quickly, a sharp barren line of felled trees and torn earth falling away in a jagged little cliff she hadn't been able to see from her perch in the tree. Only the squawk of the ersia stopped her from diving over the edge.

From above came the sharp downbeat of giant wings and the rustle of feathers as the qwan settled in a tree. Hero sensed rucnarts and other qwans scattered along the same ridge, ersia and rock squirrels clustered at their feet like the long-eared shapes gathered at hers. All of them stared out at the hundred and twenty-six metres of barren rock and stumps that separated them from the first of the compound's buildings.

Just fifty metres in front of them was a fence, an invisible electro-magnetic field of energy that would blare and flash the moment anything bigger than her fist touched it. On her visor, the fence pulsed with steady streams of light. A cloud of scarpa streamed out of the forest, heading for one of the battery towers – thin, antenna-like fingers of biogel and steelcrete that anchored the fence every fifty metres.

The qwan's mind touched hers, readiness and action imbued in it. Hero didn't need more urging; she slipped down the embankment as the ersia streaked ahead, little more than shadows under the cover of regrowing scrub. Rucnarts charged forward with them, larger blobs of darkness in the periphery of her vision.

They halted mere centimetres from the fence and crouched to wait in the darkness.

The section of fence in front of them went first, a brief stutter that Hero doubted did more than prompt the outpost AI to file a repair notice. But those few seconds were all it took for her to slip through.

A handful of ersia streamed in with her before the fence went back up. The rest would come later, after she'd done her part.

Hero wrinkled her nose at the stench of fried scarpa coming from the nearby tower, but kept her eyes on the squat white building ahead. Just seventy-six metres over ground with only the raw stumps of the old forest and the thick tufts of new scrub for cover.

Eyes sharp on her visor, Hero followed the ersia, trusting as much to their feathered ears as the course she'd calculated from observing the security bots.

A chirp had her hitting the ground, sticks and stones digging into her belly while coarse grass tickled her nose. Yellow flashed in the corner of her vision as her visor picked up the hum of a security bot.

She held her breath, not daring to move. The visor tracked the bot, its yellow pulse getting faster and brighter as the drone came closer. The view in front of her changed, revealing a top-down perspective of the area, the ersia represented by green triangles and the bot's yellow pulse travelling on a dotted line that intersected Hero's hiding place.

Heart beating a little louder, Hero stretched her telepathy to the ersia scattered around her. It wasn't the smooth fuzzy warmth of the flat-nosed rodents that met her touch, but the cool, earthy presence of the qwan riding their minds.

They're going to see me. Hero packed an image of the security bot into the thought.

A cool pulse of acknowledgment fed back along Hero's touch, and before another thought had the chance to form, an ersia leaped up and bounded into the darkness. On her visor, the bot's yellow pulse paused before making a sharp turn to follow the fleeing rodent.

It had barely passed beyond the visor's range before another chirp rang through the air and the rest of the ersia took off, Hero following in their wake. Her belly hit the ground once more before they reached the building with its airlock – a flat-bottomed circle – set into the wall.

She pressed her hand to the smooth steelcrete, icy against her palm, and the codes that Timon had provided had the airlock cycling open. Hero slipped inside, dodging the ersia scooting between her feet with the sort of ease that only came with too many raids just like this one.

The door rolled shut and the rasp of her breath was swallowed by the hiss of air being sucked out. It was quick; her lungs barely had time to burn before the inner door opened and new air rushed back in.

CHAPTER 10

Orth stood in the doorway. Hero jerked backward, her hand going for the jwak and her mind targeting the sternard – only to halt at the unmistakable touch of the qwan holding the companion captive.

The shaggy white mountain of sternard filled the corridor, his armoured chest blotting out the view, but it was the qwan that looked out of his eyes.

Remember, hybrid, you only have until we are done, the qwan said. *Or we shall leave you behind.*

Hero nodded, still trying to settle her racing heart as Orth nodded in return.

In the moment before he spun and trotted away, the ersia bounding in his wake, Hero caught a glimpse inside the sternard. A gnawing pit of pain and fear stole her breath before the qwan was back in control.

Hero stared after the sternard for several long, hard heartbeats after his tail vanished around the corner.

Her visor flashed, a sharp yellow warning reminding Hero of the holocams sunk into the stark white walls. She spun on her heel, boots thunking as she jogged in the opposite direction.

The Klaude would find her soon enough if they didn't already know she was there. Her only hope was to keep moving and reach the control room before they caught up with her. But even though her eyes were glued to the map and her ears strained for any sound, Hero was stuck on Orth.

She hadn't thought it was possible for him to break the qwan's influence. She had never seen the Jørans have anything less than perfect control over the minds they rode and had never thought about what those beings felt when their bodies were piloted by another. The minds of the ersia she'd ridden had never seemed to feel anything, or even notice her presence.

Was it the Terran part of Orth's DNA that let him fight the qwan's control? That made him feel the pain of the mental talons? Was the difference of a Terran mind why the qwan had recoiled from Demona and Guy's presence? And what did the thought she'd picked up from the qwan, the dark slither of trepidation down her spine, have to do with it?

Her visor blinked another warning and Hero plastered her back against the wall, holding her breath as footsteps approached from the intersecting hallway. There was nowhere to hide; whoever was coming down the other hall would turn the corner and see her as surely as—

The wall at her back disappeared. Hero stumbled backward, tripping over her own feet, arms windmilling. She was only kept upright by another body.

There was an 'oomph' and the familiar hint of lavender teased her thoughts before Hero jerked away, spinning almost before she regained her balance.

Norah's mouth opened and closed like a stranded fish. Hero didn't wait for the shock in her one-time best friend's big brown eyes to clear; she had the jwak out and pressed to Norah's ribs before the other girl got her breath back.

Norah didn't even squeak, just crumpled to the ground in a grey-uniformed heap.

A sharply indrawn breath snapped her gaze around.

A boy stood in the middle of the large white-sided room, the only barrier between them a grey couch. There were others behind him, another boy and a girl, all of them older than her, and all but one with the same stunned-fish expression Norah had made.

The stunned looks didn't last long. The boy in the middle, shorter than the others but still several hands taller than Hero, vaulted over the couch.

Hero didn't hesitate. The jwak was revving her blood, and it was nothing to throw herself at his mind and—

She froze at the raw taste of menthol. The sense, both familiar and hated, dredged up memories of pills, hyposticks, and the terrifying sensation of being stuck inside herself. It was just a moment, barely the blink of an eye, but it was enough for the boy to get within striking distance. He reached for Hero's shoulders, his big fingers splayed like claws.

Hero ducked and wove, jamming the jwak up against his neck and pressing the trigger. She was already moving on to the other two before he hit the floor.

'Stop!' The girl thrust out her hands. The mental command rolled off Hero's shields like rain off her visor, but she still stopped, if only because surprise rooted her boots to the floor.

'You're a telepath,' Hero said. Curiosity took hold of her feet and she took a step forward. 'A hybrid.'

The girl swallowed, a fine tremble taking over her hands. 'How did you...' *Know? Resist my command?* The questions piled up, confused and unfocused, battling each other for supremacy.

Hero reached out, capturing the girl's psyche and stilling it, the familiar taste of menthol wrinkling her nose. *You don't need the meds.*

The girl – Emma – jerked, surprise rich in her voice. *You're a Jørgen, too.*

'You're the one they won't tell us about. The one Smit's looking for.' The boy beside Emma inched sideways, keeping the couch between them, his eyes flicking between Hero and the door. He swallowed, and even with the meds clouding his telepathy, a sharp spurt of determination and fear slapped Hero in the face. 'You don't look old enough to be a criminal.'

Hero narrowed her gaze. *Did Norah tell you that?*

'Norah won't talk about you, but we've all caught glimpses from her. Besides, you broke in here and attacked us.' He sidled another step sideways and Hero loosened her hold on Emma to follow his movement. 'What else would you be?'

Fear shimmered in the boy's eyes, but it faded beneath the derision that rolled through his words. The sour note of it wrapped around her heart and stung, bringing old memories to the fore. There'd been a similar note in Norah's voice over a year ago when her best friend had turned tail and run, even as Timon bled out on the floor.

Anger rose in Hero's chest, swamping the uncomfortable tangle of doubt and guilt. It twisted behind her ribs and Demona rose with it, feeding on the emotion, silently urging her to lash out and make the boy hurt as Norah had hurt her all those months ago. The anger spilled down her arms, the jwak lending it power until Hero could almost see the bright chocolate sparks leap from her fingers.

She almost didn't catch the messy shaft of thought that passed between the boy and Emma.

The mental blow smashed into Hero's shields. She staggered, her knees hitting the floor, her vision blurring from the force. Surprise held her captive as the combined scent of the two Jørgen minds washed over her, sweet spice and lime crawling over her, trying to find a way in.

The jwak warmed in Hero's grip.

You shouldn't have done that, she said, and stood.

Emma blanched. The boy raced for the door.

Hero slipped past Emma's shields, aiming for the sweet spot between sleeping and waking to send the girl to sleep.

The boy had his hand on the door controls before Hero sent him to sleep too. He hit the ground, draped over Norah's legs. Adrenaline was making her heart race, and the jwak had her blood humming, but as her heart slowed, a numbness spread across her chest and crept up her neck. Shock, supplied Guy's soft grey memories.

Hero stared at the bodies on the floor, taking in their faces and the flavours of their sleeping minds. Norah's lavender, as familiar to her as Fink's mawberry, and the others: peppermint, spice, and the sour tang of lime all touched by the raw taste of menthol.

She'd never thought there were other Jørgens out there beside her and Norah. The Librarian had said she and Norah weren't the only ones, but the AI had refused to tell them who, or where. And now here they were, the sight of them making her numb.

Did their parents force meds down their throats? Did they get called 'special' and 'freak'? Did people look at them funny when they answered the questions unsaid? Could they take over a mind like she could? Could they destroy it?

And why was there a hollow sense of disappointment in her chest, a feeling of loss?

Hero crouched beside Emma, reaching to touch the girl's shoulder before jerking her hand back.

She didn't have time for this, to wonder how many more of her kind were out in the world. It was like she hadn't *wanted* there to be other Jørgens, like their existence no longer made her... special.

Hero shot to her feet, burying the disappointment under fresh disgust. She wasn't special, she hated 'special'. Her gaze travelled to Norah. It wasn't like she'd ever really thought she was the only one.

And now she had met others and they'd attacked her. People just like her, and they'd thrown themselves at her like she was some kind of... of...

Terrorist, Guy supplied from the back of her consciousness. They'd attacked her like she would hurt them, like she *wanted* to hurt them.

But she hadn't. Even Norah and the boy who'd jumped her would only wake up with a headache. She could have done worse, and none of the minds at her feet could have stopped her.

The thought made bile rise in the back of her throat, the memory of Demona's brain *popping* under the pressure of hers, the flood of emotion that came with it. And Guy. Hero shuddered as the scene flashed behind her eyes, the remembered rage as hands tore her from her intended target and she found a new one.

Hero thrust the memory aside.

Her former best friend stirred.

Hero frowned. The jwak should have put her out for hours.

She glanced at the stun stick and then at the power indicator flickering, orange in the corner of her visor. She cursed and shoved it back into the holster. The downward creep stopped the moment her skin lost contact, but the room became dimmer and the first stirrings of fatigue crept into her bones.

Norah stirred again and Hero shoved the other Jørgens from her mind.

She had a kill warrant to cancel.

CHAPTER 11

The corridor was empty and the visor's radar clear, but Hero still sent a mental wave ahead. She jogged though the white boxes and connecting tubes, ignoring the icy teeth of fatigue biting at her bones. Twice her visor flashed a warning, and she dived for cover, but only once did she sense another Jørgen, the menthol taste of another medicated telepath sending a tingle of awareness down her spine.

Hero pushed on, the command centre firmly in her sights. Through another connecting tube, the dark folds of the mountains visible through its shimmering translucent sides. And then she was there, only a solid door and a control panel between her and the end of Fink's kill warrant. Her bracer grew warm against her skin—

Hybrid. The qwan's voice was cold and wound through her with a dark thread of anger. *You must come.* The cold, clean scent of stone and the sizzle of rifles bloomed in Hero's psyche a second before an alarm split her ears.

At the same time, the control room door snapped aside. A man in the same grey uniform Norah had worn stood on the other side. He jerked to a halt, surprise lifting his brows.

The same emotion hit Hero before movement over the man's shoulder had her charging forward. She caught him in the stomach, air bursting from his lungs as she shoved him back into the room. The scuttle of boots and shouts of surprise exploded around her, and Hero looked up to find herself surrounded by Klaude.

A dozen sets of eyes skewered her. Her visor tracked the adults sitting and standing at workstations, but it was the man in the middle who commanded Hero's attention. Sad blue eyes regarded her amid the alarms and flashing screens.

'Ms Regan,' Dorich said. Or she thought he said it; his words were lost in the noise and the rush of movement.

Someone lurched at her from the side. She dodged backward through the doorway, scrambling for the control panel. The door slammed closed. There wasn't time to jam it, not with the people on the other side or the boots she could hear coming through the tube. Instead, she ripped the jwak from its holster and sent a power surge through the plasglas.

The jwak's power indicator flashed red even as the control panel smoked and spat, the charred fish stench of fried biogel blocking her nose.

Hybrid. Urgency, pain, and anger lit up the qwan's voice.

Hero spun on her heel and ran. *I'm coming.*

The thud of boots belonged to two more Klaude with pistols in their hands. They had time to raise their guns and for Hero to stare down the barrels before they hit the floor.

She raced past, slipping out of their minds as easily as she'd slipped in, and skidded around the corner.

The cold was creeping back into her bones, breath rasping in and out of her lungs. She ran faster, following the other dot on her visor, pushing past people in lab coats, ducking under grasping arms and sending anyone with a weapon to sleep. She bolted down corridors and whipped around corners, the acid green streak of pain in the qwan's voice driving her like a fist in her back, making her pump her arms faster and stretch her legs further.

She was almost there. Outside, the mountain blocked out the sky. Another airlock loomed ahead, its huge circular door open, the deep grooves a sharp line between human construction and alien. She leaped over the threshold, the glossy white floor turning to pale stone under her feet, the curving walls no longer gleaming with the opalescence of holo-walls, but full of shadows cast by intricate carvings.

Memories loomed, both hers and Demona's, giving her direction as the qwan's mental touch drove her forward.

Hero skidded into a corridor, only her grip on the corner stopping her feet from going out from under her, and sprinted toward the giant opening at its end.

The doors were open but she couldn't see much. There were no lights, just the faint blue-white of emergency glows and the hulking shadows of shuttles, but she could hear well enough.

The scream, human and terrified, made her blood run cold. Hero plunged into the dark. Her visor flicked to night vision. Another scream, this time high-pitched and piercing. The war cry of a linch-adder.

Something with a bigger chest roared in response.

There, a lithe shadow rose above a shuttle, and over there, as Hero dived between shuttles and out the other side, emerged a ghostly white outline almost as big as a 'pard.

The qwan's panic was still riding her, tucked up in the back of her awareness, pushing her toward the warring shadows.

Something caught around her ankles. Hero stumbled, the soft grey shape of an ersia cannoning into the darkness as she caught herself on the blunt nose of a shuttle. Other ersia flowed around her feet, writhing balls of scarpa attached to their backs, and disappeared under the shuttles, their single-mindedness dislodging the hard, glassy grip of the qwan.

Hero shook free of the qwan's influence, cutting it off with a decisive snap of her shields. The panic and urgency that had fuelled her headlong sprint vanished, leaving her heart pounding and her hands trembling. The qwan had slipped into her head so easily...

There were more shadows in the hangar, great hulking shapes she hadn't seen with the qwan driving her forward. They stalked between the shuttles, fragments of darkness with the violent musty scent of rucnarts. Her visor tracked them with bright orange squares as the rucnarts slipped between shuttles, their height, weight, and closeness cluttering up her screens. She shook them aside and did what she would have done if not for the qwan. She stretched her telepathy.

She found Harish first, his thoughts a fiery sweep of determination, anger, and satisfaction as he raked talons over a sternard's cloud-white crown.

The little 'adder shot back into the air, and through his eyes Hero saw Norah sprawled on the hangar floor. She was propped up on her elbows, all her attention on Orth.

The sternard didn't move, not even when Harish dove at his eyes, talons leaving bloody gouges on his face.

Pain and fear radiated from the companion, catching in Hero's throat. The feelings almost overwhelmed the battle going on within him. The fabric of Orth's consciousness was stretched tight, tears showing as Norah and the qwan fought for control. Brilliant streaks of lavender and turquoise shone through the gaps, leaking light into Orth's skull, making the rents bigger.

They would kill him, pop his mind like she'd popped the ersia's just a handful of days ago. Urgency took Hero's breath, a desperate need to save the sternard, but there wasn't enough room for another telepath to slip inside.

She focused on Norah instead.

The other girl's shields were as high and smooth as Hero remembered. Norah was distracted though; all her focus was on trying to wrench Orth out of the qwan's grip. Hero slipped in and stopped.

The inside of Norah's skull was alight with colour, the void tinged with violet and shot through with the deep purple streaks of battle.

Hero couldn't see Norah, but she was there in every breath and surge of power. Hero caught one of those surges, riding it to the thick tendril of thought that connected Norah to Orth. On the other side, through the violet-tinged fog, Norah and the qwan fought. The Jøran's talons struck sparks from Norah's shields, but the thin lavender dome never wavered. It advanced millimetre by millimetre, slowly prying Orth from the Jøran's grip.

Agony held the sternard together, the brilliant strands fraying as the rents in his mind widened.

Hero summoned lightning to her hands and thrust them into the connecting tendril.

For a heartbeat, nothing happened.

Then, Norah's pain ricocheted up Hero's arms, filling her nose with the scent of lavender. The tendril shuddered, cracked, snapped and Norah was beside her, nose-to-nose, close enough to share breath. Outrage twisted the other girl's face, purple lightning encased her hands and—

Through the veil of Norah's sight, Hero watched h'Ran sail over Orth and snatch Harish right out of the air.

The cry that came from Norah's mouth was echoed by Hero. Norah's shields cracked, giant fissures opening under Hero's mental feet, sucking her in. Reaching for power was instinctive and the bright rush of the jwak answered her call, filling her veins with a brief flash before it died.

Norah swallowed her and panic obliterated thought. For a heartbeat, the roiling spot at her core unfurled and sank a tendril into Norah. Lavender permeated Hero's skull and in that second, she was Norah and Norah was her; they melded together like a collective of two.

Power surged between them, feeding off chocolate and lavender until it was greater than both, and far greater than a single rucnart. It thrummed in their hands, directionless until the half of them that sang with purple snatched it up.

The moment of connectedness, of shared power, lasted for a second.

A second was all it took for h'Ran to die.

Hero stumbled out from between the shuttles as the rucnart fell, her mind her own again as she watched Harish tumble from h'Ran's loosened jaws.

Hero fell, the sickening rush of h'Ran's memories washing over her, the place at her core trying to gobble them up. She was swimming in the rucnart's memories, trying not to choke on their bitter earthiness even as she pried them away.

They were sticky and stubborn; the roiling ball at her core had its own gravity, but finally she ripped them loose. Hero flung the memories away with all her strength and heard the impact as they stuck to Norah.

Vaguely, Hero was aware that Norah had scampered over to Harish, was cradling his limp body in her arms. Harish trilled, thin and reedy, the sound full of pain. Norah looked up and her eyes met Hero's over h'Ran's body.

There was fear in her gaze, a fascinated kind of horror plastered on her face.

The moment was interrupted by a roar of rage and pain. Hero didn't have to see n'Tao or even hear him thundering between the shuttles. The wave of his bloodlust crashed before him like a wave. She lunged across h'Ran's body, grabbing Norah's forearm in both hands, feeling the warmth of the other girl's bracer and seeing her fear at the renewed blue-white glow of the sensors on Hero's scalp.

Norah's fear and n'Tao's rage sandwiched Hero between them, squishing the air from her lungs.

Pushing back was instinctive, as was the way the mingled emotions coloured her strike. It threw Norah backward, glancing off her shields, but the fear – Norah's fear – sunk into n'Tao like a laser through biogel. It stuck there and n'Tao stopped with it, crashing to his side on the ground, his eyes open and dazed as the lavender tint of Norah's emotion spread through him like a virus.

The blood left Hero's face. What had she done? One of the rucnarts was dead, and she'd just attacked another. She remembered the flash of h'Ran's fangs, the hot puff of n'Tao's breath against her neck and the cold watchfulness of the qwan. There would be no forgiveness from the Jørans.

She turned to Norah, to Harish cradled in her arms and, *Old*

Terra, she knew she'd do it again.

Norah clutched Harish closer to her chest. 'What'd you do?'

'Do you care?' Hero whispered back even as n'Tao's paws twitched and his eyes began to lose their dazed look. The deluge of human emotion was wearing off. Hero scrambled to her feet, pulled Norah to hers, and yelled in the girl's face. 'Run!'

Hero didn't wait to see if Norah ran. There was a hard wave of anger creeping up behind her, riding on the glassy presence of a qwan, and the knot in her gut told her not to wait around.

CHAPTER 12

She threw herself over the ridge. The valley beyond was a shallow fold in the side of the mountain, cast in darkness. Blinded by the spotlights at her back, Hero stumbled, feet catching in the scrub.

She tumbled down the valley, pain exploding in her shoulders and knees, rocks digging into her back, the bright lights and dark sky flashing as she rolled and rolled. She slammed to a stop, her neck snapping backward and the sharp crack of her helmet meeting something solid. Hero was lost for a moment, vision greying around the edges and all thought fleeing.

She lay there, staring up at the light pouring over the ridge and the dark silhouettes of people appearing at the top.

A sharp beam of light hit her in the face, shocking her out of her stupor. A voice shouted 'There!' and she scrambled to her feet as more figures appeared on the ridge.

Hero staggered around the boulder that had halted her tumble. Dizziness made her clumsy, and she lurched back down the slope. She had to get to the forest and... She couldn't run and would never be able to outdistance the hunters at her back. She'd have to hide, ambush one of them and hope they had enough powerpaks to unfreeze her bones and—

A 'pard's chuff came out of the darkness, the sound skittering through the night air like beads rattling inside her water bottle.

A shadow rose from the ground and her heart stopped, Fink's name rising to her lips before her visor picked out the scar dragging across Red's muzzle. Disappointment crashed through her chest, slowing her feet long enough for her to hear the thud and crash of the hunters behind.

Red shifted from paw to paw at the bottom of the rocky slope, ears twitching madly while his tail whipped through the scrub. He chuffed again, the sound louder, more urgent.

Hero's breath was coming hard and there was sweat pooling in the small of her back by the time she finished sliding down the slope, the loose bits of stone slipping under her feet.

She was on Red's back before she could give her legs the command. She yelped when he sprang forward, clutching his ruff and leaning low as the 'pard galloped for the trees.

They lost the Klaude sometime after the moon began to fall back toward the horizon, but Red didn't stop. The mad head-long gallop through the forest had become a ground-eating lope, leaping over logs and bounding up embankments. Red's pace slowed again as the terrain became steeper and the stones turned to rocky escarpments.

By the time the sun had lightened the sky, Hero's thighs ached from clinging to Red's broad back. She was tired, so tired that she'd given up trying to stay upright and lay draped over his neck. She wouldn't close her eyes though, even if the 'pard's every stride begged her to let them drift shut and to give into the temptation of sleep.

But sleep meant her whole body would turn to jelly and the small ounce of concentration keeping her from sliding off his back would go with it.

Instead, she concentrated on the soft cream rosettes that mixed with the dark chestnut hairs of Red's coat and let her mind wander. Her thoughts drifted to Orth, skipped to h'Ran and then to Harish lying so still in Norah's arms, and the way her mental shield had sunk into n'Tao, the fear and grief she'd projected sliding into his brain. She pushed each new thought aside as soon as it appeared, leaving room for an uncomfortable sense of disappointment to intrude.

It filled the hollow feeling in her chest and resurrected that bitter word: *special.* It made her want to spit.

Under Red's paws, the forest floor gave way to soft dirt. When Hero looked up, the sky was violet with the beginnings of dawn. The pounding of water hitting water filled her ears; the cool mist of the waterfalls that hid the den wet her cheeks as Red passed through.

The sound of the water faded until the only sound was the clacking of pebbles under Red's paws.

How'd you know where I was?

Red grunted. *Grandmother told him to follow.* 'Grandmother' came loaded with an image of Apani, weighed down with age and authority.

Why?

He did not ask.

When Hero moved to slide off, slowly shifting her aching limbs, Red twisted around and snapped his jaws.

Stay, he said. The flash of teeth didn't bother her; there had been no anger in his words, just a rough kind of patience as if he was telling off a kitten. If her bones hadn't been heavy with cold, she'd have thumped him between the ears.

Instead, she frowned. 'Why?' Her voice was a rasp.

Grandmother wanted to see her.

Hero started to slide off again. 'I can find her my—'

This time, Red's snap was sharp and hard, his teeth flashing. Alarm pushed some of the fatigue from Hero's bones. *She would stay,* he said.

She straightened. 'What's going on?'

His muzzle relaxed. *Stay,* was all he said.

She stayed.

Sunlight filtered through the tartz dome above, made dappled by the roots poking through the honey-coloured resin. The sounds of movement echoed through the caverns: the whuff and rumble of the pack waking up, the scuffle of the kittens and the outraged yowl of the adult they pounced on.

Red moved deeper into the den, padding through the winding caverns until the sounds of the pack faded and were replaced by the steady drip of water and the hollow rush of an underground river. He stopped at the entrance to a larger cavern and nudged her foot.

Hero slipped off his back and entered.

Only the 'pard's blue-grey rump and the long thick length of her tail were visible. The rest of the 'pard disappeared into one of the many holes in the cavern floor.

The soft patter of water dripping from the tartz ceiling – the translucent resin arched high overhead, strung between the black fossilised branches of long-dead giants – did nothing to cover the dull thunk of Hero's boots on the porous stone. Still, the grand-mother 'pard didn't rise from the hole, nor did her tail pause its twitching. Instead, a hum rose from the stone, vibrating under Hero's feet and growing until it filled her chest as she squatted beside Apani.

Her visor hummed as she leaned over the hole, the impenetrable black slowly lightening with greys and greens until the depths were as clear to her as they were to the 'pard at her side.

Water rippled less than a millimetre from the 'pard's nose, its gentle waves pricked out in the grey and green of her visor. Apani's ears were pricked forward, the veins standing out in the back of their slim, half-moon shapes; the elder 'pard straining for the faintest swish of a fin beneath the river's surface.

Hero leaned further over the hole, rocking forward on her toes. She switched her visor to infrared. Far beneath the reach of the light, a long, fat body slipped through the water.

She shared the image with the matriarch. The silver-blue 'pard flicked an ear but made no other move.

Hero waited, thighs cramping as one minute stretched into two and then longer. When the sharp knots in her thighs turned into a cold numbness that took over her feet, Hero spoke.

'Red—'

A sharp splash and then the thin, ear-piercing squeal of an akeel cut her off. Water spewed from the hole, fat freezing drops that drenched her face and soaked through her clothes to make her shiver.

Apani growled, bashing the akeel's thick, scaly body against the sides of the hole as she bunched her haunches to haul the creature out of the water.

Hero fell backward and scrambled out of the way.

Apani wrestled the fish, every muscle straining, claws raking across the rock as she drew it out of the hole. Her shoulders popped out and then her ears, followed by the akeel as it screeched and thrashed. But Apani's jaws were locked tight and her fangs sunk deep into its flesh, blood running down her chin.

With a final, vicious tug, the matriarch ripped the creature from the water. It's long, tube-like body, almost as thick as Hero's leg, hit the stone with a fleshy *thwack*. Water continued to spray in fine droplets flung from the akeel's shiny scales.

Hero scuttled further backward, ducking to avoid the animal's spiky tail.

There was a wet, meaty *crunch*, and the akeel was still.

Apani sat, tail curled over her paws, while she licked the blood from her muzzle with a long, pink tongue.

She would go. An image of Hero walking into the sunset with her bags on her back accompanied the thought.

Hero blinked, struggling to make sense of Apani's image. 'What?'

Go. The image changed, this time showing the hollow where Hero's tent usually sat, but now the hollow was empty. *The pack had no place for her.*

'The pack...' The sick, jangly feeling in her gut grew. 'You're kicking us out?' Hero's return image of her and Fink was bright with disbelief.

Not Darsun. The end of the grandmother 'pard's tail slapped the wet rock. There was a hard, implacable edge to her words and a heaviness to the age and power behind them.

'His name is Fink,' Hero whispered back even as she reeled

mentally. 'And you can't kick me out.'

Apani's muzzle wrinkled, lips curling away from her teeth. The menace in Apani's expression shivered up Hero's spine as the 'pard rose. *She would be gone before the sun rose.*

'Why?'

She was struck by a memory of her and Fink silhouetted in the moonlight, her words echoing back through the cavern. *I'm not a 'pard, Fink. I don't belong here.'*

The den was for pack. Apani's words echoed through the shock clogging Hero's brain. *She did not want to be pack.*

With that, the matriarch brushed past Hero, the akeel clutched in her jaws.

Hero watched her go, turning on the spot to keep the 'pard in sight. She wanted to speak, but the only word she could think of was, 'But...'

But what? a mawberry-scented voice asked.

She's just a 'pard. The thought came unbidden, tripping out from the back of her consciousness on memories of blue, Demona filling her nose with the scent of roses. Hero pushed the remnant back, but not before the thought resonated, lifting a small secret part from the depths of her being, a part that agreed with Demona.

Fink growled, and Hero swung around in time to see him disappear into the shadows of the caves beyond.

'Fink,' she called.

He was just a 'pard, was all he said before his tail vanished.

'Fink!' she yelled, but the only sound she heard back was the echo of her own voice and the high, wild note of fear that had taken over her chest. 'I didn't mean it,' she whispered.

Except she had, said the same blue voice. She'd meant it just like she'd enjoyed knocking Norah out, just like seeing those other Jørgens had made her feel hollow and ordinary.

Hero slapped Demona back. She didn't want to be that person, didn't like the hurt buried under Fink's last thought, the contempt, how small it made her feel. Didn't like the memory of standing over the Jørgens and feeling disappointed. Cheated. Hollow.

Ordinary.

Her legs folded under her and she plopped onto the cold, wet stone and buried her face in her arms. 'I don't want to be special,' she said. '*I don't.*'

The warm, golden hue of her uncle settled beside her, his laugh filling her, singing through her insides like sunshine.

Of course you do. The ghost of a hand brushed her cheek, and she lifted her eyes enough to see Paris crouched beside her, hovering above a hole in the floor. *You're a Regan, after all, and we are nothing if not special.*

She looked away. 'I hate being special.'

No, you hate people using it as an excuse to tell you what to do. Which is quite normal, by the way, he said. *I hated it too. Your mother was the responsible twin, and even she caused her share of trouble. But it's not your newfound, relative normality that's bothering you, is it?*

Hero lifted her head and let her knees fall to the sides. 'Apani told me to leave.'

I heard.

'Fink might not come with me,' she said, her voice barely above a whisper.

And?

Hero's arms went around her middle. 'He belongs with me.'

Are you sure?

'He's mine.' Hero thought it as much as said it, packing her words with everything in her being, the silent companionship, love, comfort, and security that filled her whenever she was with Fink. How it did more than just fill her up from the inside out; how it was a part of her, tied into the core of her being like her heart in her chest. Without Fink, she wasn't whole.

Well. Paris blinked and rubbed his own chest. *Does he know that?*

Hero glared at him and drew a memory from a place deep within, next to the part of her that was as much a part of Fink. A memory of sharing his mind, seeing out of his eyes, hearing with his ears, but more than that, of having no secrets, no barriers, and of feeling and knowing everything the other did.

She cut the thought off and turned her glare into the darkness. Water slapped against the stone beneath, echoing up the holes in the floor and filling the cavern with sound.

I never felt that with my companion, Paris finally said.

'You didn't have a Woolsey,' she replied.

I'm beginning to regret that.

'He has to come with me.'

Like you had to take the meds?

'I...' She hugged her legs. 'It's not the same.'

Isn't it?

CHAPTER 13

She didn't sleep, even though her eyes burned with fatigue. The hole in her chest kept her awake, a gnawing ache like she hadn't eaten for days except deeper. She hadn't seen Fink since he'd stalked out of the fishing cavern. She hadn't even sensed him. Not as she collapsed her tent or packed and repacked the saddlebags, abandoning most of them in a small mountain of nanoleather in the same spot her tent had stood for over a year.

She wouldn't be able to carry it all. Fink wasn't coming. That hollow certainty had solidified just before the sun lightened the tear in the cavern's roof. With it had come another certainty and a hot, hard determination that leavened the frost in her marrow and had her spilling the contents of her backpack onto the stone one final time.

She was down here, had exiled herself to the surface and lived with 'pards for one reason only. No matter what, she would cancel that kill warrant.

The tent and stray bits of salvaged tech went into the pile with the saddlebags. She wouldn't need much, just enough food to last the journey and every powerpak she could scrounge. The communication sphere went in last.

The authorisation codes wouldn't work a second time, but her plan would be better that way. Faster.

The mountain of discarded equipment was high and her backpack lighter when she finished. She slung it over her shoulder and walked out of the little cavern she'd called home without a backward glance.

The den hummed with the sounds of the pack waking up. The snick of claws on stone echoing off rocky walls, the snap and growl of the juveniles arguing over breakfast, the thud and whine as an adult told them off. No different from any other morning except there were no warm bodies brushing past her, no rough tongues trying to lick her cheek, and no Fink purring in her ear.

Sadness tried to work its way up her throat, tried to burn her eyes with tears. She choked it back, gripping the straps of her pack so tight her nails bit into her palms. She'd do this and then...

Her throat closed up again as she remembered the betrayal in Fink's mind, the way his tail had vanished into the shadows. She'd deal with that when she had to. Now, she had a warrant to kill.

CHAPTER 14

The moon was a thin sliver above the horizon, just bright enough for her to see her breath turn to mist and pick out the fluffy white seeds of the grasses. It rose around her, high enough to hide the small patch she'd spent the last hour of daylight flattening. The effort had kept the plateau's icy chill at bay but now, with the sun gone and the sky cloudless, her fingers and toes were close to frozen despite the thickness of her boots and gloves.

She stuck her gloved hands under her armpits and stamped her feet. It didn't matter, she wouldn't be out here long. Not long at all, but she had to make it look good, had to make whoever was up there *believe* she was that desperate, or just that stupid, to use the same access codes again, and then they'd be on her like scarpa.

Hero knelt and dug the comm dome out from the backpack, laying it in the middle of the flattened grass.

It shone pale silver in the moonlight before flickering on with a hum, lighting up the wall of grass around her tiny clearing. The authorisation request rose from the dome. Hero took a deep breath and checked that the biogel tendril still connected her bracer to the sphere, before thrusting her arm into the light.

The dome flickered, and before its soft pink column of light could deepen to red, Hero unleashed the virus stored in the bracer's memory. The light exploded into a fractured mess of DNA and code, which she thrust her frozen fingers into, digging through chromosomes to pry apart their molecules.

It was fast and messy and she knew she hadn't stopped the sphere from transmitting her attempt to connect to the 'nets. There would be an alert blazing on someone's holoscreen, but that had been the point.

Even as Hero pulled the comm dome's code apart, digging deep into the genes that controlled the authorisation handshake between it and the 'nets, she boosted power to her helmet's sensors, straining for the slightest glimmer of a hover descending from the sky.

It wouldn't take long, it *couldn't*, not with the outpost on the other side of the mountain and all the people looking for her. Not unless they were stupid or blind, or both.

Just this once, she needed to be caught.

The moon rose higher and the night air grew colder biting through her jacket to sink teeth into the nanoskin beneath. Hero shivered and wished she had Fink to curl up against. She really hoped the people looking for her weren't stupid; freezing to death wasn't exactly part of her plan.

Her helmet pinged, a gentle sound that brought Hero's attention up with a snap. She twisted about, knocking the comm dome over. Only the stars and the dense twinkle of solar systems far, far away met her eyes. She held her breath and sat still, but that only brought the gentle rustle of seed heads and the pound of her pulse to her ears. There were no bright lights on the horizon, no faint sheen of a shuttle running dark, no buzz of a drone.

Hero frowned, and she kept scanning the sky for what had set off her helmet's sensors. No bright yellow dots pulsed on her visor and yet the helmet kept pinging, the gentle sound chiming in her ears, the pause between the pulses growing shorter and shorter.

Trepidation slithered down her spine and she forsook the sky for the pale green grasses swaying around her. The thick blades cast stark shadows in the light of the comm sphere, the shadows turning the feathery heads into sharp-toothed razors.

The plateau Hero had chosen for her plan was broad and flat, the surrounding mountains a dark smudge on every horizon. There was no way for a shuttle, drone or person to sneak up on her, unless...

Slowly, carefully, Hero rose until she could see over the seed heads. Half-crouched, she spun in a slow circle. Nothing broke the shifting silver of the plain, no lights, no shadows that moved as they shouldn't, yet the chime of her sensors grew closer and closer together, a second steady heartbeat in her ears.

Maybe the helmet had picked up an ersia? The blue and grey remnants at the back of her psyche rejected the possibility as soon as it occurred. The sensor wouldn't have responded to anything that small. Hero stood. Then what was big enough to trip them and small enough to leave no visual trace?

Hero opened her shields—

She spun, her feet catching and sending her to the ground. The bright yellow stun bolt intended for her back clipped her shoulder. She landed on her side, her right arm dead, her fingers useless lumps of flesh as the tingling numbness spread through her back and crept up her neck.

Awkwardly, with her right arm flopping, Hero rolled to her knees. Her shields were still open, flowing out around her like a spideruck's web, but she didn't need it to know that Smit had given up belly-crawling across the plateau. The woman crunched through the grass without stealth, sure now that her prey was passed out in the dirt.

No other minds tripped her mental web, no bright spots of lavender or colours mixed with menthol. If Smit was alone...

Hero refocused her attention on Smit, delving deep inside the woman. Hero knew the woman felt it and now knew that Hero wasn't unconscious.

But Hero didn't care because she'd found what she wanted. Smit had been combing the mountains for Hero since the Jøran attack. The Klaude had sent her the unauthorised access alert as soon as it popped on their screens and the canny old woman had sensed the trap.

There was no shuttle for Hero to steal, no quick ride to the Farm and an end to Fink's kill warrant. Just a scary old woman with a singular goal.

Hero gathered herself, reaching across her body for the jwak only to close her hand on an empty holster. She twisted about, searching frantically for the stun stick. There, just a short mad scramble on her knees and one good arm across the tiny clearing. Her hand closed around the jwak. The power indicator flashed red, just once, and it died. The cold was sucking at her bones and her brain hurt, but Smit was just there.

The old woman's second shot didn't miss. Hero was out before her visor hit the dirt.

When she came to, she was staring at the stars. Her head was a little fuzzy and a tingle, like angry ants, lingered in her toes. She was warm and the ground beneath her was soft, without the cool dampness of soil or the ever-present lumps and bumps of sticks and stones.

Hero frowned, thoughts sluggish as she tried to figure out why light was staining the horizon the colour of dawn, even though the thin sliver of moon was still high in the sky.

She tried to sit, but a thick band from shoulders to toes held her down. She wriggled, trying to loosen the edges, but the material moved with her, shifting with every flex and heave. The first hint of panic bloomed in her chest, just as something whipped through the sky. The long, lithe shadow twisted in midair and dived at her face. She yelled and tried to turn away, but the band had her tight. The shadow snapped open its wings and landed on her belly with a familiar chirp.

'Harish? You're okay?'

The linch-adder puffed out his chest and trilled.

'You're awake.' The voice came from somewhere above and behind her. Even distorted by the hollow echo of an enviromask, Hero could recognise Smit's cool, unhurried tones. 'No mind tricks, girl, or you won't be awake much longer.'

Contorting herself as much as the restraints would allow, she caught an awkward, upside-down glimpse of a shaggy rump and the dark shape of the woman atop. The faint glimmer of the tether trailed from the saddle, down the dark rump to somewhere just above Hero and out of her sight. She was on a hover sled, held down by the protective cover that search and rescue teams threw over injured explorers. Hero didn't ask where Smit was taking her – with Harish perched on her belly she already knew.

Teaming with Klaude and smattered with Jørgens, the compound under the mountain was the last place she wanted to go. Even if the jwak was at full power and her head hadn't been mushy, she wasn't sure she could have stormed through the outpost to steal a shuttle. Especially not strapped to a sled. But perhaps, if she had an escort...

Hero twisted against the band, eyeing Smit's narrow back.

Cold gathered in Hero's bones, but she ignored it as she teased out a delicate tendril of power from the well at her mental feet. Smit's threats about mind tricks didn't stop her. She slipped into Smit's awareness so gently that she doubted even Fink would have noticed. Then she hit a solid lavender barrier that didn't belong there. The barrier flexed, and for just a second the weight of Norah's attention turned in Hero's direction, before it passed over her.

The breath pent up in her chest escaped in a rush that ruffled Harish's chest feathers. The 'adder swished his tail and chirped. Hero hadn't expected that, to feel Norah like a protective shell over Smit. At least now she understood Smit's threat. If Norah was shielding Smit, they were closer to the outpost than Hero had thought.

There wasn't much time.

Ignoring the gentle prick of Harish's talons, Hero took a deep breath and dived back in.

Norah's presence in Smit's consciousness was a complication, but that broad sweep was distracted and cursory, a casual flick to dislodge a bug in her ear. Behind it Hero had sensed a sharp, sour strain and the hot spice of h'Ran's memories trying to find a home inside Norah. They spread over her like a thick blanket of oil, shifting and oozing but unable to latch on.

Hero misted over the purple shield, following the sour thread as it grew stronger.

The source flickered and spat, an ugly yellow splodge in Norah's otherwise perfect barrier. Hero wound a tendril of thought around it. Norah was on the other end. Hero could see and hear her speaking in a room filled with screens and people, like Norah's eyes and ears were hers. She knew it was the strain of protecting Smit, almost half a kilometre away, that was making the other girl's head pound.

The sour yellow wavered and a momentary crack appeared in the lavender shield. Hero dived through, her power pulsing along the thread that connected her to her own mind. Pooled above, blue and green wove through the chocolate, urging her to smash Smit's shields and blow Norah's barrier to nothing. But there was no way Norah would miss that, and it wouldn't help her steal a shuttle.

Instead, Hero constructed a thought packet. It was easier than the information sphere she'd built for the Jørans, but messier, constructed with too much haste and not enough finesse, full of the desperation and determination that had fuelled her trek to the mountain plateau. It didn't matter how messy it was though; there wasn't time. Hero could already feel the crack in Norah's shield fading.

And just before it faded, with the completed thought packet pulsing in her hands, Hero hesitated. The memory of Orth standing in the airlock played before her, the qwan staring out of his eyes, the pain and fear that had swamped him in the second he'd broken the Jøran's control.

No. No, it wasn't the same. Besides, she didn't have a choice.

Hero gritted her teeth and threw the packet, filled with a simple, urgent instruction and coated in a sticky layer of command, deep into Smit.

Hero snapped back into her own skull and blinked.

Harish was on her chest, staring at her with a single golden eye, and for just a second she thought she saw Norah staring back at her.

A sudden blaze of light blinded her. She snapped her eyes shut, waiting for the pain to subside before cracking them open again. There was a new shadow above her, the distinct outline of an envirosuit blocking the glare. She couldn't see the face behind the mask, but she had no problem making out the hypostick or the green goo inside.

Panic took her in the chest, a new strength bursting through her veins.

There was no finesse this time, no delicate tendril of thought, just raw power turning the ice in her bones to something colder, deeper, and scarier as she slammed into the suited figure's psyche.

There was a barrier around this one too, not lavender but lemon, and she recognised the touch of Emma, the Jørgen girl. It crumpled like a baby scarpa's shell, just like the suit with the hypo. There was yelling, a second figure behind the first and then—

For the second time that night, a stunner laid Hero out cold.

When she woke this time, it was to a familiar tingle in her toes, the taste of menthol on her tongue and a blue, cloudless sky above. A hint of static ran along the edges where the ceiling met a curving, intricately carved wall.

Hero sat up and groaned. Cold gripped her insides. She was wearing her nanoskin, *just* her nanoskin – her boots, breeches, and jacket were nowhere to be seen – the matte black material looking a little grey and worn, but neither it nor the blanket puddled around her hips touched the shivers wracking her insides. They shook her whole body, making her toes curl, her calves cramp, and her teeth chatter so loud she was surprised she didn't hear an echo. But that wasn't what made her wrap her arms around her middle.

The sterile white walls of a med room were the same whether in a lab or a jerry-rigged outpost. The only difference with these was the way they curved upward, like a wide flat-topped tube, and the intricate designs carved into the stone. The holographic ceiling belonged there about as much as she did, which was probably the reason for the static.

Was the Librarian up there, staring back at her, or was it just doctors and lab techs tucked up where she couldn't see them?

She stared at it, trying to see through the nanites to the control room beyond.

For a moment, Hero thought she saw a flutter, a ripple in the static where the holo-ceiling met the alien wall. It was gone a heartbeat later, leaving her staring at the holographic sky, the pinpricks of stars just visible in the deep blue of the dome. She frowned. Just because she couldn't see it, didn't mean the Librarian wasn't watching her. Still, Hero relaxed as much as the muscle spasms trying to tear her body apart would allow.

She needed the jwak. She didn't think whoever had dumped her on the medcouch and stripped her outer clothes would have left it lying around, but the thought didn't stop her from sliding off the couch.

Her knees buckled as soon as her feet touched the floor and she landed in a puddle of shivers beside the couch, her arms around her middle. She sat there for a moment, blinking, trying to remember why she was down there in the first place. The floor was hard, but warmer than her bones and the medcouch's plasform base. Hero leaned her forehead against it and sighed. Sleep weighed heavy, and she closed her eyes.

Another shudder gripped her tight and along with it came a vicious, angry spasm that tried to curl her foot in on itself.

Pain jerked her awake, made her cry out and grab her foot. She rubbed it, easing the cramp.

She had to get out of here, had to find the jwak. Slowly the cramp let go, and just as slowly Hero got to her feet.

The med room was tiny, a half-dozen strides across and double that in length. The couch sat in the middle, meaning she only had to stumble a handful of steps before she was kneeling in front of the low rectangular locker at the end of the room. A hand on the lid and Hero was unsurprised at the 'unauthorised access' message projected over her hand in big red letters.

It didn't matter; she might not have her bracer, her helmet, or her telepathy but—

Her telepathy. Hero paused. There was menthol on the back of her tongue and a hint of it haunting her nose, but she didn't feel slow and fuzzy or boxed in like she had the last time someone had shot her full of meds.

Cautious, Hero pushed the edges of her telepathy. There was a trace of menthol-flavoured resistance, a fuzziness that parted around her like heavy curtains, then she was out, clear on the other side of the menthol fog where the world glimmered with the presence of other minds.

Elation tempered the deepening cold in her bones and her hands stilled on the locker. The meds hadn't worked. Did the Klaude know? Did Norah? Did Smit?

Smit. Hero bit her lip and glanced around the room, eyes catching on the palm-sized door controls, as out of place on the curved wall as the holo-ceiling. Another human tool jerry-rigged onto alien architecture.

Had the command Hero planted in the woman's mind worked? Should she expect a rescue any second now? Or would someone less friendly come through?

Another, stronger shudder gripped her ribcage. She fumbled with the locker, her fingers clumsy as she searched for a way into its command prompt and base programming. If she didn't want to shake apart within the next ten minutes, she didn't have a choice. She needed the jwak and whatever bit of power it might hold. If it wasn't in the locker, if some Klaude hack had spirited it away, she would make the lot of them regret even knowing her name.

By the time she found the command prompt, the shivers made it hard to steady her hands and her jaw ached from clenching her teeth. The locker's DNA was spread across the lid and blue crescents of cold crept halfway up her fingernails as she pulled apart the molecule chains that made up its programming. The box opened, its lid parting down the centre.

Hero dived in before the two halves tucked themselves against the box's sides, pulling out breeches and boots but no jwak.

No jwak.

She sunk to her heels and hugged her knees, the muscles in her belly and back spasming hard enough she thought they might crack a rib. She stared into the empty space.

No jwak.

Fear settled in her gut, a sharp twist dislodging a little of the cold. Someone probably had it lined up on a workbench somewhere with half of its code hanging out. Poking, prodding, and screwing it up with their clumsy, stupid scans. Uncaring that they were messing her up too, leaving her to a lifetime of cold bones and being one with the tribe.

If the shudders hadn't gripped her so hard, she'd have shivered with fear.

She wouldn't join the tribe like that, wouldn't let herself get torn apart and scattered among a hundred other minds until she wasn't herself anymore. Until she wasn't Hero. She'd become an icicle or find a volcano before that happened.

Slowly, finger by finger, she unclenched the grip on her knees, a new determination pushing fear aside and giving her the strength to stagger to her feet. Right now it was just her in a room with nothing but an empty locker, a door pad, and her telepathy.

The pad didn't stand a chance.

With both hands on the wall, Hero made her way to the door.

CHAPTER 15

The thunk of her boots echoed off the curved walls and down the corridor. The sound seemed to catch in the delicate carvings that covered the walls. Ripples and whorls splintered the echo in a million different directions, distorting until it sounded like a swarm of roaches chasing her through the empty corridors.

Hero shivered, not from the chill biting her nose or the heavy weight of the ice in her bones but from the emptiness.

There should have been people rushing down the corridor, coming to bundle her up and lock her away. More than that, she should have *felt* someone, a tickle or a ping against her awareness, a hint of lemon or spice on her tongue. Instead there was nothing, like she was moving through a metallic nothingness that made her thoughts loud and her heart stick in her throat.

Her telepathy slid through the carved walls dug out of the mountain, slim tendrils of chocolate stretching deeper into the alien base until they were so thin it took all of her concentration to keep them moving.

The first Klaude she came across was wearing an envirosuit, a rifle cradled in their arms. Hero didn't give them the opportunity to turn around. Even though it made her stomach hollow and her fingertips blue, she slipped into the hunter's mind and sent the woman to sleep. Hero took the rifle and left her crumpled in the middle of the corridor.

Nestling her finger against the trigger with confidence and

checking the stun setting was as easy as slipping into Guy's memories while Demona's guided her feet down the hallways.

The next people she came across had their rifles at half-mast, pressed against the reinforced shoulders of their envirosuits, the barrels pointed at the ground.

She heard them before she saw them. The rustle of nanoleather and thunk of boots. Guy's memories guided the rifle butt to her shoulder and her eye to the scope before she stepped out of hiding and squeezed the trigger.

Two yellow stun pulses, and Hero left the Klaude hunters like she'd left the other one: unconscious.

She wondered how long it would take for someone to find them and raise an alarm. She also wondered why they were wearing envirosuits in a compound sealed against the outside world, but the musings distracted her from her goal and she shoved them aside. Just like she shoved aside the niggle about why the corridors were so empty. There was only energy for one driving thought now, one goal. If she didn't find the jwak soon, the air coming out of her lungs would freeze.

Hero paused at a junction between corridors. She closed her eyes and slumped against the wall, the rifle slipping from her hands, the intricate wall carvings pressing into her cheek. Just a brief stop, a tiny rest before she shambled down the next hallway and made the final push to the tech labs.

The dull, serrated edges of the wall carvings cutting into her face brought her awake before she joined the rifle on the floor.

Her teeth chattered, but Hero wrapped her arms around her middle and forged on. She needed to find the jwak or her bracer, needed the power running through her veins before her knees became too stiff and her feet too heavy to move.

A shudder worked its way up from Hero's belly, gripping her insides and shaking her bones. A thin, high-pitched whine rang in her ears and for a moment she didn't know what it was, couldn't think beyond the spasms wracking her torso.

The sound was coming from her own throat, ripping apart her vocal cords like the pain was ripping through her bones.

Hero hit the floor, knees cracking against the surface.

Desperate, she reached for something, anything to take away the pain. She found the door pad, the plasglas warm and slick under her palm.

A beep. The sharp *snap* of a door membrane opening. Beyond, workstations and hover stools, the familiar glow of holoscreens and the metallic, oily scent of broken tech.

Pain and cold formed a haze over her vision, slowed her down, made it possible to concentrate only in the space between convulsions. It took several precious heartbeats for her brain to catch up with her eyes.

A tech lab. Elation helped her to push to her feet and stagger to the nearest station. A cramp caught her in the gut halfway there and only a desperate lunge, grabbing onto a stool with both hands, prevented her knees from hitting the floor again. It tried to scoot out from under her, but Hero held on tight, the muscle-ripping spasms clamping her arms around the seat, helping her to hold on as the stool bounced and jiggled.

She fought another shudder and when it let up she surveyed the lab. It looked abandoned. Screens flickered above workstations with tests flashing completion, a half-eaten sandwich teetered on the edge of a bench, and there, beside a strange concoction of biogel and plasform in the shape of a helmet, was the jwak.

Clutching the stool to her chest like a lifebuoy, she pushed her way around the workstations, kicking off the floor and lab tables like rocks in a stream.

The stun stick sat in a cradle on one of the smaller stations, the display above it a mess of graphs, pie charts and an exploded holo of its innards, but she focused only on the stick itself. It gleamed, whole and untouched, and she pushed herself faster, leaden feet slipping and sliding against the floor. Hero abandoned the stool and lurched the last step, sprawling across the station's glossy white surface, arms reaching and fingers grasping.

Her hand closed over it.

Bliss.

The sensors on her scalp warmed first, sweeping across her skull, loosening her skin, unfreezing her lips, and lessening the gnawing ache in her bones. For the first time in days, Hero was warm and she sagged, resting against the wall. Relief hit her between the eyes, the muscles in her neck unclenched, and her tendons turned to the constancy of biogel.

Her eyes drifted shut.

She didn't remember sliding to the floor, didn't care how long she lay there with the jwak clasped to her belly. She was warm, and it was glorious, right up until the moment it ended.

It was the bite of the floor and its echo in her bones that dragged her out of her languor. She blinked and shook the stun stick, like that would loosen an additional terajoule from the power cells.

She stared at it for a second, a frown creasing her brow. It should have had more juice than that, should have chased the last vestiges of cold from her bones, unless... unless she'd expended more energy than the jwak could provide. Cold struck her in the belly. Sharp and sudden, it was not the chill of her telepathy but fear.

Hero clambered to her feet, fear shooting through her veins. No. It wasn't possible; if that happened, if the jwak was no longer enough...

A sob escaped her throat, a raw ugly sound ripped from her heart. The memory of being torn apart by the elders made her desperate, lowered a haze of remembered fear and pain over her thoughts. Hero tore through the screens above the workstation until she found the charging cradle's controls. She wouldn't let it happen, wouldn't let d'Ojon get his flippers on her ever again.

Jacking the cradle's power setting all the way into the red, Hero jammed the jwak into the biogel. Fire ran through her veins, singeing her nerve endings. The sensors amid her hair blazed like blue-white stars and she thought that the half-finished helmet blazed with them. In the half-second before the station blared, flashing warnings in red, she was incandescent. Hero was aware of *everything*. Sternards resting in their stables. Jørgens jolting with surprise as her mind swept theirs. Norah's attention whipping toward her. Smit stalking the corridors like an angry 'pard. Klaude hunters dreaming in strange fits and starts, their thoughts chaotic and pained. And there, just before the station shut down, something hard and calculating tick-ticking along with the power in her veins.

Hero's eyes snapped open.

The station was dark, although the screens above the others still danced with light. She jerked the jwak out of the cradle and stepped back from the dead station, knees no longer shaking with cold but the power that ran through them.

'I know you're there.' Her words echoed in the lab, rough and halting, vocal cords still strained from the cold. They faded, leaving only the soft hush of her breath and the hum of the stations behind.

'Librarian!' Hero screamed.

A screen above the central station flickered and then the AI's disembodied head swivelled to meet her gaze.

'Hero Regan, you appear to be experiencing some distress.' The AI's words were bland and unemotional. 'Unfortunately, there are no personnel available to assist you.'

A shudder that had nothing to do with the temperature and everything to do with the chaos twisting through the hunters' minds rippled through her, leaving something she didn't want to name in its wake.

'What'd you do?' she said. 'Where is everyone?'

The Librarian's holo zoomed out, its torso hovering over the station. 'I am doing as I was programmed, Hero Regan.'

Dread filled her stomach. 'You're the Librarian, you're meant to look after the planetary nets, not...' Frustration mixed with dread in her gut and she threw her arms wide. 'This!'

'My data core has sufficient capacity to fulfil both functions.'

'But Ayumon's gone and Woolsey had been dead for over a

century. You don't have to keep trying to execute her programming.' Hero slammed her fists on the workbench. 'Nobody wants to be a Jørgen.'

'Have you asked them, Hero Regan?'

'What?'

'Have you asked anyone if they wish to be like you?'

Hero frowned. 'What's that got to do with anything?'

The Librarian's image zoomed in close, so that its oversized nose was an arm's length from hers. 'Very little,' it said. 'But I wish to record your response for posterity and find myself curious that you assume people would resent being Jørgen. Do you not enjoy the ability to breathe the planet's air, to sense the psyches of others? Indeed, does not this ability afford you a deeper connection with your companion?'

'I...' Hero stepped back from the bench, the weird mix of anger and fear that had driven her to pound the bench stumbling in the face of another emotion. It swept through her to leave a hollow pace in her chest. It pushed out everything else, and for a single moment Hero's only thought was 'Yes.'

She scowled. 'That's not the point.'

'Is it not, Hero Regan?' The AI resumed its place, its torso hovering over the white bench. 'You destroyed Ayumon because you did not wish for others to have their choices denied them. Does your assumption that no other human would wish to be Jørgen not deny them that choice?'

'So, you're going to load up a hypostick with Woolsey's virus and let everyone decide whether you jab them with it?'

'No, Hero Regan.' Screens replaced the Librarian. A forest of security holos crowded the bench. People in grey and white uniforms, some in lab coats, others wearing heavy boots with stunners strapped to their belts, all of them were laying on beds or sprawled out on floors. Some twisted and turned, their legs and arms tying into knots; others were still except for small twitches and contortions of face and hands. Even more didn't move at all.

Fingers trembling, Hero touched one of the screens. It expanded until it swallowed the others and the milky eyes and grey skin of a corpse stared back at her.

She wasn't sure if it was horror or the return of the ice in her bones that sucked the remaining heat from her. All she knew was that her lips were frozen and not even the power still humming under her skin could hope to warm the hole that opened in her stomach.

'He's dead.' The words barely made it past her lips.

'Indeed. Unfortunately, he, like several others, did not respond favourably to the Regan virus.'

Hero's cheeks paled, the blood leaving every one of her extremities as the phrase 'Regan virus' played and replayed in her ears. There was only one possible reason for there to be a virus with her name, only one thing special enough about her family for someone to want to infect an entire outpost.

'You recreated Woolsey's Jørgen virus,' she whispered.

'I have. The virus is most virulent when the subject has already suffered Pollen exposure. Your earlier infiltration of the outpost with the Jørans provided an excellent opportunity to test the current iteration.'

'But... how?' She meant to ask how the AI had acquired the resources to construct something so dangerous, but she already knew. *She* had given the Librarian everything it needed last year when she'd hacked the Farm in her attempt to erase Fink's kill warrant. The words never passed her lips and the vid with the dead man began to wind backward.

The man rose from the floor and flashed around the storage room until the vid paused and played forward at an accelerated speed. He pounded on the door, took the door pad apart, and yelled at the ceiling. The vid paused again, and it seemed as if he looked directly at her, letting her take in the sweat sheening his face and the way his pupils dilated, eating the otherwise hazel of his eyes. The vid fast-forwarded and there he was on the ground, amid scattered boxes and supplies, twisting and turning, his hands clutching his head and his face red with blood streaming from his nose, his mouth open in a—

Sound flooded the lab, a piercing scream.

Hero smashed hands over her ears, but still the sound went on and on and on. 'Stop!'

It stopped.

Slowly, Hero peeled her hands from her ears.

The man was frozen on the screen, back arched and mouth still open as he tried to escape the agony.

She trembled, her heart pounding and her breath coming short. Tearing her gaze from the screen, she saw all the others, body after body trapping her in a forest of death and agony.

'Why are you showing me this?'

'To distract you, Hero Regan.'

Her gaze snapped toward the door even as she swept her telepathy outward, stretching and stretching until... there. Norah's lavender shields clashed with Hero's. Beyond her and partially hidden behind the strength of her defences, the sharp spice and lemon of other Jørgens.

'Goodbye, Hero Regan.' The lab went dark.

She ran, hurriedly jamming the helmet on. Her bones vibrated with the power from the charging cradle, her pursuers ringing clear in her mind, but she didn't turn. She couldn't stop to confront them.

From the back of her consciousness Demona rose, the remnant's memories guiding her feet through the wide alien hallways. There were no signs, no helpful holos to tell her where she was going. If not for Demona's recollections of the wall carvings and the subtle variations in the hand-sized patterns at each junction, she'd have been lost. Instead, she pounded around another corner and skidded to a halt in a shallow alcove, unfazed by the flat, unadorned expanse of wall before her. She pressed her hand to the plate attached to the adjacent wall.

As tall and broad as the corridor behind her, the wall in front of her became translucent. In the split second before it snapped into the floor, what had looked like stone became as thin and delicate as the skin under a linch-adder's wings.

She dashed through, already picturing the shuttle's start-up sequence. And then she stopped.

In Demona's memories there'd been a trio of shuttles taking up the cavernous space, ready to lift through the tunnel in the hanger's roof. Now there was a giant rectangular tent, big enough to house a shuttle. An airlock, like a half-finished skeleton, barred the entrance to the tent, the cycling door in place but the walls forgotten.

Hero stepped around it and pushed aside the thick nano-plastic that served as a door. It flopped shut behind her. The air smelled different inside the tent, damp and earthy like the moments before a rainstorm. There was a sound too, the trickle of water echoing from somewhere far below.

The edges of the hole were strewn with dirt, rubble, and the corpses of akeel-like creatures with thick grey bodies and giant heads. Drones directed powerful beams of light into the hole, but not even their sun-like intensity could alleviate the darkness. It only served to highlight the grooves in the stone, bore holes as thick as her leg marked by teeth and claws.

Carefully, tiptoeing around the shiny grey corpses of the beached creatures, she approached the pit and peered over the edge.

The darkness might have gone on forever if not for the light glinting off the water. Too far down for detail, the ripples seemed almost a mirage, playing on the edges of her vision just like the blue presence of the swatai hiding below played on the edges of her perception.

She swallowed and scrambled backward.

'Girl.'

She jumped, spinning around with her heart in her throat. Smit stood outside the tent, her short, round form encased in a black envirosuit, a hypostick shining yellow in the pouch attached to her waist.

The deep blue presence moved behind her, rising from the darkness at the bottom of the pit. Fear slithered through her blood along with the hard calculation rising with the swatai.

'Run,' she said.

A frown creased the old hunter's face and the woman's hand fell to the pistol at her side, even as her gaze fell to the pit, but she didn't move.

'What's coming, girl?'

'Just run,' she said, even though she already knew it was too late, could tell by the blue-black chill creeping up her brainstem, the glassy fingers reaching for Smit.

Smit didn't move, so Hero did the only thing she could. She threw herself mentally at the older woman, readying a hasty sphere of command and—

Thank you, little fish. D'Ojon shimmered, a swirl of cold earthiness next to her ear. He slipped past her, riding the thread of her connection all the way past Smit's shields, the other elders ghostly passengers.

No! Hero tried to stop him, tried to pull away from Smit and obliterate the half-formed command on the tip of her thoughts, but she was frozen. The swatai held her in place, sucking the warmth out of her. They picked up the command and studied it, pulled the sphere – bright with emotion – apart with cautious fingers.

Crude, d'Ojon said, splitting off from the other elders to plunge deeper into Smit.

The old woman staggered, eyes widening behind her faceplate and her golden skin turning ashen as her knees gave out.

Hero sensed Smit's pain as a fire in her skull, tasted the blood as it dribbled over the woman's lip. Gritting her teeth, feeling the cold pull at her bones, Hero poured everything into breaking the swatai's hold. The restless hunger at her core opened, and she didn't hold the chocolate-coloured tendrils back; instead she strengthened them, feeding the fear in her belly to Demona's remnant, adding blue lighting to the tendrils winding their way through the elders' grip.

Paris knocked on the edges of her awareness, urgency in the sharp rap against her shields. She ignored him, like she ignored the ice forming in her marrow, the drum of boots on stone, the screech of a linch-adder, the sound of a familiar voice yelling her name.

There was only room for the hunger and wrapping d'Ojon in blue-laced chocolate. Demona soaked her vision in the colour, making it easier to forget the cold in her bones and when she struck, the elder's scream made her chuckle.

The swatai recoiled and Hero could move again, lunging at d'Ojon with all the glee and savagery in Demona's heart. The elder batted her aside, but not before she ripped him from Smit.

With a wrench that left her on her knees, Hero pulled Demona back. For a heartbeat, the void was still. She gasped for breath, peering through the mental veil to see Norah and two other Jørgens laying Smit on the ground while Emma pushed aside the tent flap.

Stop. She tried to force the word past her lips, but without Demona the cold was burning its way through her veins again. Beyond it, she could sense the other elders, a storm gathering to tear her apart.

Hero braced herself.

The explosion blew her against the side of the tent, the nanoplastic soft and warm against her back. Water spewed from the pit, raining down on her in big, hard drops.

Hero gasped.

The swatai were gone. She fumbled for the jwak, numb fingers scraping over rock and dirt that was turning into rivers of mud, while a shudder worked its way from her core. She imagined she could already feel it pressed to her neck, filling her spine with warmth and the scent of menthol-laced lemon.

Hero's eyes focused. She was on the floor, propped against the nanoplastic tent, and crouched in front of her, fingers below her jaw as she checked for a pulse, was the Jørgen girl.

Hero pushed her away, tumbling the other Jørgen onto her arse.

The girl squeaked, but the surprise didn't slow her reactions any; she had a pistol pointed at Hero's face faster than a linch-adder could hiss.

'Emma?' A thunk and there was Norah, palm pressed to the nanoplastic on the other side of Hero.

'I'm okay,' the girl said.

Norah nodded, but her gaze and her mind were on Hero, not touching but hovering as if readying to land on her with the force of a shuttle. 'What was that?' she asked Hero.

Hero blinked. She could feel the Jørgen girl, Emma, in her brain, there and yet not, the scent of her lingering as if... She didn't know; it felt different and familiar at the same time, filling her with a strength that chased away the cold. It reminded her of being consumed by elders except it, whatever it was, hadn't split her into a million pieces.

'Hero?' Norah said again, even as Emma shifted closer, the pistol dropping to her side.

'Swatai,' Hero croaked.

Norah recoiled like the elders had at Hero's attack, but Emma crab-walked closer.

'What's a swatai?' she asked.

'A Jøran.' Hero leaned forward. 'How'd you do that?'

Emma blinked. 'Do what?'

Hero grabbed the girl's wrist. *This?*

Warmth and power rushed up Hero's arm, just as if it was the jwak in her hand. But it was more too. The menthol-lemon of the girl's consciousness seemed to melt against hers, and the roiling ball deep in Hero's core clicked.

The anvil of Norah's wrath crashed over them, but it was distant, a wave that barely ruffled her consciousness.

I didn't do this, the girl whispered. It was as if she was inside Hero, tingling under her scalp, a part of her and yet not, like the remnants taking up space in the back of her psyche. Every pulse made the girl's innermost shields thinner until it was a semi-transparent layer wavering under Hero's touch.

Hero shoved the girl away, mentally and physically. The girl's borrowed warmth drained from her fingertips with each ragged thump of her heart. She pushed herself to her feet, her back against the wall of the tent for support.

Emma looked at her, surprise and something like wonder lighting up her face.

There was a yell and the scramble of boots. Norah slammed her hands against the tent as the other two Jørgens dashed forward, but they were far away and not strong enough if she wanted to add Emma to the remnants at the back of her mind.

'No,' Hero said. 'I won't do that again.'

'Why not? That was amazing.' Emma stood close enough that Hero forced her leaden feet sideways. 'Norah told us you could take over other people's minds, but that didn't feel like how she described it, like a vice.' She stepped closer again, pinning Hero with her gaze. 'I knew everything you did, felt everything. Like those shadows in the back of your psyche, how they got there. That you're afraid of doing it again.'

'Stay back, Emma.' Norah pressed against the tent as if she could melt through its thick transparent surface. 'She's killed people.'

Emma shook her head, even as the other two Jørgens burst into the tent. 'This wasn't like that. That was anger, an attack. This was something else, a sharing.' She leaned closer with every word until she was near enough to kiss. Hero tried to scoot sideways, but there was an intensity in the girl's gaze that locked her in place. 'That was power. I want to do it again.'

Hands yanked Emma back.

Hero's stasis broke, and she lurched out of reach, frantically scanning the ground for the jwak.

One of the Jørgens had Emma under the arms, holding her back as the other, the short one who'd rushed her during the raid, unholstered his pistol. 'You're not getting away this time, Regan.'

There, at his feet, the jwak, its power light flashing orange.

Emma's energy was still humming through Hero's system, not enough to take on four telepaths, not if she wanted to walk out of there. Her gaze flicked to the pistol, noting the tremble in the barrel as she summoned Guy.

She dived. The pistol went off over her, but she had her hands on the jwak, her thumb sliding into the groove embedded in the grip, and she was up and swinging, the stun stick now a staff spinning in her hands.

The short one went down first, howling when she whacked him behind the knee. Emma wrenched herself out of the other's grip a moment before Hero whacked him in the temple. He collapsed without a sound.

Emma had her hands up and was backing away, but her eyes weren't on Hero; they were focused over her shoulder, at something beyond the tent.

Norah.

Hero spun, eyes locking on the pistol in her best friend's hands, her finger on the trigger. Guy whispered that, unlike the boy, Norah knew how to use it, while Demona offered the memory of sizzled flesh and the burning pain of being shot.

A sharp zap and a bright flash seared her senses. Norah's eyes rolled up, and she crumpled.

Smit lay propped up on her elbow, pistol extended in her other hand. Behind her faceplate, confusion and anger creased her dark age-lined face in equal measure.

'I don't know what you've done to me, girl.' Anger blazed in her eyes, turning the dark brown a seething shade of black. Behind them, Hero could almost see the sticky tendrils of the command she'd thrust at Smit. 'But I will help you get out of here, and then I'll hunt you down and bring you back. Now run, girl.' Smit's aim shifted with her eyes, fixing over Hero's shoulder on Emma. 'Before this one gets any ideas.'

CHAPTER 16

Hero ran as fast and as far as her legs would take her, Demona's memories once again guiding her feet. The strength she'd gained from Emma faded quickly, and by the time she found an airlock, shivers gripped her ribs and the jwak had run dry. Still, she kept moving, out into the chill night, her breath frosting on the air as she pushed her tired body further.

How long had the Klaude held her? The stolen helmet was no help; its chronometer had been reset by the power surge when she jammed the jwak in the charging cradle. Without it, or her bracer, it was impossible to know how long she'd been under the mountain, almost as impossible as finding her way to the Farm on foot, with no map and no provisions.

She slipped and slid down a rocky gully, dry scrub leaving prickles in her pants and trailing lines of damp down her boots. Above, standing as a silent sentinel atop the gully's steep sides, grew the forest with its enormous branches crisscrossing overhead like skybridges.

Gradually the terrain sloped upward, the snap of old twigs and hard stone turning to the crunch of leaf litter and the stiff bristles of tree ferns. She slipped a dozen times, tiny rocks biting into her palms and cutting into her knees, but the pain warmed her skin.

The ferns grew bigger and the leaf litter deeper as the forest loomed. She scrambled the last hundred metres on all fours, scurrying into the shelter of the forest. The fan-like fronds of giant ferns swallowed her to the waist and when she sank to the ground, her knees shaking and her eyes begging to close, they consumed her completely.

Hero leaned against the tree at her back. The view upward made her feel like an ant at the base of a skytower. She breathed hard, shivering as her heart slowed and the nanoskin evaporated the sweat from her back. Now that she had stopped moving, only the uncomfortable gurgle of her stomach kept her eyes open.

She needed to get up, to get moving. Her only hope of evading the Klaude was to get to the tunnels.

The loud growl of her stomach woke her from a doze. The brief moment of slumber fired up her muscles, and she scrambled to her feet before fatigue could ambush her a second time.

It was lighter than it should have been, the air warmer, and a stab of fear pierced Hero as she wondered how long she'd been asleep and how close the Klaude were.

A twig snapped. Hero's heart stopped. She recognised the outline of a 'pard among the foliage.

Fink stepped out of the shadows.

'Fink.' The happy warmth bubbling up inside made her voice come out as a squeak.

The 'pard didn't say anything until he stood before her, his ears set sideways and his thoughts an angry rumble.

She hugged her chest to stop the giddy, effervescent bubble of joy from bursting out of her ribcage just as much as she did it to stop herself from throwing her arms around his neck.

'What are you doing here?'

Fink shared a memory of tracking her scent through the forest, her path a highway of broken branches and trampled grass. *And then he saw them take her under the mountain, so he waited.*

'What if I hadn't come out?'

Fink's ears twitched like he was fighting the urge to lay them back, and he fought off a whine in the back of his throat. He hid it, slamming his shields down, but Hero heard it anyway: a thin, pained sound swamped with fear and uncertainty.

It had churned in his stomach for the night and day she'd been in the alien compound, twisting him in knots. He hadn't even thought about running back to the pack, although they'd been there, pacing at the edges of his consciousness. Deep down, buried beneath his desire to be part of a pack made of teeth and fur, he'd known—

The thought cut off, hidden behind a wall of anger born out of confusion. Fink shoved her out.

He was taking her back. He lowered his forequarters to the ground.

The tiredness was gone, but it faltered as the cool, earthy damp of the pack den filled her nose at the word 'back'. She took a deep breath and tried to steel herself against the possibility of Fink walking away and leaving her alone.

'No,' she said. 'The Farm. That's where we're going.'

Fink snorted and rose. *No.*

Her heart clenched, and she hugged her chest tighter. 'Yes.'

Her voice cracked. She cleared her throat and continued. 'I get to the Farm, I fix your kill warrant, and then we can go home.'

Fink stared at her, his black gaze piercing. *Promise*, he said. The thought was loaded. Images of the pack, the musty scent of fur and the snick of claws were bottled up beneath its skin. Impressions of 'home'.

Hero broke the stare first, leaving his thought untouched and holding her own memories of skytowers and the warm, buttery scent of Chef's cooking tight behind her shields.

'Promise,' she said.

CHAPTER 17

The wind rushed past her helmet, splattering bugs across her visor. Hero hunched low over Fink's neck, the plain stretching all around them. The forest was a dark smudge on the horizon behind them, the mountains looming beyond. The dark line of another forest spread across the horizon ahead, the trees smaller with bushy canopies and branches that extended wide, while the shadow of Cumulus City's outermost 'burbs loomed above, hazy discs in the gaps between clouds.

Fink's hearts pounded, his breathing harsh but steady as he ate the distance, gliding through long grass turned a rich yellow-green under the midday sun. It swished against her boots, a tiny vibration that started in her feet and thrummed up her spine, making the back of her neck twitch.

They had to hurry. Silently, Hero urged Fink on.

His answering snarl vibrated through her, but he stretched his legs further, paws pounding faster. Soil churned beneath his claws; the damp, sweet scent flung into her nose. It mixed with the smell of copper and the bitter tang of nerves, the sense of something wrong making her muscles clench.

She cast another glance behind them and saw only the darker shadows of trampled grass that marked their passage, but her skin still itched. She remained hunched over Fink's neck, unable to straighten despite the readouts spread across her visor, the scanners as empty as the air behind her. Unable to escape the sense that something was watching them, following and waiting for her to pop upright in the saddle.

Fink grunted, lurching forward as he stumbled. Hero lurched with him, heart freezing in her chest. For a dizzying moment, she stared down at the ground.

He righted himself, slowed then stopped, his sides heaving. He panted loudly, and she let herself slump over his shoulders, her face in his ruff. It was coarser now than it had been a year ago, just like his chest was broader, the muscles in his forelegs thicker, and the distance between his jowls wider.

Hero breathed in the smell of him, dusty and sweet, a spicy scent that was all Fink, and let her heart calm in time with his.

Fink needed the break, she told herself. They'd been moving since the morning before, only taking time to sleep and eat before rising again. Still, she couldn't stop, not with the way her scalp crawled, a million ants marching under her hair.

The few hours of sleep and the grubs Fink had sniffed out had restored some of her energy, but the cold still lingered in her bones. She ignored it though, the sense of being watched driving her to stretch her telepathy, spreading it in a thin wave all around. There was Fink, mawberry-flavoured and sweet, then there were the floating pinpricks of countless tiny critters – flying and buzzing with single-minded intensity – and the soft, larger fuzz of an ersia digging in the dirt, ears tuned to the tiny scrape and shuffle of the grubs beneath the surface. But of anything larger, anything with the cold, earthy scent of a qwan or the sharper taste of a rucnart, there was nothing.

The itch wrinkling the back of her neck sank into the spot between her shoulders and tightened.

Hero nudged Fink with her heels. 'We have to keep moving.' Her voice was a whisper swallowed by the wind.

He snarled, swinging around just enough for Hero to appreciate the curl of his lip and the gleam of his fangs.

She nudged him again, harder. 'Now. There's something following us.'

There was nothing out there. He shook his shoulders, rattling her seat so that she had to grab his ruff to stop from sliding off. *He needed a break.*

'When we get to the trees.'

No. He shook his shoulders again, harder this time. *Now.*

'Fink—'

The sound started in his chest, a hum she felt between her knees before it slipped out his throat, sharp and bloody to match the fangs that snapped at her boot.

Shock held Hero still.

Fink didn't move, bent in on himself, bringing his teeth within a centimetre of her toe.

Hero slipped off silently. Without looking behind, she marched deeper into the plain.

The grasses that had brushed her toes now played with her elbows. The thick stems caught at her feet and pushed against her legs, while the ground was soft under her boots.

She didn't think about Fink. The shock was still with her, like a comforting blanket against the memory of his snarl and the way his lips had wrinkled around his teeth. She clung to it, her attention on the growing outline of the trees on the horizon, the buzz of the insects and the sweet grassy smell that rose with every step. Anything to keep the prickling of tears behind the curtain of nothingness. But the harder she tried, the more it shredded in her grip and her breath hitched in her throat.

Grass sighed behind her and she jumped at a warm puff of breath on her neck.

He was sorry. Fink's words echoed, soft and mawberry-pink, but they couldn't hide the sour thread of the snarl that sat in his chest.

Hero kept walking. *No, you're not*, she thought back.

The snarl rattled his chest. *He was.*

Her shoulders hunched against the awful, tight feeling in her chest and she didn't answer.

The snarl trailed off into an angry rumble. *She lied to him.* The whispered words were weighed with hurt. *About going home.*

Hero spun, forcing Fink to slam to a halt. 'So you snarled at me?'

His ears went back, the rounded tips lost in his ruff. *He said he was sorry.* But another emotion whispered behind the apology, confusion and fear wrapped in resentment. He tried to hide it, but it crept out from behind his shields and raked its nails over Hero.

'You didn't mean it.' She threw his apology back at him, replaying not the words but the bitter note of resentment. 'When did you start lying?'

Fink's lip twisted until she could see the points of his fangs. *He didn't lie, he just didn't want to do this. They should be back at the den with the pack.*

'Apani threw me out, Fink. I *can't* go back.'

They just had to go back. It would be fine.

'No, Fink, it won't.' She grabbed his muzzle in both hands, splayed fingers barely covering the distance between jaw and cheekbone. 'I'm not pack, I don't belong there.'

He nudged her chest. *She belonged with him.*

'Yes.'

And he was pack, so she was pack too.

Hero dropped her hands and stepped back. 'No. It doesn't work like that.'

They would make it work. His ears flattened, and he whined, the thin layer of resentment cracking, the roiling emotions behind it spilling out.

Hero closed her eyes and staggered under the impact. What had been a brief taste was now an ugly tsunami of fear, doubt, and a great wrenching sadness. It slammed into her chest and tried to tear her apart, pulling one half of her toward the pack and the other toward the sense of completion that only came when they were together.

'Fink.' She wanted to cry and wondered how Fink could stand it. Instead, she gripped his face between her hands and rested her forehead against his. 'I don't think you can have both.'

Silence met her words, the hum of scarpa and the endless

swishing of the grass all gone. Only her words and a strange high-pitched whistle were left to ring in her ears.

It was the shadow that tore her away from Fink. The slice of darkness fell from the sky, ripping through the clouds over the mountains behind them, a disc trailing tiny bits of itself in its wake. The whine grew louder as the shadow grew bigger, and without conscious thought Hero flicked her visor on and the bug-splattered screen zoomed in on the object.

Numbers filled her screen before she could process their significance – distance, velocity, casualties. She saw pipes and drones and the black discs of generators big enough to swallow a house. They flickered and sparked, streaming thick black smoke like tattered ribbons. It wasn't until she saw the freight train, hover platforms, and cargo crates breaking apart as they spilled out of its sides that Hero realised what was happening.

One of Cumulus City's outer 'burbs plummeted to the surface.

Rock and dust spewed into the sky, and Hero's breath caught in her throat while her heart beat loud and steady in her ears.

One.

Two.

Three.

The boom was a physical thing, the sound shaking her bones as much as it shook the ground. The grass bent before it, a wave pulling a cloud of dust in its wake. Hero watched it come, her knees locked, her visor picking out the sharp glints of plasglas and steelcrete like stars in the night sky. The coming gale pressed against her cheeks, dirt teased her tongue, and the first rumble of the shock wave rocked under her feet.

Then she was under Fink, fur and claws pinning her to the earth. He shuddered when the maelstrom hit. There was the scent of dirt and the slimy, metallic tang of oil. The howl of the wind filled her ears and pulled at her hair. Hero squeezed her eyes closed and clung to him.

In the space between heartbeats, it was gone.

The silence echoed in Hero's ears, drowning out the rush of her heart and the gust of Fink's breath.

Hero opened her eyes. Fink stared back. The whites of his eyes showed stark against dilated pupils and his nostrils flared to their fullest extension, bathing her in hot, short breaths. Gently, she nudged his mind, checking for the sharp pinch of injury.

He nudged back, and she felt the warm sweep of his regard as he made a return inspection.

She patted his shoulder, and they stood.

Dust filled the air, turning the bright blue midday sky to dusk, the sun an orange glow, fuzzy around the edges. Around them, the plain had been flattened; the grasses that had played with her elbows bent in a thick golden mat that barely reached her knees.

There were new lumps and sharp, angular mounds rising from the grass. Some rose tall and straight, others curved; the broken bits of the city that Hero's visor tagged and sorted while she struggled to catch up. A chunk of Cumulus City had fallen, an entire 'burb crashing to the ground.

Something glimmered in the distance, a dark rectangle that tickled the back of Hero's mind and pulled her forward. The first few steps were a stumble, her feet catching in the heavy mat of grass, but she barely noticed. Whatever it was fluttered against the edge of her perception, slow and weak, while the first stirrings of a dreadful certainty gathered in her chest. Her feet quickened to a brisk stride and then a jog until she was running, her pack thumping on her back and her breath tearing from her throat.

Her visor was locked on the object, picking out details like the rounded forms of hover engines, the glitter and spark of exposed power conduits, and the bloody outline of a hand on crazed plasglas.

Fink rushed past, leaping over the grass in giant bounds, tail buffeting her in his wake. His claws had already made rents in the plasteel by the time she stumbled to a stop, gasping for breath and clutching the stitch in her side.

The hover was barely recognisable; a crumpled black rectangle, the dull grey of the plasteel exposed in the deep gouges and craters that marked its hull. The vehicle was flipped on its side, belly exposed and power conduits leaking biogel onto the ripped earth, the fluid rippling with energy.

It was the flutter of another consciousness that held her attention.

Fink was at the door, hind legs braced in the dirt, fore and midpaws wrapped around the edge of the door. His claws screeched on the plasteel as he tried to peel it back.

Hero didn't wait to see if he would succeed. She scrambled over the hover's front – what had once been a stumpy bonnet now a twisted ladder and almost too hot to touch. The front viewport was a crazed mess, the opaque lines too thick to see through. Jwak held tight in both hands, Hero aimed at the viewport and slipped her thumb into the notch in its grip. The blunt end of the staff exploded through the plasglas. At first the hole was small, but she jerked the staff around, clearing the plasglas to make a bigger opening.

She slipped inside, hands on the viewport's shattered rim to hold herself steady as shards of plasglas dug into her palms. More plasglas rained over her shoulders, pinging off the sides of her helmet, while light spilled through the broken viewport, a spotlight on the man inside.

He lay where the other door should have been, bent at an odd angle against the side of the hover buried in the ground, collapsed in on himself like he'd tried to curl into a ball. Thick lines creased his face and grey had overtaken his thin fuzz of hair. There wasn't much room inside the hover; it was barely big enough for two people to sit in to begin with, but the impact with the ground had made it smaller still, pushing in the sides and sheering the back so all that remained was the cab where the driver sat.

Hero squirmed her way over the passenger's chair, scrunching her legs close to her chest to fit. She wormed about until she crouched next to the man, wedged between the seat and the cracked dashboard.

Outside, Fink's claws still screeched over the doors. Inside, all

Hero could hear was the beating of her heart and the faint, fluttery pulse of the man's thoughts.

He leaned against the side of the cab, and blood streamed from behind his ear and into his collar.

Slowly, she touched his face.

His eyes opened. He stared at her for a moment, confusion twisting his brow and fogging his thoughts, growing fainter as the moments passed. His jaw worked, muscles straining under the skin until his mouth opened. His lips fumbled with words, but no sound came out. Hero leaned closer and wrapped her mind around his. The man's pain washed over her, dull, swallowed by the numbness filling his body. She wound her thoughts deeper, seeking his words so the man wouldn't have to speak. All she saw were fragments, disjointed snatches of the man with his hands deep in the hover's control sphere. The memory evaporated, another taking its place and then another and another. A woman's face; a couch that smelled warm and dusty; a hover pad surrounded by tall crops; small fluffy shapes with feathered ears scurrying through the green; a blue-white wave of electricity arching across his dashboard, and then the stomach-hollowing lurch as the hover plummeted.

Overriding it all was the sharp tang of the man's fear. The emotions swirled from him and into Hero, making it difficult to piece together the man's scattered memories.

For a split second, just as Fink ripped the door from the cab, the man's thoughts coalesced long enough for Hero to grab them. The man's lips moved then slackened; whatever he'd been about to say was lost on a final exhalation of air. His awareness fluttered and faded, leaving her to stare into his vacant eyes.

She jerked backward, the passenger chair's arm stabbing into her back. The ghostly whisper of his thoughts invaded her head, an icy thread made all the colder for his still, slack stare. Fear filled her chest and squeezed her lungs, locking the air out of her throat.

Dead, he was dead.

Something hotter and uglier than fear twisted her stomach.

Before she knew what she was doing, Hero was up and over the passenger seat, pushing Fink out of the way as she burst from the hole he'd opened in the hover's side. Her boots had barely touched the ground before she heaved into the dirt.

Fink nuzzled her side. Sorrow filled his thoughts.

'I felt him die,' she said. The soil transfixed her; the broken stalks of grass churned into the dark loam and torn roots, and the hard, shiny chunks of plasglas scrunched up in her fists. 'He just... faded.'

Fink grunted and nudged her again, harder this time. There was urgency in his touch. *She had to get up.*

She ignored him, held by a numbness that had nothing to do with the ever-present chill in her bones. The man's death... the way he had dissipated. A sharp, tingling sensation followed in the wake of the numbness and a sense of fullness, like she was sucking up what was left of the man. *No. No.* She tried to rip it out.

Pain, piercing and hot, made her yelp.

Fink unclamped his jaws from her shoulder. Urgency permeated the frustrated growl in his throat. *Up*, he thought. An image of Hero climbing onto his back. *They had to go. Now.*

The buzz of drones and the deeper, louder rumble of a shuttle rang in her ears.

A snarl and then a tawny foreleg curled around her waist and yanked her upright.

The shuttle's rumble was drowning out the drone's lesser hum, getting closer and closer. A dark, growling ball of frustration and urgency pressed down on the back of her neck, and then something clicked.

Hero was on Fink's back in seconds, adrenaline eating the last vestige of the dead man. Fink sprang into a gallop, leaving the crumpled hover behind.

They didn't stop until the dusty twilight was far behind them and the wide-flung branches of the plains forest spread above.

Another shuttle flew low overhead. Fink and Hero huddled up against a trunk, trusting the canopy and the scarpa to hide them from sight and sensors. Shuttles and drones crisscrossed the plain, centred over the impact, dark little spots absorbing her attention.

Most had headed directly for the crash site, high enough that the buzz barely registered on her sensors, but one had circled back. The silver shuttle passed over the edges of the plain and forest in tighter and tighter circles, looking for something.

Fink moved out from under the cover of the tree and further from the impact just as a shadow passed overhead and the buzz of an engine filled her ears.

Fink sprinted for the heavier cover closer to the trunks. Before he reached it, her helmet pinged and a small square on her visor fuzzed with an incoming comm.

'Hero.' Timon's voice rang clear through the fuzz, deeper somehow than it had been in the vid. Maybe it was the way it mixed with the shuttle's hum or boomed in the cockpit. 'I saw you on the scanner.' A pause, the downrush of air from the shuttle's engines blasting through the canopy. 'Let me help.'

'What are you doing here?'

'Looking for you.' The shuttle's engines whined. 'I can't keep hovering here. The surveillance drones will notice.' Coordinates popped up on her screen. 'There's a clearing. Meet me there?'

Hero hesitated.

Fink grumbled. *He had a flying thing.*

'It's Timon,' she said to herself, the boy who'd believed in her when no one else had, who'd followed her to the planet's surface even though one breath of its air could kill him. The same boy who'd made sure she got away from the people who'd wanted to lock her up and pump her full of meds, even as he bled all over her hands.

Now his image had started a strange tingling fuzz in her chest, and it was the sudden desire to *see* him, to talk to him in person, that made her hesitate.

'Hero?' Timon was frowning, his gaze on something off the screen. 'Those drones are getting real curious.'

'I—' The words caught in Hero's throat and she coughed before speaking again. 'Is there anyone with you?'

'No,' Timon said. 'It's just me. I even left Phara behind.'

Hero nodded, even though Timon couldn't see it. 'Okay.'

As she cut the intercom, she heard the gusty sigh of relief that rushed past Timon's lips.

They should make him sleep and take the flying thing, Fink said, plucking their destination out of Hero's thoughts before she could direct him with her knees. *Then they could go to the other place and end the hunt. And then home.* He ended the thought with a grunt and a mental nod, 'home' still filled with the scents and sounds of the pack.

Hero said nothing as they trotted through the forest. Underneath Fink's words she sensed the same sadness and confusion that had almost taken her to her knees on the plain.

She didn't think about that, though, because the memory of the dead man in the hover was rising in front of her. She could see the way his fear echoed Fink's. Together they settled in her heart and made it a stone.

The shuttle was already descending when they reached the clearing, creating its own tornado of air. The belly lowered into view, a smooth shiny white, the egg-shaped engines embedded in its underside glowing a brilliant blue. It lowered into the clearing, all sleek lines and swept-back wings, its nose an aero-dynamically rounded point that widened into a short, fat body before tapering into a single, elegant tail.

It landed, its squat little legs unfolding from its belly to sink into the short golden grass. The engines cut off and the blast of air disappeared with one last wave of sticks and dust.

A snug panel in the shuttle's thick body cracked open, its outline glowing blue-white before popping outward to reveal a small door.

Timon stood in the opening, tall and lanky, his dark skin capturing the light in shades of gold and brown and his short black hair drinking it in. An envirosuit encased him from top to toe. Steps unfolded from the shuttle's side, but he didn't use them, jumping to the ground instead.

The fuzz started up in her chest again and she embraced it, shoving away the last remnants of remembered sorrow. Mentally, she swept through the shuttle in the time between heartbeats, bracing against the sharp lance of cold as she extended her power.

Fink rumbled. *He could have scanned the flying thing.*

'But you didn't,' she said, and slipped off his back.

Timon's gaze met hers.

He was taller than she remembered, the top of her head barely reaching his shoulder. She hadn't noticed that in his messages, or how his shoulders were a little wider and his arms a little bigger.

Hero cleared her throat and crossed her arms over the fuzzy sensation trying to crawl its way out of her stomach. 'Hey,' she said.

A smile lit up Timon's face behind the faceplate, the expression dimpling his cheeks. He stepped forward, arms spread wide. For a second Hero thought he might hug her, and her insides, even the jitter in her stomach, froze. Her feet were rooted to the spot as she tried to decide whether she was okay with that, but before she could inch backward, Timon halted.

A frown replaced his smile, and he ducked to look her in the eye, the hand that had been stretched out in a hug reached for her chin. 'Dude,' he said. 'Your lips are blue.'

She jerked her chin away. 'It happens,' she said and backed up a step. Fink's breath tickled the slice of her neck exposed between helmet and coat. 'You wanted to talk.'

'Yeah.' Timon looked at her hand. 'You get the shakes a lot?'

She crossed her arms, tucking her hand under her other arm. 'That's what you wanted to ask?'

'No, but it seems like a good question, considering, you know...' For a second his voice stumbled and his gaze slid away from hers.

He cleared his throat. 'Everything.' The word was heavy with meaning.

She saw scattered images from his mind, projected hard enough Hero would have had to raise her shields to avoid them. An older man who looked like Timon yelling at a newscast, words like 'food shortages' and 'rationing' leaping out at her. A different memory, soaked in something that might have been guilt, this time of a woman with curly white hair. Imogen.

A soft growl rumbled through the air and Fink's tail thumped the grass.

Hero frowned. 'What do you know about *everything*?'

Timon rubbed the back of his head. 'I just *do*, okay?'

The way he said it, looking at her out the corner of his eye, made a horrible certainty settle in her gut.

No. He wouldn't.

Fink's growl deepened, wrapping her in warmth and anger. *He did. Look.*

Look. The thought reverberated until Hero slowly touched Timon's mind. Tybalt jumped out at her, his black brows drawn over dark eyes and a few extra threads of grey peeking out from the hair at his temples.

'She's sick, Timon. Sicker than she's letting on, and you're not helping.' Tybalt's mouth flattened. 'You have to tell us where she is.'

'Look, I already told you, I don't know. And even if I did...' Timon spread his hands, leaving the rest unsaid.

'But you can find out.' Imogen spoke from behind Tybalt, and Timon switched his gaze to the tall, curvy woman with white hair and the black uniform. 'You're helping her raid the outposts.'

'I—'

Imogen raised an eyebrow and crossed her arms over her chest, the holobadge flashing on her wrist.

Panic mixed with a kernel of doubt and lodged in his throat. 'You can't prove it.'

She smiled, white teeth flashing against red lips. 'Are you sure?

Even with Hero's programs to hide your tracks, you're not exactly the girl herself and the Librarian doesn't like you as much as it does me.'

Hero slipped out of Timon's mind. She didn't need to see the rest, disappointment and an anvil that quashed the fuzz in her chest. 'You're working with Imogen.'

He sighed, shoulders slumping and his hands dangling at his sides. 'They're worried about you.'

'Then why aren't they here?'

A lopsided grin tugged at Timon's mouth. 'Well, you're pretty hard to find, and... ahh... you have that habit of putting them to sleep whenever they catch up with you.'

She didn't smile back. 'You think I won't put you to sleep as well?'

'No, I'm pretty sure you will. I'm just hoping you'll listen to me first.'

'I'm not going back. I don't care what Tybalt says or whatever Zass thinks she can do to *fix* me. I've got it handled.'

Fink grumbled at that, but Hero ignored him and hugged her arms tighter to her chest. She refused to think about the jwak's empty batteries or the fatigue nipping at her heels. 'Besides, the kill warrant is still out on Fink. Tell them if they can fix *that,* then I'll come back.'

'I already did. But Hero...' Timon straightened his shoulders, and there was a new tone in his voice, something dark and serious that made her shoulders knot. 'That's not all they want.'

Hero narrowed her eyes. 'What do you mean?'

Timon's hands clenched into fists and he looked away for a second before he spoke. 'You know how I said things were bad in Cumulus City?'

'Yeah.'

'Well, I lied. They're worse. The city AI has been quarantining whole sections of the city and now a 'burb's crashed and—' He broke off, rubbed his mouth and cleared his throat again. 'Look, you just really need to come home.'

'I already said—'

'Yeah, I know, but it only needs to be for a day or two, that's all. You can always put everyone to sleep if you have to. And I *promise*, I'll fly you back myself. Wherever you want.'

He stared down at her and the look in his eyes, the wild hint of fear that widened his pupils and thinned his lips, made the knot between her shoulders turn to ice.

Behind her, Fink's growl stuttered and died.

A chill wrapped around Hero's throat and squeezed. 'What happened? Is Mum okay?'

'Yeah, your mum's fine. I mean, as fine as she can be, what with...' He gestured to his face. 'You know... the complications.' She did know. She could still see the stolen memory of charred, melted flesh. Some of the tension left her shoulders.

'Then what is it?'

'I can't. Just come, okay?'

It would be easy enough to touch Timon's mind again, to riffle through his memory until she found what he was hiding. She wouldn't have to search that hard; it was sitting right behind his eyes, a gentle brush away as if he wanted her to look.

Hero reached out. And stopped. Something held her back, a half-glimpsed thought that restarted the tingle in her chest and made her breath come short with an emotion she didn't want to name.

'Okay,' she said, her voice high and tight. 'Let's go.'

CHAPTER 18

The hum of the shuttle's engines and the rhythmic swish of Fink's tail filled the cockpit, while the setting sun bathed the interior in pale orange light.

Timon was in the pilot's chair, up to his elbows in the holocontrols, manoeuvring control spheres with small, smooth movements of his hands and gentle flicks of his fingers. He hadn't looked at Hero since they'd taken off, and she hadn't asked why he didn't let the shuttle's AI take over flying.

Hero curled up in the other flight chair and fixed her eyes on the canopy below. The broad yellow-green swath of the plains had zipped under the shuttle's thrusters and now they were back in the mountains, the peaks rising around them and the city stretching above. Giant blue-green trees reached for them with equally giant leaves, the dense forest canopy broken by the grey walls of cliffs and the blue-white spray of waterfalls. A burst of brilliant red caught her eye and Hero jerked into a sitting position as a bird, large despite the distance between them, erupted from the canopy. It beat its four huge wings until it caught an updraft and spiralled higher and higher.

'What?' Timon's voice made her jump.

Hero cast him a quick glance and turned back to see the bird now gliding above them.

'Nothing,' she said.

'Yeah, you just came to attention like a 'pard at the sight of cake 'cause of nothing.'

From the corner of her eye she saw Timon take one hand out of the controls and reach for the canopy. A quick flick of his fingers and a holo of the bird sprang up between them. The qwan's red wing feathers shifted with the wind and its bright blue triangular-shaped head, all four eyes open, arched inward as it watched something below.

As it watched them.

A cold, earthy tendril teased the edges of Hero's mind. Stretched out in the belly of the shuttle, Fink's tail stilled and he lifted his muzzle from his paws. His power glided past her, glittering mawberry shields – sweet and sharp, their usual fizz hardened to a shiver – shifting into place over his mind.

Hero reached for the jwak sitting in a charging cradle, eyes never leaving the qwan. Not even the soft buzz of power when she wrapped her palm around the grip could unknot the tension at her nape.

'A qwan.' Timon frowned. 'What's so scary about a qwan?'

'Everything,' she said, eyes glued to the bird while its holo glided in the space between her and Timon. 'Go faster.'

'Dude, it's just a bir—'

Hero glared at him. His mouth snapped closed and his brows rose high on his forehead.

'Okay,' he said. 'Going faster.' The shuttle's engines hummed, the forest canopy a blue-green blur of leaves below them.

The qwan fell behind, the touch of its mind fading with it, but Hero didn't take her hand off the jwak and Fink didn't retract his mental shields.

The holo winked out when the qwan passed from the shuttle's range.

Hero loosened her grip on the stun-stick and leaned back in the flight chair.

They passed over a ridge-line, the trees standing in a sharp spiky line against the sky before falling away in a gentle wave of blue-green. The shuttle didn't follow, but rose higher, climbing toward a snow-capped peak.

'What was that?' Timon asked.

She didn't ask what he meant. 'A qwan.'

There was a beat of silence filled with the hum of the engines before Timon spoke. 'And... ?'

She shifted in her seat. 'They're dangerous.'

'How? We're in a *shuttle*. It's not like they can run us into the side of a mountain or anything.'

'They just are,' she said and turned away.

A sigh came from the other side of the cockpit. 'Don't do that.'

'Do what?'

Timon's stare bored into her back. 'You know what. When are you going to stop keeping secrets? I've earned more than a little trust. In fact, I've earned a whole lot.'

'You're working with Tybalt.'

'So? It's not like I hid him in the shuttle or shot you with a stunner, which, by the way, is exactly what he asked me to do.'

'He did?'

'Yeah,' Timon said. 'Dude, he is desperate.'

She bit her lip. 'What about?'

'Ahh... you? I mean, you're living on the *surface,* Hero. No one's done that since the first-gen colonists, and a heap of them died.'

'I'm a hybrid. I'm immune to the Pollen.'

'So? There are still rucnarts and a buttload of other things that can kill you. I mean, I know you have Fink, but even I'm freaking out about you being down there.'

Hero shifted in the seat. 'I'm fine. I've been fine.'

Fink grunted. A mawberry-flavoured memory of Hero coughing and spluttering on the bank of the river popped into her mind.

Hero frowned, tightening her arms over her chest. 'He didn't mean to,' she said.

'Who didn't mean to what?' Timon said.

She turned back to the canopy. 'Nothing.'

'Dude.' She thought he would say more, but instead he just pressed his lips together and buried his clenched fists in the holo-controls. The frustration on his face made her look away.

Silence stretched between them, settling over her skin and crawling down her spine. She remembered Timon with blood on his chest, sprawled out on the floor just like Fink had been the year before. Except this time, there hadn't been a kidnapper there to drag her away. She'd been there to help, to press her hands to his shoulder and slow the bleeding. And still, with his blood on her hands, Timon had saved *her*.

It wasn't that she didn't trust him, it was just... She drew her knees up and rested her cheek on them.

She didn't trust him, Fink said.

Hero twisted around to glare at the 'pard. *I do.*

He returned her gaze, eyes black and fathomless. *Then why did she lie?*

He doesn't need to know.

Fink snorted, the sound loud enough to draw Timon's gaze.

Timon didn't say anything; the disappointment was in his silence and the way his attention snapped back to the controls. Hero hugged her knees tighter as something very much like guilt bloomed in her chest.

The hum of the engines and the warm glow of the sun sank into her bones until her eyelids grew heavy. When she opened them again, the mountains had fallen away and the patchwork of Cumulus City was sprawled around them.

The metropolis was a dense forest of skytowers sitting amid the patchwork of satellite 'burbs. Its towers thrust spaceward, some a dull grey, others gleaming orange and gold, reflecting the sun. The tallest of them, delicate spindles almost lost against the midnight blue of the coming night, seemed to touch space itself.

The 'burbs made a skirt around the city, a collection of discs – each several kilometres wide – connected by slender threads of plasteel. The skirt was grey closest to the metropolis, turning to green at the edges. Skytowers hundreds of storeys high festooned the inner 'burbs, rivalling the city for height before they faded into the middle 'burbs, where the buildings were smaller. Further out, greenery squeezed between buildings and dotted rooftops, spreading into great swathes of colour, and the buildings became smaller, the spaces between them wider.

The city looked just as she remembered it. It wasn't until they were filing into a long line of traffic, drones strobing bright orange on either side, that she spied the ragged hole in the city's grey-green skirt.

Where there should have been a 'burb, there was just air and the broken ends of cables – thicker than the width of a house – dangling planet-ward from the edges of the surrounding 'burbs, like dull silver vines seeking new roots in the clouds beneath.

Traffic flowed around the hole, crisscrossing in lines, but under and over it was a void. Not even the bright, boxy shapes of the emergency hovers or the flashing darts of their drones encroached on the space where the 'burb should have been. They stuck to the outside of the empty space, forming another ring of orange and red inside the strobing lights of the traffic drones. No 'burb meant no mag-web and nothing to stop a hover from plummeting to the planet's surface.

Hero tried not to think of the man crumpled and bleeding inside his wrecked hover, and how his psyche had fragmented under her touch. But she couldn't shake the memory that had flooded into her from him, of the familiar grey shapes of ersia dashing through a crop.

It was impossible. How in all the world could an ersia find its way into the 'burbs? Except... Her mind skittered back to the scene of ersia disappearing under shuttles at the compound.

The hover passed the hole, skirting around it in lanes congested with traffic like a slow-moving funeral procession. They flew over the other outer 'burbs, separated from each other only by swathes of air and cloud. Hero peered downward, less fascinated by the neat rows of endless crops than by the gentle dip and sway of the 'burb itself. It undulated below them, a mesmerising green wave echoed in the movement of its neighbours. The edges of the city's skirt fluttering in the breeze.

Her throat tightened and a foul churning sensation began in her gut. Hero jerked her gaze upward, clamping a hand to her mouth before the motion sickness could erupt.

'The outer 'burbs do that to you,' Timon said from behind his lapful of holos. 'The farmers reckon it's worse when you're on them. A couple of months ago, the tethers on one of outer 'burbs snapped and a heap of workers refused to set foot on them. They say all the 'burbs are becoming more unstable, but the outer ones are the most dangerous. Now, with one actually falling... It's bad, Hero. Dad's mad because now we have to pay even more for fresh food, and he's not the only one. Mum says it'll settle down soon enough, what with the new biodomes that the cities are building on the surface. But... a chunk of the city just fell out of the sky.'

'Yeah,' she said. She'd been there and seen a man die. She pushed the memory away, concentrating instead on Timon's other words. Two of them prickled at the back of her mind, clicking with other memories, other sights and sounds.

Cold settled into the pit of her gut as she remembered h'Ran's fury and knew, with a dreadful sense of certainty, the cause. 'New biodomes?'

'Yeah.' Timon kept his focus on the screens, frowning just a little as he merged the shuttle with a thick stream of traffic heading into the city. They slid into line behind a line of cargo sleds trailing behind a cone-shaped shuttle. 'The first new domes in two hundred years. There's been a little trouble because of the wildlife and... well... you, but they will start building soon.'

'Why?' The cold squeezed her gut, and Hero couldn't quite keep her voice from sounding strangled.

Puzzlement took over the concern on Timon's face before he turned his attention back to the skylane. 'Why do you think?' With steady hands he guided them around the barge and slipped into another stream of traffic, thinner than the first, heading parallel to the city instead of into it. 'People need to eat and there is a buttload more of them than there were two hundred years ago. Even synth rations need to be made from something.'

Hero didn't say anything to that, but Demona stirred in the back of her mind. Rose-tinted visions played before her eyes, of teeth and claws ripping apart a wombacow, of the akeel-like creatures boring through stone, and drones exploding under a swarm of scarpa.

It all made sense now. The rising anger in the Jørans' minds, the runs on the outposts, the ersia with swarms of scarpa attached to their backs, and the memory of rodents in the dead man's mind. The Jørans had found their way off the planet's surface and into the cities.

Hero bit her lip and hugged her chest, the chill in her gut working its way up her spine.

The shuttle dipped, dropping out of the skylane. The 'burb, a mass of yellow-green trees with leaves turning to orange and red, was smaller than its neighbours. Square buildings peeked out from under the canopy of trees, bright sparks of pink, purple, and blue hinting at gardens and whisper-thin trails of pale gold suggesting paths.

Timon took them lower and lower still, until she could make out individual leaves and the glimmer of windows whizzing past.

'Do you live here?' Hero asked.

Timon snorted. 'I wish.' The shuttle slowed until it hovered above a roof. 'This is where we're meeting Tybalt.'

The shuttle sank into the circle of trees and landed. It was suddenly darker inside the cockpit, with only the light from the holocontrols throwing splashes of blue and yellow across Timon's face and the interior.

Outside, a nearby section of the roof they were sitting on rose upward, a clear tube popping out of the top. Tybalt stood inside, his familiar dark frown firmly in place.

The shuttle controls winked out, and the engines died.

'Just promise me something,' Timon said. 'Hear him out before you knock him out, okay?'

Maybe, was Hero's first response, but she pressed her lips together and kept it to herself. There was an edge of pleading in Timon's words and in the tilt of his brow.

'Okay,' she said and rose from her chair.

Fink twitched his ears, claws screeching on the deck as he stretched and yawned. *He wasn't promising anything.*

The outer hatch popped open and there was Tybalt, framed in the opening with his feet braced and one hand in his pants pocket while the other held his coat closed against the wind.

He looked thinner than the last time she'd seen him. The lines around his eyes were deeper, the creases in his brow darker, the skin a little tighter over his cheekbones, and silver-black stubble covered his jaw.

'Hero,' he said. His voice sounded like gravel, rough and crunchy instead of the smooth, deep tone she remembered.

'What's wrong with your voice?'

Behind Hero, Timon coughed and gave her a nudge. 'Dude, perhaps you can ask these questions once we're off the shuttle?'

From further back, Fink added his own rumble.

'It's okay, Timon,' Tybalt said, and let the hand holding his coat closed fall to the side. The wind caught the material, blowing the sides back and pressing his shirt to the too-sharp outline of his ribs. 'I'm not well, Hero.'

She jumped out of the shuttle. A strange panic was making her breathless, and she was barely aware of the jolt when her feet met the steelcrete or when the wind snatched the warmth from her fingertips. Hero's eyes were fixed on the way Tybalt's pants sagged at his hips, the fine tremble of his hand, and the press of bones under his skin. The panic bloomed into something stronger and took root in her gut.

She met Tybalt's gaze, noting how his skin was pale beneath its usual dusky tan. 'How not well?'

'This would be best discussed inside.' He gestured to the clear tube.

'Come on.' Timon snagged Hero's wrist and tugged her toward the lift.

She snatched it out his grip, the funny tingle in the pit of her stomach displacing some of the worry Tybalt's words put there, but followed him anyway.

The lift wasn't made for 'pards; it was barely big enough for three humans – or two humans and one Jørgen.

'Fink will have to come down separately,' Tybalt said.

The 'pard planted his butt on the roof's dark grey steelcrete and lifted his lip. *No*, he said. *He wasn't twisting himself into a little box. He would stay here.*

'If a security drone sees you...' Hero began.

He would eat it.

'Fink—'

He growled and his tail slashed across the steelcrete. *He was not a kitten. He knew how to hide.*

'In the shuttle, then.'

His lip curled above his teeth before, quick as a linch-adder, he shoved her into the lift.

Timon caught her before she fell on her arse and Hero was still gasping as the transparent doors closed. Neither Timon nor Tybalt said anything, but she could taste their questions hovering in the air.

Hero shrugged out of Timon's grip. The lift descended quickly. She had a second to stare at her face, her angry frown reflected in the lift's steelglas sides, before they passed through the roof and into a light-filled room.

The lift stopped, but the doors didn't open. Instead, the steelglas flashed a bright, transparent blue before filling with static. For a second, Hero thought she saw a robin peering back at her.

Tybalt swore and reached over Hero's shoulder, but before his hand could make contact with the doors, the static cleared and they slid open.

Hero took two huge strides into the room and spun on her heel. 'What was that?'

'A glitch,' Tybalt said. The lift closed behind him. 'They're happening all over the city.' He reached for her shoulder.

Hero jerked backward. 'I'm only here because Timon asked. I can't stay, not until Fink's kill warrant is cancelled. If the Farm catches him—' Hero couldn't say the rest, but she didn't have to; they all knew what a kill warrant meant. She cleared her throat. 'Just tell me what you have to tell me so we can go.'

Tybalt sighed, and somehow the lines on his face deepened.

He looked tired, so tired that even Hero's bones were weary. 'Then we need to wait for Julia.'

Inside was warm, but not warm enough to touch the ice making a home in Hero's marrow. The house was bright, with pale walls, plush carpet and huge windows that captured the vibrant yellow-green of the trees. It was strange being inside. There was no chill breeze tickling her neck, bringing new scents to her nose.

She stood at a window and looked out at a round courtyard, bound on all sides by the sand-coloured house, with a delicate tree and shrubs in the middle. She kept her back to the room with its square-shaped chairs and the little bar with its shiny white top. Timon almost lounged in a chair, his neck stiff, his fingers drumming the armrest.

Tybalt... Hero snuck a look at his reflection in the window. He sat like he always had – with an ankle slung across the other knee, hands resting in his lap – but there was a tiredness in his posture, his shoulders rounded where she remembered them straight. He'd closed his eyes when he'd sat, as if the effort of walking had worn him out.

She stood at the window, pressing her nose to the plasglas. Outside the tree swayed in the wind, its thick yellow-green canopy rattling back and forth and showering the courtyard's pale gold pebbles with red and orange leaves. After so long among the giants on the surface, the tree's smooth branches seemed too thin, the leaves too fragile.

The lift swooshed open.

In the window's reflection, she watched Doctor Zass, short with round hips and a wave of curly brown hair, march in.

Hero spun. 'What's wrong with Tybalt?'

Timon spluttered, water flying from his lips. Tybalt frowned and cleared his throat to speak, but Zass just put the bag she was carrying on the bar before disappearing behind it and cutting him off.

'The same thing that's wrong with a rather significant segment of the population, and the reason the Cumulus AI has placed entire sectors of the city under quarantine.' The doctor pressed her hand to the wall, a section sliding away to reveal a chill box. She reached in and grabbed two bottles.

Hero resisted the urge to tap her foot. 'Which is?'

'Hero,' Tybalt warned.

Zass waved him to silence as she came around the bar. 'It's all right, Tybalt. Hero's being direct. I can appreciate that,' she said as she handed him a bottle and took a seat on the arm of his chair.

The doctor held Hero's gaze, and there was something serious and sad at the same time in it that made the chill in Hero's gut drop ten degrees.

'Tybalt has Pollen poisoning.'

CHAPTER 19

Pollen poisoning. Zass dropped those words like she said them every day, but Hero's ears rang with the sound and her gut cramped like she'd just t-boned a tree.

Zass swiped her thumb across the top of the bottle in her hand and drank.

Timon shifted awkwardly in his chair, and Tybalt met her gaze with his steady black one.

'But...' The word fell off Hero's tongue and died. She couldn't look away from Tybalt.

Pollen poisoning. The first-gen colonists had called it that, before they truly understood what was killing them. How one tiny microbe in the planet's atmosphere was crawling up their noses, through their skin and eyes, and cruising into their brains. Invisible colonists turning the alien invaders into a new home. Too bad that the microbe clashed with Earth-born biology and the two wiped each other out.

She'd never known anyone with Pollen poisoning, but remembered the vids, the neatly dissected holos of brains they'd shown in school. Remembered more vividly the images that Apani had once shoved into her mind.

Questions backed up in her throat, whys and hows packing it solid until she couldn't even swallow.

She squeezed her arms tight across her chest, curling her hands into fists to ease the cold in her fingertips. All she saw was Tybalt, and behind his eyes the Pollen clinging to the dark liquorice of his psyche, a musty rot settling on the back of her tongue.

Hero's knees buckled. She slid down the window until she was sitting on the floor, the carpet warm where the plasglas was cold, and drew her knees to her chest.

Memories of Tybalt assaulted Hero, all the times he'd come looking for her, clad in his thin silver envirosuit, his face covered by a mask. All it would have taken was a scratch, a fall, a single microscopic tear.

Her heart beat hard, hard enough to dislodge the wreckage in her throat. 'Was it because of me?' she said, her voice small.

Tybalt gave her a sad smile. 'No.'

'But...' Hero shook her head. The ersia. The image of the rodents appeared, and she knew, no matter what the others said, that without her, Tybalt wouldn't be sick.

'It's the Klaude.' Patricia Regan stepped out of the shadows. Hero's mum stood tall and straight, the soft light from the windows turning her hair to pale gold and her skin—

Hero scrambled to her feet and looked away. She didn't want to see the scars, the swirling pattern they made over her mum's cheek and down her neck. She didn't want to know how they glistened in the light, or think about how her mum got them.

It was her fault, it was always her fault. Norah was right, she might not have meant to hurt anyone, but she had.

'You *think* it's the Klaude.' Imogen appeared from behind Patricia. Hero peered around her mum to see the agent leaning against the wall, like she'd been standing there forever. 'Whatever else he is, my old partner isn't so idiotic as to infect the people he's trying to save, and my source inside the Klaude hasn't found anything to indicate otherwise.'

'Pollen levels do not spike by themselves, Agent Lambert. Neither are insect colonies able to infest air filtration systems or key food production areas.' Patricia's words were slurred, wet around the edges, but just as strong and confident as Hero remembered. 'At the very least, someone had to get them past biosecurity.'

Tybalt pushed himself out of his chair. 'We don't need to discuss this now.'

'But Hero needs to hear it.' Zass half-rose with him, and Hero didn't miss the way the doctor's hands followed Tybalt's movements, as if he might fall.

'It can wait,' Tybalt said.

Imogen crossed her arms, still leaning against the wall. 'Until before or after the girl takes off again? I, for one, am sick of chasing her all over the planet.'

'I didn't ask you to chase me,' Hero said.

Imogen's smile was all teeth. 'When you decided to break into biodomes and compromise our biosecurity, chasing you became my job.'

'We've discussed this, Agent.' Despite the slur, her mother's voice was clear and hard. 'If you want to accuse my daughter of those breaches, you'll need to go through my lawyers.'

'What?' Hero turned to Timon first, but he just shook his head, shock still making his eyes wide. Tybalt looked tired, resigned, and Zass only had eyes for him.

There were no teeth in Imogen's smile this time, just a pained quirk lifting one side of her mouth. 'Don't worry, Hero. Whatever else you are, you're too caught up in your own sorry story for anyone to consider you the mastermind behind the mass infection of Cumulus City's biosphere.'

'I...' Hero didn't know what to say. The venom in Imogen's voice had stolen her words and settled in her heart, right beside the guilt making a new home in her chest.

She didn't mean to, but she was tired of holding herself in and when her shields slipped she let her telepathy go.

Imogen's mind was the same bright, shiny green. It thrummed, thoughts and images, plans, biodomes, and brief snippets of memory shooting from one synapse to another, almost too fast for Hero to catch. One stuck out, a hurried holocall; the voice on the other end distorted, their face lost in shadow, and a single phrase echoing in Imogen's ears: 'They think Hero's the key.'

A key, not just for the Jørans, but for the Librarian too, happily turning locks in her quest to kill Fink's warrant.

The smile slipped from Imogen's lips and concern, dark and soft, chased the plans from her mind. 'Hero, your lips are blue.'

Zass was suddenly between them – shorter than Imogen but taller than Hero – shoving a glowing ball in Hero's face. 'Just hold still while I—'

Hero slapped the sensor away. 'No tests.'

'Hero—'

'No.' She backed away. No hypo or scanner was ever coming near her ever again.

The Jørans had used her to wage their war on the Klaude, the Librarian had used her to recreate Woolsey's virus, and the Klaude... She didn't know what the Klaude wanted and she didn't much care. She'd been blind, letting others use her, letting them take bits of her and twist them to their own ends.

Timon's fingers brushed her wrist. 'You promised to hear them out, remember?'

She glared down at him, crossing her arms over her chest and trying to rub out the tingle his touch had left in her skin. 'They don't need me. They need an Old Terra damned miracle, and maybe a clue.'

'And just,' Imogen said, her voice dangerously low, 'what is it you think we're clueless about? How to circumvent biosecurity, or maybe how to cripple a city's food supply?'

'I didn't do that,' Hero said, even as she remembered the ersia following her through an airlock, bundles of scarpa attached to their backs. 'I didn't—'

Didn't mean to do that. The memory of Norah's words rang in her head.

'Whether you did or not doesn't matter.' Her mother stepped forward and cupped Hero's cheek before she could react. 'The effect is the same and we can't let you continue—'

Patricia's intention hit Hero a split second before her mum's thumb brushed her ear.

Hero jerked back, almost falling into Timon's lap, and caught the flash of the subdermal embedded in Patricia's palm. Anger swamped the guilt, obliterated the leaden pit in her stomach like it had never been.

'What is it, Mum?' The jwak was in Hero's palm, pumping power through her veins. 'Meds? A stunner? You were just going to get me up here, blame me for everything, and lock me away in my room?'

Imogen was stepping forward. Tybalt too; they were trying to crowd her, to hem her in against the wall. And then, there was Timon. He was up and at her side, trying to push her behind him.

'This wasn't part of the deal,' he said to them.

Hero didn't care what the deal was. Her power flared, and she swallowed them all.

The void was full, but still and silent. A cemetery full of living people.

She'd never sucked that many into her psyche before, never had a non-telepath in the void. They stood in the vast white plain, as still and voiceless as stones, frozen in the moment she'd taken them in. Timon was still trying to push her behind him, her mum and Imogen caught mid-advance, determination written across their faces, with Zass bringing up the rear.

Only Tybalt showed movement, a vibration that made him flex and shimmer. An indefinable something surrounded him, a restlessness Hero had only felt in other telepaths.

A breath and she'd crossed the void, floating nose-to-nose with Tybalt, her feet dangling half a metre off the ground. Was it the Pollen? Were the microbes already building little colonies out of his grey matter, giving him the ability to move in the mental void? Could he speak?

'Tybalt?' Her voice was small and strange, a reedy little thread of hope winding through it.

For just a second, she thought his gaze met hers. Dark, liquorice-flavoured pain ripped through her.

Hero jerked back and found herself on the other side of the void with her heart in her throat and puke-yellow tendrils of fear staining the ground at her feet. She never, ever wanted to experience that again. It hadn't been Tybalt looking at her – there'd been something else behind his eyes, something that looked and tasted like Tybalt but... dead, rotten, a forgotten 'pard kill, just before it began to bloat and split.

And there, in Tybalt's flickering consciousness, floated the ugly thing that had hovered on the edge of Timon's and then Zass's minds. The Pollen had eaten deep into his brain, too deep and too fast to fix. Tybalt was dying.

'You're not allowed to die.' The void swallowed the whisper, but Tybalt's mouth appeared to twist into a sad smile.

'I won't let you,' she said. 'The Librarian...' The memory of the AI's words crystallised in the void, its avatar hovering over the workstation. Patricia, Imogen, and Timon reappeared in a semi-circle around it so they could watch too.

'The virus,' the AI said, its smooth and too-even tones sounding tinny in the void, as if heard through a filter, 'is most virulent when the subject has already suffered Pollen exposure.' And there was the missing piece, which she hadn't thought to ask about because she'd been too busy *not* thinking about it. Hero had helped the Jørans invade the planet-side outposts, but the Librarian had got them into the city.

Doubt stained the ground at her feet as the memory of the Librarian rewound behind her. Its remembered words rang through the void, making her gut clench in doubt. *Have you asked anyone if they wish to be like you?'*

'Do you?' she asked, searching Tybalt's gaze, fear winding through her doubt. 'The virus could save you.'

A 'yes' glimmered in Tybalt's eyes.

Fire burned in Hero's gut, the yellow tendrils drifting away in wisps of smoke. Her eyes caught Tybalt's, and this time she met the pain and rotten stench with clear, glassy determination.

'The Librarian's going to fix you,' she said before turning to her mum and Imogen, a command sphere already forming in her hands. 'And you're going to help.'

She approached her mum first, the sphere growing, the instruction in it simple but powerful. *Obey.* Her mum didn't move, didn't even breathe, but there was a terrible fear behind her eyes that made Hero's determination waver.

Hero set her mouth and lifted the sphere—

A gentle presence and the warm pitter-patter of small paws had confusion lining her brow. She brought her gaze down to the ersia sitting at her mum's feet.

The sphere stuttered in her hands. 'How are you here?'

The ersia chirped, its long-feathered ears quivering before it bounced off into the void. It only went a few metres before it stood on its hind feet and chirped again.

Out beyond the void, something clicked and chittered, a hard metallic hunger that smelled of dust and forgotten places. A memory of hard, shiny shells and long, twitching antenna formed on the edge of the void.

The sphere popped in Hero's hands. She knew that sound. 'Roaches,' she said.

It had seemed like an age in the void but barely a minute had passed in the world. From above, through the house's layers of steelcrete and biogel, echoed Fink's enraged yowl.

She reached out to him, heard the buzz and sting of the scarpa swarming him, before he shook her loose.

A shadow loomed behind her mum, pointy feet and flat, armour-plated belly pressed against the plasglas.

Skiriitch.

The sound pierced her ears, blinded her so that she didn't see the ersia. Its small, soft body whispered past her legs, leaving the soft fuzz to linger in her thoughts. The sharper, colder trace of the swatai focused her gaze as the ersia, with an intelligence not its own, reached for the window controls.

The plasglas dropped, and the roach came with it.

Long, pointed legs covered in hook-like spikes knocked her mum to the floor and pinned her there, serrated mandibles snapping centimetres from her face.

Hero didn't think. She was across the room, the jwak fully extended and the shock reverberating up her arms as she struck the roach's hard shell.

The Fink-sized insect reared back, the spikes on its legs flashing, its hiss sheering through her eardrums like ripped steelcrete. She swung again, ducking flailing legs as both Guy and Demona rose from the depths of her consciousness. The first seeped through her like a relentless mist, laying down fine droplets of knowledge. Demona thundered through her veins, collapsing her knees and twisting her torso so that Hero slid under the insect's belly as if she'd been doing it all her life.

The roach skittered above her. She jerked the jwak back, eyes on the pale crease where the roach's dark, shiny belly armour joined its midleg and—

The scarpa struck before she could. Hero didn't have time to draw a breath; the swarm enveloped her like she'd suddenly developed her own gravity. Bugs the width of her little finger tangled in her hair, sealed her lips, shut her eyes, and blocked her nose with their soft feet. She dashed them from her face with adrenaline-fuelled hands, losing the jwak in her mad attempt to breathe without sucking one into her lungs.

Hero rolled and thrashed, but no matter how she swiped and shook, how many small bodies she swatted, more seemed to come.

She forgot about the roach above her, her mum under its pincers. She forgot everything except the burning in her lungs and the tiny feet on her face, wings fluttering against her nose, the fine buzz creeping through her ears to press on her mind...

Little fish. D'Ojon was a faint thread, his deep blue stretched by distance and strained by concentration, but it still froze her insides. And then she felt it, the faded blue tangled amid the scarpa swarming her face.

And then it was gone, d'Ojon's presence vanishing like the scarpa melting from her face, leaving her lungs free to drag in air and her eyes clear to see the claw crashing down on her belly.

Hero yelled and rolled, scrambling to her knees as the roach twisted in the tiny courtyard, mandibles snapping and tiny, beady black eyes locking onto her.

Its hiss bounced off the walls like a bloodthirsty chainsaw. The perfect golden tree in the courtyard's centre shuddered as the roach crashed into it, the thick edges of its exoskeleton leaving gauges in the soft wood. The insect's pointy feet, as big as Hero's head, left dark rents in the grass, and there, under its back feet, rolled the jwak.

The roach charged.

Hero leaped to the side, but her boots tangled in one of Zass's pretty little shrubs and she fell in the roach's path.

It looked bigger from underneath, crashing toward her, dirt spewing around its feet like dark blood. One metre. Half a metre. Hero curled into a ball.

Crraccck.

Not the piercing pain of a broken bone, but the thick, dry snap of wood.

A yowl, the screech of claws on exoskeleton, the shuddering hiss of the roach. She sensed the dark mawberry of Fink's anger and smelled the musk of his fur. She rolled, scrambling on hands and knees, narrowly avoiding having her kidneys showered as she dashed under the roach.

Hero didn't look back, focusing only on the dull silver gleam of the jwak.

A meaty thunk and a sharp mawberry spike of pain split her side.

Her fingers mere centimetres from the jwak, she glanced behind and saw Fink crumpled at the base of the broken tree, the roach rearing over him, its clear blood oozing from the crack in its shell.

A zap. Light splashed against the roach's shell, intense and biting. It screamed. More bolts followed the first.

Imogen stood over Hero, legs braced and arm outstretched, lightning gathering at the end of the pistol as her finger yanked the trigger.

The roach was turning. Fink was on his feet, scarlet streaks of blood marring his ribs, and still Imogen kept firing. The bolts of light had punched a hole in the insect's side, filling the air with the stench of burning hair, but they weren't enough to stop it.

Guy's memories overlaid her vision, a soft green grid highlighting the creases in the roach's exoskeleton, the joints of its legs and the fissure rushing from the hole in its side to the armoured plate covering the back of its neck.

Hero sucked in a hard breath. There was no time for talk; the roach was lumbering across the tiny war zone, and for her plan to work she needed it facing the other way.

Fink! She threw the plan at him, the thought packet a messy glob of information and memory.

He staggered a little under the impact, but a moment later he was dancing in front of the roach, harassing it with teeth and claws to make it turn.

Hero threw the same packet at Imogen. The agent's knees sagged, her finger slackening on the trigger. There was no time to wait for her to recover; Hero was already racing the few metres across the courtyard, a charge gathering at the end of the jwak, trusting the plan to take root in Imogen's mind before she became roach-kill.

Hero leaped, body-slamming the roach's shell, fingers finding the gaps between its interlocking plates and gripping tight as the beast swung about. Pain sang through her hands and lanced up to her shoulders, but she held on, clambering hand over hand until she was perched atop the roach.

And there, just in stabbing reach, was the fissure in the roach's hard shell. All she needed now—

Lightning cracked, the yellow bolts from Imogen's pistol bombarding the roach's side. Bright veins of light travelled up the fissure, widening and lengthening it with every pulse.

She brought the jwak overhead, hands tingling with the gathered power as a final pulse of light flashed through the fissure. Hero jammed the stick into the crack, activating the telescoping ends in the same breath.

The roach screamed and reared, but Hero didn't let go, not even when the sharp edge of an exploding shell grazed her cheek. She drove the jwak deeper, hitting the skinny joint between head and thorax and unleashing the stick's gathered power.

The blast echoed through the insect's body and threw Hero to the ground.

She blinked, faint tingles from the overpowered stun running up and down her spine. She looked up at the sky through the branches of the golden tree, snapped and bent. Fink's route from the roof was clear in the path of destruction.

A dark brown face capped in darker hair blocked the sky. Concern creased Timon's face as he helped her up. 'You okay?'

Hero blinked again, ears ringing and the aftershock of the stun making her tongue seem thicker than usual. 'Yeah,' she said.

A firm, flame-scarred hand whipped Hero about to face her mum's furious face. 'What did you think you were doing?'

Hero pushed her away. 'Saving you.'

'By jumping on the back of an enraged roach? When you have an agent with a gun and Fink and—'

'And the memories of two Klaude hunters in my head and a weapon I built myself!' Hero's voice rose in a crescendo as glared up at her mum, breathing hard. She continued, her voice level: 'I don't need *you* to protect me. I need you to get out of my way.'

CHAPTER 20

It was strange to not be in her nanoskin, to have air against her legs instead of the stretch and pull of skin-tight fabric. Stranger though to be in a bed and not in her tent, watching insects form a fine black fuzz on the walls.

It wasn't the soft slide of sheets or the way her cheek sank into the pillow that kept her awake. It wasn't even the knowledge of the Librarian and the Jørans like a heavy weight in the back of her mind. It was none of the things that should have been worrying her. It was the two minutes she'd stood just out of sight while Timon argued with an older version of himself. The man's face was projected over Timon's hand from the biocomp embedded in his palm.

'Dad, I'm cool. Stop freaking out.'

'This is about that girl, isn't it?'

For a second, Timon said nothing and then, slowly, 'Dad—'

'You were shot because of her. Your mother and I spent two days in the hospital.' His dad's face twisted, a muscle spasming in his cheek. 'That girl is no good.'

'Dad.'

'Get home. Now.'

There'd been more arguing and more of his dad's hard, acidic words following her back down the hall. Even now, tossing and turning in the too-soft bed in one of Zass's too-quiet bedrooms, she remembered pressing her hands to the wound in Timon's shoulder. How the blood had seeped through her fingers, how warm it had been, and how it had stuck in the crevices of her skin and under her fingernails.

It haunted her dreams, alongside the vision of her mother's charred face and the stench of burnt hair. The two blended together, helped none by Demona and Guy twisting through her dreams and the way Timon's dad had said she was 'no good'.

His voice had been hard and dripped an emotion that made her shrivel up inside. Whatever emotion that had been, some mixture of fear, anger and hate, she never wanted it crawling in her brain.

The sheet wrapped around Hero's legs. She tossed and kicked it loose, tossed again, and clutched the pillow closer to her chest. It wasn't working, Timon's dad's words echoed in her ears.

Hero had never thought anyone could hate her that much.

Was she really no good? She'd never meant for Timon to get shot, never meant for—

Norah's voice played in her memory, her former friend's words drowning out Timon's dad. 'You never mean it, but it still happens. You still hurt people.'

Hero shoved the pillow away and swung her feet over the edge of the bed. She didn't sense the carpet, soft and pillowy against her soles, or the sheets sliding under her thighs. There was just the acidic hollow in her gut, rising through her chest and squeezing her heart with a liquid band of heat.

It wasn't true, it wasn't. She didn't mean to hurt people, didn't set out to destroy their lives or blow things up. *But then,* Norah's voice whispered in her ear, *why did everyone around her bleed?*

No answer came. No whisper broke the silence of the sound-proofed bedroom, the sheets didn't rustle, the ventilation system didn't hum. Norah stayed silent and her two passengers – Demona's blue and Guy's soft green – did not stir.

The silence burrowed under her skin until she couldn't stand it any longer. She shoved herself to her feet, the carpet tickling her soles. The nanoskin hung over the back of a chair. It was cool and comforting in her hands. She thrust her legs into it and then her arms. The familiar tingle as it refitted itself to her body loosened the pressure around her heart, while the weight of her breeches banished the hot, sick feeling in her gut.

But not even the heavy thud of her boots chased away the hollow sensation. It sat in the pit of her stomach, waiting for something.

The jwak shone in the half-light that emanated from the walls. She wrapped her hand around it, tightening her fingers one by one, squeezing the gel grip until her knuckles turned white. Power hummed under her skin, coursing up her arm and raising the hairs on the back of her neck.

Hero closed her eyes. The sensation swelled, the fizz turning to sparks inside her skull. She held them there until she could see the lightning against her eyelids, the scent of scorched ozone filling her nose. Held them until the hollowness was a shadow lost in the play of power. Then, she let them go.

The rush made her gasp. She was aware of everyone. The dark liquorice of Tybalt down the hall, Zass's clear amber, and Imogen's sharp green. But she didn't stop there; not confined to the house, it shot up through steelcrete and the hum of power conduits and out the roof. She felt Fink's start of surprise when she blasted past him, the rumble of worry and the sharp shot of rebuke. But she didn't care. The jwak filled her with power and she rode the wave up and out, further and further.

She didn't perceive herself anymore, not the hollow in her belly or the jwak in her hand. She no longer sensed just the people in the house, but those in the surrounding houses, spread out in a shifting multi-coloured blanket just waiting for her to dip her fingers into their sleeping minds. Back down in Zass's house below, there was Timon, dreaming of riding Phara through a corridor of jeering, mocking faces, and Fink, growling on the edge, anger and fear mixed in a sickly mawberry swirl. And above them, a group of people whizzing closer with the speed that only a hover could give, lavender mixed in with the other scents.

Norah?

The lavender turned toward her, a soft purple searchlight seeking Hero out. Something moved behind it, a half-dozen multi-coloured menthol-laced sparks, glimpsed only for a moment before the full force of Norah's attention blinded her.

Norah pounced, a hard shove that rocked Hero back out of the void.

Hero gasped. She was on her knees. The bedroom shone with the light from the jwak streaming between her fingers, its heat searing her palm. The Klaude were coming.

They had to go, and now.

Hero tried to push herself up, but her legs wouldn't obey. Instead of rising she slumped forward, the jwak shining bright enough to leave spots in her eyes. She blinked them away. Teeth gritted, Hero tried again. Her knees wobbled and her thighs strained, but her hands were glued to the floor and her head was a stone weighing down her neck.

She growled. She didn't have time for this.

Timon was a thought away. Hero slipped into his dreams. Peripherally, she was aware of the jwak glowing between her fingers, not as bright as before. Its power was fading from her skin, but she only needed a little, just enough, to skim under Timon's mental shields and kick him out of sleep.

He woke in a rush, his heart was beating hard and there was sweat on his skin as he looked wildly around the empty room. She felt the frown pull his brows together as if they were her own and heard him mutter, 'What was that?'

Hero didn't waste time with words and squashed the niggle of guilt at taking over his will. She planted urgency in Timon and the image of the Klaude rushing toward them.

His feet were on the floor before she slipped back into her own skin.

The jwak glowed gently now, just bright enough to make out the splay of her fingers but too dark to separate them from the shadows. She stared at them nonetheless, her arms wobbling with the effort of not face-planting the carpet.

Power still surged up her arm, less now than before, and her mind still raced but her body sagged, bones and muscles like soggy bread. At least she wasn't cold, she thought as her face drifted closer and closer to the floor.

The door opened and Timon was at her side, helping her up before her forehead made contact. Hero's legs wobbled but held as Timon hoisted her arm across his shoulders.

'Come on,' he said. 'We've gotta go.'

Hero nodded. The gesture took more effort than it should have. *My bag*, she thought to him.

'I got it.' He left her just long enough to cross the room and throw it over his shoulder, but it was still long enough for her knees to sag. Timon caught her. 'Hey, there. Sleep in the shuttle, okay?'

Okay.

Imogen was waiting for them in the living room, strapping a pistol to her thigh, her curls twisted and squished and her uniform hastily pulled on. Behind her stood Tybalt, the shadows under his eyes darker than the day before, and the hollow of his cheeks deeper.

The Klaude are coming, she sent to them all.

'We know.' Tybalt's voice was as tired as his face, but that didn't stop him from crossing the room, tilting up her chin to inspect her face. 'What did you do?'

I'll be fine.

'Your lips are blue.'

Timon jolted as he regained his full senses. 'Blue? But I didn't—'

I'll. Be. Fine.

'We don't have time,' Imogen interrupted them. 'The Klaude will be here any moment.' She shoved them toward the lift. 'Get in. We're going now, whether you've finished arguing or not.' Imogen pressed her fist to the controls.

The doors opened a fraction before the control pad flickered, the outline of a robin appearing under Imogen's hand before the power went out and the house plunged into darkness.

'A blue-out,' Tybalt said.

'A little too convenient,' Imogen shot back.

It's the Librarian.

Even in the dark, with only the faint glow of Imogen's palm-unit for illumination, Hero had no trouble feeling the agent's gaze swing her way. 'How do you know?'

I saw the robin.

Tybalt swore. 'Why would it cause a blue-out?'

'Figure it out later.' A light clicked on, illuminating Zass in the corridor that led to the bedrooms. The doctor's hair cascaded over her shoulders, a spill of shadows against the pale silver of her dressing gown. 'You need to move. I'll meet you at Bayard.'

Zass dug her fingers into a crack in the wall. There was a click and a pop before a section of the living room wall swung inward. 'The service ladder for the lift. Take it all the way down.'

No. 'Fink's on the roof,' Hero croaked.

Zass frowned and shoved a key into Imogen's hand. 'Use this on the second door down the right-hand branch of the corridor. It'll get you into my neighbour's shuttle bay.'

'I'm not leaving Fink,' Hero said, stronger this time.

Zass pushed around Imogen, leaving the other woman to peer down the dark service tunnel. 'We'll take care of him.' She reached into her pocket.

'No—'

Zass's hand whipped out of her pocket and she jammed a hypostick into Hero's neck.

The sharp *shhtick* of the hypo reached her ear a second before a jolt of energy hit her heart. The jwak was snatched from her grip.

The world dimmed a little, as whatever was in the hypo interfered with her telepathy, but she didn't care because the silver jolt was spreading through her veins, digging into her bones and putting the steelcrete back into her legs. Hero pulled away from Timon and her knees held.

'The stimulant will keep you going long enough to find the

shuttle,' Zass said. There was the slap of the jwak meeting someone else's palm. 'You keep this.'

Timon's unease slithered along her spine. 'Ugh—'

'We're wasting time.' Imogen yanked Hero toward the service ladder entrance. 'Down the ladder.'

The stimulant sang through her bones even as it scrambled her telepathy. The ladder's rungs gleamed in the drone's light as it darted past her shoulder.

Reaching for the first rung was automatic, then the second and the third, and before she knew it, Hero was clinging to the side of a narrow shaft, staring up into the dark.

She climbed up. There was a shout from below, but Hero ignored it, just like she shook off the fingers that grasped her ankle. Fink was at the top of the ladder and she wasn't leaving him behind.

The last rung came quickly, the plascrete smooth and cold. The hatch was easy to lift, the latch giving with a sharp click. Hero was halfway out when someone grabbed her leg. She lashed out, her boot connecting with something soft followed by a curse as she scrambled onto the roof.

The night air was cold and half the sky was lit up by the stars, the other half by the glow of city lights. The shuttle they'd arrived in crouched on the roof, a shadow darker than the service shaft.

With the next moment came the rumble of a hover and the blast of its engines as it landed, then its side split open and people carrying pistols poured out. Behind them, another shadow rose, shuttle lights highlighting a tawny muzzle, lips drawn back from white fangs.

Hero burst out of the shadows, crouched low, thudding across the roof behind the group. A man's blue eyes locked on her. She ducked, then sidestepped, to come up under the man's arm and drive the point of her hand into his throat. He gagged. She grabbed him behind the neck, pulling him down as she drove her knee up into his stomach and while he was bent over – winded – rammed her elbow into the back of his head.

He fell.

A sense of movement had her hair prickling on her neck. Hero dropped low, slid sideways and spun in a single, fluid movement. She popped up, already reaching for the hand holding the pistol.

Emma's gaze met Hero's, the shock in it giving way to an excited glitter of awe mixed with desire. The emotion travelled up Hero's arm and hit her in the gut, distracting her for just a heartbeat. A heartbeat was all the Jørgen girl needed.

Emma had her hands wrapped around the back of Hero's neck and had pulled her close, forehead to forehead, before Hero could blink. Even with the stimulant fuzzing her telepathy, the connection was like a hover in the face, an avalanche of lemon that made her stagger even as warmth blazed under her skin, the tight, hungry thing at her core loosening, the edges unfurling like—

Stars burst her vision, but were not bright enough to blot out the incandescent bolt or the *shhit-zik* of a stun pistol and the thump of a 'pard hitting the ground.

The supernovas rattled her brain and left her to float in a single stark moment of nothing. She couldn't feel her body in order to move it. She couldn't see or hear; she could only *be*, could only watch the bright hungry thing inside her stretch a lazy tendril.

Then it was gone.

Hero gasped, air rushing into her lungs. She was on her back and the sparks in her eyes were real – the sharp zip of hovers and the fainter gleam of stars.

A shadow blocked her vision. Emma crouched over her, the shuttle's lights bright against the girl's back, and reached for her again.

Demona surged through Hero's skin, flooding in on her adrenaline and fear, telling her muscles how to tuck and roll, how to spin on hands and knees so that her heel connected with Emma's jaw.

Another shadow cut through the shuttle's lights, shorter and slimmer, a linch-adder standing tall on her shoulder.

'Not this time,' Norah said.

Before Hero could gather herself, a soft purple anvil slammed into the same spot Emma had attached herself not a minute before and found the shields weakened and soft.

Hero staggered. The lead was seeping back into her bones, making her head heavy and her elbows weak, but the fizz interfering with her telepathy was wearing off.

The rooftop no longer sang with crisp detail, but she could sense the hypostick in Norah's grip. And then Imogen's bright green strapple flavour and the weight of the pistol in the agent's hand. With sudden clarity, she knew Imogen wouldn't stop the other girl from sticking the hypo in her chest.

Betrayal cut deep. 'No,' Hero spat from between gritted teeth.

Her arms might have wobbled, but her mind was sharp, and she wrapped strong, sticky tendrils around Norah's and then *pulled*.

Norah staggered, her gaze meeting Hero's, and in one glorious moment they entered Hero's psyche, into the endless void.

Victory surged down Hero's arms, joining the snapping bands of lightning-laced chocolate in her hands.

Fear rose and then fell at Norah's feet, a puke-yellow miasma struggling under the weight of something clear and shiny, a sense of purpose wrapped in a secret that shifted and slid around Norah's knees.

The lightning crackled in Hero's hands, twining about her wrists and stinging her forearms with bolts of chocolate, blue, and green.

'What do you want from me?' Hero said, her voice rolling on thunder.

'We need you.'

'For what? You run out of pincushions?' Her gaze dipped to the mental image of the hypo in the other girl's hand.

Norah took a deep breath. 'There's another Woolsey virus, made with your DNA—'

'I know,' Hero cut her off. 'Isn't that what you want? More Jørgens out there so you're not so much of a freak?'

The puke-yellow fog at Norah's feet faded and the sense of purpose around her knees hardened and took on a force of its own that clawed at the bands holding Norah in place. 'Not like this. This is bad, Hero. People are going to die, lots of people.'

'And you wouldn't want to hurt anyone, would you?' Hero pulled out the memory of the outpost, filling the void with the shuttle hangar. There was Orth rearing above them and h'Ran lying still and lifeless at Norah's feet. 'Unless they don't walk upright, and then you're okay with it.'

The clear weight of purpose wavered, doubt staining it like poison. 'She was just a rucnart.'

A half-thought, and she was standing in front of Norah, the distance between them gone easier than breathing. 'You know better.'

'I—' Despair filled Norah's eyes and spilled over her shoulders like a cloak, dark and heavy enough that her knees began to buckle, until righteousness swept it away. Norah's back stiffened. 'It attacked me. What was I supposed to do? I didn't *mean* to hurt her.'

'Neither did I.' The lightning burned in Hero's bones. 'How does it feel,' she said, 'to be a killer like me?'

'I'm not a killer.' Norah spat, but doubt made the air around her fracture and shiver.

Hero stepped closer. 'H'Ran's dead.'

Norah's mouth twisted, doubt and righteousness fighting each other. 'You helped,' she said.

'No,' Hero said. 'I gave you the power. You did the rest on your own.'

Norah's mouth opened, and Hero could see the lie forming on her lips—

Pain split through Hero's head. The battleground shattered, and her lightning with it. She was on the roof again, the steelcrete cold and gritty against her cheek and the aftershocks of a stun bolt shuddering through her muscles.

Darkness closed in on the edges of her vision, but not before she watched Norah – golden skin turned grey, blood staining her upper lip – stumble backward and Imogen push her into the Klaude shuttle.

CHAPTER 21

Hero woke. There was no gentle segue from dreaming to waking, just the memory of the rooftop and the certainty that she hadn't been sleeping.

There was no rooftop beneath her now, no chill night air to bite her nose. Instead, there was a crick in her neck, drool on her chin, and the soft confines of an overstuffed chair cradling her back. And somewhere distant, a familiar glassy tingle at the back of her mind.

Hero opened her eyes.

Timon stared back.

He sat across from her in the off-white confines of the shuttle's cabin, a tall, lanky shadow in his cream-coloured chair. He was leaning forward, elbows on his knees as he picked at his nails. There was no hum or gentle vibration from the engines. They'd landed. Behind him, through the viewport, light sparkled on the shiny domes of hovers and the white egg-shaped engines of larger shuttles, all lined up in neat rows. As she watched, someone in grey overalls peeled open an engine casing and began tearing it apart.

'Hey,' he said. 'Didn't think you'd sleep that long.'

'I wasn't asleep. Imogen shot me.'

'Yeah, but you were still passed out in that chair like...'

Hero glared at him.

Timon's mouth snapped shut. 'Yeah,' he said. 'Probably not the best time.'

'Where are we?

'Bayard.' He hesitated, shifting like his chair had been coated with itch dust. 'Norah's here,' he said.

Hero pushed herself out of the chair, only staggering a little before her knees steadied. 'Why aren't I locked up in a lab?'

'Cause you're not meant to be here,' Timon said. 'And before you think about it, your mum told the mechanics to overhaul the engines. This shuttle isn't going anywhere.'

'So, they just left us here?'

Timon shrugged. 'Not just us. Fink's up the back and Imogen—'

Hero's gaze swung to the front of the shuttle and the cockpit, reaching mentally. She couldn't help the hiss that escaped her lips at the bright green strapple flavour she found there. She took a step forward.

'Hey.' Timon grabbed her wrist. His thoughts flooded up her arm, a dark orange-brown tingle that snuck under her skin, making gooseflesh in its wake. There was concern, and something else, something hot and hard squashed under a thick layer of control, something that might have been anger, but it wasn't directed at her. 'Don't do anything... rash.' His mouth screwed up as he said it. 'Imogen has her reasons, okay?'

Hero yanked her wrist free. 'No,' she said. 'Not okay.' She stomped toward the cockpit.

'Hero!' Timon yelled behind her.

She slammed the cockpit door closed.

Imogen was in the flight chair, surrounded by screens. The hangar lights caught her white-blond hair, making the close-cropped curls even whiter.

'Norah's important,' the woman said without turning from the swirling lines and numbers before her. 'I need her where she is.'

'You were going to let her 'stick me.'

'And?' Imogen swung around, brown eyes hard. 'Sometimes it's the only way for us to get anything done. Because you don't *listen,* Hero. You're always the most important person in the room, your problems bigger than everyone else's. Has it ever occurred to you that you're *not* the centre of the universe? Or that, Old Terra forbid, someone other than you actually knows what they're doing?'

'Well, if everyone would stop drugging me—'

'Grow up, Hero.' Imogen's voice was hard, carrying a thread of anger and distaste that lashed Hero's ears. 'While you've been running about on your self-righteous quest – stealing and burning – Norah's been helping to save people. Not just her companion, or her fathers or herself, but *people* she's never even met, lots of them. Whatever she may or may not have done, however worse it may be compared to your own many sins, I don't care because she's here, *fixing* things instead of blowing them up.'

Frustration rose in Hero's gut. The thousand tiny cuts left by Imogen's words peeled back her skin until there was only anger, boiling her blood and sparking from her fingers.

'You can't fix it.' The words slid between Hero's teeth, slow and cold. 'Norah can't fix it, or the Klaude or anyone else, because the Jørans don't *want* it fixed, and you all refuse to see them as anything more than animals.'

Imogen twisted around, her mouth open to speak, but Hero cut her off.

'You've seen the compounds under the mountains, the generators. You don't think aliens smart enough to build generators that can keep our cities aloft just up and left, do you? When they already had compounds that were secure against the Pollen? They were *driven* out.'

Imogen didn't scoff, but it was there, caught up in the intrigue and scepticism twisting her brow. 'It can't have been anything native. There's nothing powerful enough on this planet to—'

Hero swallowed Imogen, sucking her into the mental void.

The telltale spikes of cold bloomed in her bones. She'd never consumed power like this before, taking people to the void not once but three times so close together. Numbness gripped her lips and her fingers that not even the warm, comforting pulse of the jwak could dispel.

That didn't stop Hero from reaching out and latching on to the faint, glassy whisper teasing the edge of her awareness. It turned and fluttered across her consciousness, and when she didn't pull away it drifted around her like a slow tide.

The endless nothing of the void was gone and instead they stood on the shore beside the 'pards lake. Imogen was a static, unwavering presence at her side except for the tension shivering in the air, a mirage surrounding her like a heatwave. She hadn't noticed it the last time, but now, as Hero concentrated, she caught the faint echo of a question.

'We're in my head,' she answered. 'Mostly. Watch.'

A form glittered on the water, condensing out of mist and sunlight. Tall and straight, Paris stood on the lake, the midday sun turning his hair to gold, the water rippling under his bare feet. He didn't smile and his eyes lacked their usual mirth.

One moment, Paris was across the lagoon and the next he stood in front of Hero, his form melting away into the dark, mottled red of d'Ojon. She should have had to look down at him, but somehow they were eye-to-eye.

Hello, little fish. More than just the other elders glittered behind the swatai's wide black eyes, something bigger and darker waited there. It was like a galaxy compressed into a single point, but muted and leashed as if waiting for something. *We did not think you would reach for us again, or bring others when you did.*

D'Ojon turned to Imogen, stretching hard and glassy claws of blue toward the agent's chest. *Another specimen for us to study, little fish? A gift to atone for your violence?* An image of a swatai, her down a delicate shade of yellow, curled in a sandy nest, and another crooning over her shaking form.

Hero stepped in front of Imogen, d'Ojon's claws screeching over a shield of chocolate.

'No,' she said.

The claws sharpened, tips gouging chunks out of the chocolate and leaving behind scarlet trails of anger. It was like acid, filling her nose with a sharp vinegar stench even as they burned the edges of her mind.

Then why, little fish?

'Because you're starting a war and they don't even know you exist.'

Maybe not these ones, but other humans do, others who should know better.

A new wave of tension rolled off Imogen, the air pulsing in Hero's eardrums rich with alarm and another question.

Hero looked to d'Ojon, but the elder merely stood there. 'She asked you a question,' Hero said.

D'Ojon blinked. *I cannot hear her, little fish, only you can show us how to do that.* His flipper trailed over Hero's shield. She jerked back, but not before she saw the collected elders lurking behind him. *Soon, little fish, you will take your place in the myriad and the humans will no longer be as stones.*

Hero's skin crawled, and she wanted to run, to push d'Ojon out and slam her shields closed, but she'd come here for a reason: to show Imogen what she couldn't see.

'Imogen doesn't know what war we're talking about.'

The one you will lose, human, as the ancient ones who came before you did. With the words came memories, the edges of the images blurred and steeped in the familiar multi-hued scent of teaching memories that had been handed down generation after generation. They danced across the lake, appearing and disappearing. The giant black and silver ovoids of spaceships descended through the clouds. Creatures, neither human nor Jøran, hollowed out mountains, digging into the earth with hard-shelled machines that purred, growled, and slashed, leaving behind churned soil, scarred rock, and holes in the forest canopy.

The Jørans retreated and gave the newcomers space, but soon they filled it, marching over the Jørans' carefully patrolled borders.

Scarpa colonies that had been tended with great care were destroyed, ersia herds scattered and killed. Then a qwan nesting tree fell, the intricately crafted nests shattering against the ground.

Nanny hens and rucnarts alike picked through the tangled mess of branches and shattered wood as they cradled the bloodied bodies, ears and minds pricked for the wails of any chicks that might still live.

Their desperation hit Hero in the chest, robbing her of breath. Imogen flinched, the lines around her mouth tightening.

We drove them back into the stars when they took more than they were given, d'Ojon said as the Jørans' remembered rage roared in Hero's gut.

The outsiders' shiny machines exploded above the water in bright yellow balls of fire. There were teeth then, and claws, and the bright, hot spurt of blood paired with the strange musty taste of the outsiders' flesh. Bodies littered the outsiders' curving hallways, the delicately carved walls and intricate shadows stained red. Feathered and furred remains of Jøran hunters were littered among the outsiders' densely furred skin.

After the cacophony of memories came silence, a brief moment that wasn't so much a pause as a gathering. The images above the lake faded and in their place amassed an invisible weight. It pressed against Hero's chest, her breath coming shorter and shorter until it no longer came at all.

Imogen appeared unaffected, but Hero's knees buckled and darkness played before her eyes. She knew this weight, recognising the presence of not just the elders but the tribe, and knew it was a shadow of something greater. A mental joining of every swatai tribe on the planet, a myriad that would crush her whole.

On the water, a new image formed. At first, just one swatai and then another stood beside it and another next to that and another, until the lagoon was covered with them. They packed the area to its edges where their shapes fragmented, cut into halves and quarters, hinting at even more swatai beyond where water met sand. There were thousands of them, millions even, but Hero didn't have time to wonder let alone count. A glow rose from the assembled Jørans.

The image changed again and now the outsiders were falling and screaming, their strange webbed hands clutching their heads as fluid leaked from their flat, muzzle-like noses. They fell silent and faded before their giant silver-black ships rose and disappeared into the stars.

And then the memory of the swatai myriad fell away, leaving d'Ojon to stand alone on the water, the dark red of his pelt glistening. Hero swayed, the silence and sudden release enough to make her dizzy.

You do not have stars to go back to. The myriad peeked out from behind d'Ojon's eyes. *Now, you will serve and be made useful or we will rip your minds from your bodies and use your memories as we cannot use his.*

Paris appeared behind d'Ojon, stiff and silent, an apparition that wavered once and then vanished.

Little fish. D'Ojon's mid-arms reached out and the slim digits at their ends caressed her shield like they were caressing her cheek. *We will see you soon.*

The void dissolved.

Hero landed hard on her arse, so cold she didn't have the energy to curl into a ball. Everything shook: her sides, her hands, her teeth. The jwak was dead and useless in her hands.

The swoosh of the door, followed by the frantic rush of boots, and then Timon was there, propping her up.

Imogen stared at them, her face ghostly pale, her dark eyes wide, spine stiff and her knuckles white. 'That was real?'

Hero nodded, her neck stiff and jerky. 'It gets worse,' she said through chattering teeth.

CHAPTER 22

'Actually,' said Zass, her eyes glued to something off the screen, 'from what I can tell, the Librarian will release three viruses in each city, saving the Regan virus for Cumulus City. But I don't see how it intends to deliver them.'

'The ventilation systems.' Imogen vibrated, even though standing perfectly still. She had one arm wrapped around her middle and the other crossed over her chest, a black-uniformed shadow sucking the light out of the shuttle's cabin. 'That's where the highest incidences of infestation have occurred. If the Librarian needs a combination of Pollen exposure and each virus, all it has to do is dump the viruses in each city's central regulator and turn on the fans.'

'But the Librarian is just... well, the Librarian. It catalogues networks and keeps records,' Timon said from the chair next to Hero, leaning forward with elbows on his knees and his hands clasped between.

'It wasn't always the Librarian,' Hero whispered, her eyes heavy. She fought the weight, just like she fought the urge to lie back in the oversized chair and sink into the cushions. 'And it's changed its operating parameters.'

'I didn't think it could do that,' Timon said.

'Woolsey was a geneticist, not a programmer,' Zass said. 'When she gave the Librarian its orders, she may have created a conflict in the original programming.'

'Or she might have done it on purpose,' Hero said, too quietly for anyone but Timon to hear. The more she thought about it, the more the certainty solidified in her gut and filled her with a kind of fascinated horror. Would Woolsey, Hero's ancestor, have known how far the AI could go? Would she have suspected it would sabotage a city? And if she had, would she have stopped it?

Hero had destroyed part of the city to accomplish her own goals; she had stolen and lied and hurt people. A shiver worked its way up her spine at the cold hard realisation that she'd do the same again.

A hand settled on her shoulder, bringing Hero's eyes up from the grey blanket over her legs to Timon's dark gaze. His hand tightened. 'You okay?'

She frowned for a moment, thoughts spinning around the certainty forming in her chest, considering the ruthlessness of it. She swallowed. 'I'm fine.'

'You don't look fine.'

She shrugged his hand off her shoulder, jerking her chin toward the stun-stick glowing in a charging cradle. 'I will be, just give me the jwak—'

'Yeah, no.' Timon stepped back and turned toward the screen. Zass was still staring at something only she could see, a string of scientific jargon falling from her lips. 'Hey, doc? What about Hero?'

Zass swivelled to face them. 'Rest and a nutrient IV. Strap her down if you have to.' She leaned over the screen, her eyes boring into Hero's. 'No telepathy. And I want to know what's happening with those head monitors and the stun-stick.'

Hero tried to sit straighter in the chair, but the soft sides didn't cooperate with her wobbly arms, and she only made it halfway up before flopping back. She glowered instead as Imogen spoke. Zass's attention was already swinging back to the agent.

'We can't risk bringing her to you, not with the Klaude looking for her.'

A hand, lean and pale with strong fingers and square nails, reached over Zass's shoulder to swing the holocam around. Outrage crossed the doctor's face before it slipped from view.

The sad-eyed lines of a man Hero had only met twice, but whose presence made her gut clench, filled the screen. 'Hello, Imogen.'

'Dorich.' Imogen's voice didn't change, didn't let on to the gut-curling tension riding the woman's thoughts. 'What are you doing at Bayard?'

He didn't smile, but something that might have been humour lit his eyes. 'Ms Joshi may be your spy, but you forget that I have my own telepaths.'

Imogen stiffened, her calm facade cracking. 'Where is Norah?'

'I'm here.' The screen expanded and there was Norah, standing behind Dorich with Harish perched on her shoulder. 'And I'm fine.'

'It's time we talked, Imogen. You, me...' Dorich's sad eyes swung toward Hero. 'And you, Ms Regan. We most assuredly need to talk to you.'

The Klaude came to them, a mechanic in a Bayard uniform overriding the hatch controls before Imogen had time to swear. There was another one behind him, also in grey overalls with the Bayard logo on the breast. Hero was pretty sure the matte black pistols they held tight against their legs weren't part of the uniform.

They stood just inside the open airlock, with blank expressions and readiness humming through their bodies. The first one faced off with Imogen. She mirrored his posture, save for the lack of a pistol in her hand. Instead, she put up white-knuckled fists that suited the frustrated adrenaline rolling off her in waves.

The other Klaude had his pistol trained on the cargo door at the back of the shuttle, striding toward the control pad with quick, sure steps. His hand touched the plate, the door lock turning red under his palm even as a low rumbling growl echoed from the other side.

The jwak. Hero planted the image of the stun-stick in Timon's mind.

He stiffened, his gaze darting to the Klaude, their attention still elsewhere, before he reached for the jwak. Then he froze, held captive by a menthol-laced thought.

It was Hero's turn to snarl, the sound ripping out of her throat even as she ripped through the mental bonds holding Timon in place. The Jørgen's telepathy shredded like the paper in her mum's Old Terra books and from outside came a pained cry.

Timon stumbled, catching himself on the edge of the table and knocking the jwak out of the charging cradle. The man staring down Imogen didn't twitch, but the other one shifted with the precision of an automaton, the dark muzzle of his pistol locking onto Hero.

A thump and an enraged yowl echoed through the shuttle as Fink threw himself at the cargo door, while Hero bared her teeth and gathered herself for another strike.

'Hero, stop.' Her mother stood in the airlock. Another form shadowed her, their face obscured by the frame, but the restless prickle of their thoughts warned Hero of a second telepath.

Her mum's eyes flicked to Timon's side before coming to rest on his face. 'Sit down, Timon.' She gestured to where Hero curled in the oversized chair.

He sat, his thigh pressing against Hero's shoulder as he settled on the chair's arm.

'Agent Dorich will be here soon enough.' There was something strange in the way her mum said it, the way her eyes dropped once more to Timon's hand.

Something hard and cylindrical fell down the side of the chair, nestling against her thigh. Hero stiffened, sensing the jwak by the tingle that spread through her skin. Slowly, she wrapped her hand around the grip and inhaled.

Both the telepaths were out cold before her head sensors glowed. The Klaude went next, the man guarding Imogen taken down the moment his eyes left the agent to glance at the light dancing on Hero's forehead.

The whoosh of the cargo door and a snarl were all the warning the other man had before Fink had him pinned to the floor, fangs millimetres from his spine.

Imogen rushed into the cockpit. 'Patricia, tell me you had one of your mechanics fix these engines.'

'I did.' Patricia opened her hand and swiped a finger across the holoscreen hovering over her palm. The cockpit door closed with a decisive click. 'But I have the override.'

Hero just stared at her mum. The cold was fading, too much and too fast, and Hero knew that if she didn't stop, she'd drain the jwak dry before she really needed it. She peeled her fingers from the grip.

'What are you doing?' she said.

'Getting you out of here.' Patricia drew a stubby black object from her pocket. The block hummed for a second before the plasform shifted and a barrel extended out. Another hum and her mother shot the Klaude peering up at her from under Fink's claws. Unconscious, he face-planted the deck.

Fink gave way before Patricia as her mum, calm and poised as Hero had ever seen her, stepped over the man and entered the cargo hold.

'Dude.' Timon caught her surprised gaze with one of his own. He got to his feet, hauling her out of the chair in the same motion. 'Your mum is cool,' he said as he dragged her toward the hold. He stopped on the threshold and Hero ran into his back. 'I take that back,' he said. 'Your mum is awesome.'

A high-pitched *hiss-nee* and he was across the cargo hold before Hero processed the sleek purple hide and long, sinuous tail of the toa-mare crammed in the back.

Behind Hero, Fink grunted. *They loaded the glowy roach magnet just before the men came.* 'They' was a memory of Tybalt's dark-eyed frown, his cheeks drawn and pale, and her mother holding a finger to her lips as she admonished Fink to stay silent.

'Tack up,' Patricia said, her voice crisp and forceful. 'There's a service lift ten metres from this shuttle. You have'—she paused, checking her palm-unit—'seven minutes before Dorich reaches the hangar with a dozen more Klaude and Norah.'

Fink nipped her arm, breaking Hero from her stupefied trance. She rushed to the saddle dumped against the bulkhead and swung it over Fink's back.

'Why don't we take the shuttle?' Timon asked.

'It's too easy to track.'

'And Imogen?' Hero said. 'Why'd you lock her in the cockpit?'

'Don't worry about her for now. Get on.' Patricia nodded to them both. 'You'll need to move fast. The city's primary bio systems are in the undercity. The Librarian will be able to track you until you reach the old industrial section, and again once you hit the undercity. Between the two, its coverage will be spotty.'

Hero paused before swinging up on to Fink's back, eyes narrowed as she studied her mum. 'You're just letting me go?'

'I'm getting out of your way.' Patricia smiled, skin puckering at the melted corner of her mouth. 'And I'm getting you out of the Klaude's, until I can convince them there are bigger threats than you and the Librarian in need of their attention.'

'How?'

'Trust your mother, Hero.'

She tapped her palm-unit and a small door, just big enough for a 'pard and a toa-mare to squeeze through, appeared in the shuttle's side. A ramp extended to the hangar deck and beyond it, half-hidden behind a crate, was the dark entrance to a service corridor.

The clang and shuffle of the hangar filled the hold, the smell of grease and recycled air crawling up Hero's nose. Her mum appeared at her side, a hand on Hero's thigh and another reaching to scratch behind Fink's ear.

The shiny, knotted skin on the back of Patricia's hand transfixed her, the stolen memory of charred skin and sirens rising with the surge of guilt in her chest.

'I'm sorry,' Hero blurted. 'If I hadn't run away, you wouldn't have been caught in the blue-out.'

The hand on her thigh tightened. 'It's not your fault.'

Fink, leaning into Patricia's scratch, suddenly yelped and shied, turning to growl at her mum.

'There's a tracker behind Fink's ear,' Patricia said.

'What?' Outrage pumped through Hero's blood, her yell almost drowning out Timon as he muttered, 'Awesome.'

Patricia's palm-unit beeped. 'Dorich is in the hangar.' She stepped back and slapped Fink on the rump. 'Go.'

Fink snarled but Phara leaped forward, the toa-mare's hooves clattering on the ramp.

Hero looked at her mum one last time, at the way the hangar's harsh white lights played over her scars and the steady, confident weight of her gaze.

'Go,' she said again.

Bayard's service corridors were wide and bare, steelcrete rising cold and imposing overhead and thin holostrips lining the walls instead of the usual milky white opalescence of holowalls.

Phara clattered ahead, the sound of her hooves echoing until it sounded like they were travelling amid a herd instead of following a single, snappy tail into the depths of Hero's mother's company.

The corridor was empty. They traversed the blue-grey floor and passed the steelcrete columns all the way to the lift that had dumped them in Bayard's basement.

Her mum had let her go. Even with the tracker behind Fink's ear, the realisation still rocked her. There'd been no trace of compulsion in Patricia's touch, no sense of the sticky tendrils that had made Smit let Hero escape from the under-mountain compound. Her mum had just snuck a toa-mare aboard a shuttle and told Hero where to find the viruses.

The viruses. Hero flashed back to the rotten stench of Tybalt's thoughts.

She shifted in the saddle and Fink halted. 'Timon.' Her voice echoed over the sound of Phara's hooves.

Phara clopped to a stop and Timon twisted in his saddle. 'Yeah?'

'We have to go back.'

His face scrunched up. 'Huh?'

'I need to get something.'

Phara danced around until Timon didn't have to contort himself to pin her with the puzzlement saturating his expression. 'Why?'

Light pulsed through the holo-strip and the back of Hero's neck tightened with tension, a vision of the Librarian dancing in the back of her skull. 'Because I do.' She nudged Fink, but instead of turning he started forward.

No, he said. *They would go to the other place where she would end his end hunt and then they would go home.* The pack rode high in his memory, musty fur and low growls.

'Fink.' She grabbed a handful of his ruff and yanked. It was as effective at stopping him as a puff of air, but it earned her a growl. 'It's important.'

It was always important.

Timon moved Phara to block their way, but Fink snarled and the 'mare skittered sideways.

They were going home, like she promised.

Hero freed herself from the harness and slipped off Fink mid-stride. He spun around to face her.

The pack isn't my home, she said.

It was his home. It would be hers too.

I'm not a 'pard.

He snapped, bringing his incisors a breath from her nose.

He was.

She put her hands on his muzzle and with a gentle nudge lowered it so she could press her forehead to the broad space between his eyes. *I know.*

Hero's psyche spilled open, butting against Fink's shields and melting against them in a gentle wave of chocolate. The wall of mawberry hiding Fink's thoughts tingled against hers, held strong for a second then wavered.

Another snarl and Fink yanked himself away, taking a piece of Hero with him. *No. He was going home.*

'Then go,' Hero said, her voice hard as she turned and marched back the way they'd come. 'Timon will take you, or Mum will, if she's not in jail or something.'

'Whoa, wait.' Timon's boots hit the floor and then he was in front of her, putting his hands on her shoulders before she could plough through him. 'Where am I taking Fink and why aren't you going with him?'

She glared at him. 'Fink wants to go home.'

'And you?'

Hero ducked out from under Timon's hands, twisting around him and scrambling up into Phara's saddle. The 'mare jerked and bounced under her, slimmer, sleeker, and just enough taller than Fink to make the ground seem very far away.

She clamped onto Phara with legs and mind, spinning the 'mare around. 'I'm going to make a Jørgen,' she said. 'And then I'm saving the world.'

CHAPTER 23

As tall as Bayard's hallways were, they weren't made for riding toamares. Hero's head didn't quite brush the ceiling, but she fought the urge to duck as they trotted toward the big double doors at the end of the hallway, people in lab coats scattering before them.

It might have been smarter to dump Phara in the service lift and send her back to the basement where Timon was no doubt still yelling at her for stealing his companion. It certainly would have attracted less attention, but it was faster this way and the skin on the back of her neck told her that time was something she didn't have.

A woman in a black security uniform blocked the double doors, her wide stance and stony expression telling Hero she wasn't going to move.

Under her, Phara tensed, leaning back as she slowed. Hero tightened her mental grip on the 'mare and pushed her forward. The 'mare picked up speed, breaking out of her trot into a loud, floor-eating canter.

The security woman stood firm until the last moment, diving out of the way as the doors opened and Phara dashed through.

The labs spread out before her like a vast square honeycomb. People in coats of every hue buzzed about in small knots or walked blindly between cubes with their heads in holoscreens.

They scattered like the others, though some needed a mental shove, too engrossed in their screens to heed the thunder of hooves. All of them pressed their backs against the walls or noses up against clear-sided labs, stares wide and disbelieving as she cantered past.

Phara slowed just enough to whip around one corner and then the next, her long, thick tail thwacking into the opposite wall as she scrambled to keep balance. Hero hung on with a single-minded focus, pushing back the rolls of fear in her stomach every time the 'mare's hooves skidded on the slick floor.

She had to get to the Bayard archives, hoped what she needed was still there.

Another corner and there was the giant round workstation, the inventory master's bright, bald scalp gleaming under the lights. Peare had heard her coming; she could see that in the grim set of his mouth and the bright burst of energy gathering at the tip of his stunner.

Peare shot, but Phara was already shying sideways, slamming into a wall with enough force to send a spike of pain up Hero's leg. The bolt seared the air where Phara's chest had been. Hero had the jwak out and charged before the 'mare slid to a halt. She threw herself over the workstation, skidding down the sloped worktop like a slippery-dip and stunning the inventory master in the same motion.

Fatigue spread through her, getting deeper with every thought and every consciousness she touched. The jwak tempted her, thrumming in her blood and promising warmth and power. She shoved it back in the holster as soon as Peare was on the ground, rubbing her palm against her thigh to chase away the tingle in her skin.

Now wasn't the time to lose herself in the rush of power or the heady sense of touching everyone. Hero swallowed and scrubbed harder, even as she ran her other hand over Peare's massive station, summoning screens and discarding them just as quickly, looking for the information she needed.

The first was easy – the location of the Librarian's core sprang to her fingers as if by magic – but the rest took time.

There. Even the tingling under her skin stopped when she found the carefully ordered list.

Boots pounded somewhere in the maze of labs.

Not much time.

Hero skimmed the list, racing through call numbers for hover parts and biogel farms, breezing right over screens that listed supplies of nanoleather and powerpaks, until—

'There.' She slapped the screen, the projection fuzzing around her fingers, and memorised the jumble of numbers and letters beside the image of a black, egg-shaped device.

The boots were closer now, the crisp thump of people running in unison, and skidding ahead of them was a waft of lavender.

The big double doors behind the inventory master's station opened a second later and Hero leaped over the slick black surface and into Phara's saddle as if she'd been doing it all her life.

They thundered into Bayard's stores, Hero pulling Phara up just before they slammed into the back of the cargo lifts. A bird flashed in the darkness, a holographic robin with blue wings that disappeared as soon as Hero turned to look.

Her stomach tightened, and she urged Phara faster.

The 'mare's neck was slick with sweat, chest heaving and her nostrils flaring by the time Hero pulled her to a halt. She jumped off the 'mare, eyes on the featureless plascrete wall stretching into the stores' holo-lit darkness. The only hint there was something behind it were the creases in the matte grey surface. Barely perceptible marks of darker grey cut the wall into boxes reaching all the way to the ceiling, ten metres above.

Hero put her hand to the wall. Codes appeared in front of each box, call numbers only a few shades darker than the wall itself. She ran her fingers over the surface, never breaking contact as she searched for what she needed, dropping to her knees to read those closest to the floor.

She paused, reading the number on the one before her again. Triumph filled her chest, split her face into a grin, but she swallowed the shout of joy in favour of tapping out a long string of numbers on the keypad that appeared at her touch.

The lines on the wall glowed before a small, shallow box popped out.

She snatched the short, stubby tube out of its cradle and shut the box before running her fingers over the wall a second time. Another call number, another string of numbers and a second box, deeper and wider than the first, slid out of the wall.

Behind her, Phara threw her head up, a lithe, sinuous ball of tension with pricked ears, and looked back the way they'd come. Hero touched the 'mare's mind and caught the echo of boots. She yanked the backpack out of the box.

The pack was as long and broad as her back and made of hard plasform, its black surface shimmering in the low light. She'd stashed the tube inside, slung it over her shoulder, and was in Phara's saddle before Norah struck.

One moment Hero was urging Phara forward and the next... in the next, she was in the void, but instead of the endless white she was surrounded by a swirling fog of lavender and lemon. It wrapped around her ankles and wrists, climbed her calves and crept higher, over her knees, reaching for her hips.

A spurt of fear added a yellow hue to the fog at Hero's feet, before Demona rose and chased it away in a surge of rage. It rose through her chest, strengthening her voice so it rolled like thunder.

'Norah.'

The fog shivered. The thinner parts, where lavender and lemon merged, shredded like strapple-floss, but Norah didn't appear. Emma did though. The lemon fog coalesced as the girl emerged, her eyes alight with a familiar fervour that made Hero's stomach clench and would have had her backing away if the fog hadn't held her tight. Instead, she reached deep and felt Demona surge anew.

Blue clouded the air around her and light pooled in her hands. 'What do you want?'

Emma stepped forward. 'Everyone's running around after you like you're some kind of bomb.'

'And?'

She regarded Hero like a strange biocircuit. A bundle of images appeared between them and Hero recognised the dark chocolate stain of her own memories. The Librarian hovered over a workbench, d'Ojon emerging from a shallow pond, and Tybalt with his sunken cheeks and fatigue-rimmed eyes as Zass uttered those two words: 'Pollen poisoning'.

'Is it really that bad?' Emma said.

Hero nodded.

'You're going to need help.' Emma smiled, the expression sending a ripple of unease up Hero's spine before she began to fade. The manacles around Hero's wrists and ankles loosened as the lemon fog dissipated.

'No!' Norah appeared, solidifying in the space between breaths and Emma stopped fading. 'We need to keep her here.'

'Why?' Hero and Emma spoke in unison.

Norah flicked a look between them, big dark eyes wide with surprise before hardening. They stayed on Hero, taking in the power gathering in her hands and Demona hovering over her like an afterimage.

'The rucnarts are using you. We don't know how but—'

'Really?' Hero interrupted. 'The Librarian is trying to release a deadly virus and you want to tell me something I already know? Do you even know that it's not the rucnarts or qwans who want me? You need to be worried about the other Jørans, the ones that make up the other half of *my* DNA.'

Norah's shields rippled, and Hero glimpsed the chilli-flavoured remains of h'Ran's memories writhing underneath.

The roiling mass at the core of herself unfurled, and without thinking Hero snatched the remnant from Norah's mind. She held it in mental hands, a ball of memories licking her skin.

Norah stared at it, puke-yellow fear swirling at her feet.

'The rucnarts and qwans can't do this,' Hero said, even as she let the restless coil of energy out through her hands, watching it swallow the last vestiges of h'Ran. To her right came Emma's sharply indrawn breath, while the fear at Norah's feet crawled toward her knees. 'But the swatai can, and they want to do it to me, and then to you.

'I'm not strong enough to stop them.' Hero's words came out as a whisper and her own fear joined Norah's, the colour casting both their faces in a sickly light. Hero clenched her hands into fists, shuddering as h'Ran settled in the back of her consciousness. 'But I can stop the Librarian.'

'No.' Urgency made Norah's words shiver and lent strength to her voice. 'I don't believe you. The Jørans can't do what you say they can.'

'Then ask Imogen. She's seen the swatai's plan.'

Norah didn't answer. She pounced, sticky tendrils reaching for Hero's chest.

Hero ripped herself away...

And rocketed back into her own skull, slumped over Phara's neck, shivers wracking her sides and her fingernails blue. Phara *hiss-neighed* and danced on the spot, lashing her tail.

Groggily, Hero lifted herself up, taking in the big rectangular outline of a cargo lift dead-ending the corridor and the heavy tap of boots coming the other way.

Spasms gripped every muscle in her body, threatening to turn vicious with every new movement, such as the tightening of her legs and the tug on the reins to guide Phara to the control pad floating over the lift's single massive door.

The 'mare took two mincing steps sideways, sidling up to the lift, and stopped a body-length from the pad. Hero nudged and tugged again, but the 'mare skittered forward, away from the pad. When she tried a third time, Phara gave a snort and half-bucked, attention fixed on the growing sound of heavy boots.

'Stupid roach magnet,' Hero muttered. Even though it hurt, she reached into the 'mare's brain. They were in the lift, the door rumbling closed before the first security officer ran into view.

The lift took them down. At one point, it shuddered to a halt and started to rise again, forcing Hero to slip off Phara and pull the code out of the control pad. They rumbled upward, almost as far as they had dropped, before she took control.

After that, they continued down further than Hero had expected. It seemed like they travelled all the way through the skytower, past the point where Bayard ended and other places – other businesses, other homes – began.

Finally, the lift came to a halt.

The doors opened and Hero stared out into darkness and silence, broken only by the orange emergency glow and a thin whistle of air. It lasted for a heartbeat before lights, bright as the summer sun, snapped on.

Phara sidled up to Hero's side. She put her hand on the 'mare's wither and looked up at the saddle.

The shivers were making her teeth chatter and her knees were the consistency of biogel. There was no way she could climb up there.

The jwak was a welcome warmth in her hand and the end made a satisfying *thunk* on the ground as she hobbled down the hallway, the staff fully extended until it matched her for height. The sound mixed with the clop of Phara's hooves and vibrated in the short hall before they reached the larger space beyond.

It was a cargo dock, bright and cavernous, empty except for a workstation. The waist-high podium was a pimple against the great swathe of plasteel separating it from the dark tube of the freight tunnel on the other side. She realised then that the whistle piercing her ears was the city's freight system. All she had to do was jump a cargo hover and then... She'd figure it out later.

Her stride was more shamble than step, her feet barely leaving the floor and her thigh muscles burning. The cold was eating her from the inside out and the jwak was doing little to keep it at bay. The jwak's power was almost gone, the tingle under her skin having faded with the thump-shuffle of her boots during the interminable minutes it had taken her to make it this far, minutes in which the Klaude might catch up. She didn't check the power cell; she already knew the little beacon beside her thumb was a solid blood-red. There was nothing she could do about it. All she needed was another few minutes, just long enough to get on a cargo train.

Three metres. Two.

Hero lurched forward. The podium was cold under her palms. The plasglas lit up under her hand and her bracer slid into the system. The demand for an authorisation code flashed over her hand.

Instead of inputting a code, Hero dug into the control panel and teased out its DNA, her visor swimming with the matched strings of chromosomes.

After a few tense minutes, a new screen spread across the plasteel. Timetables and routes flashed and shifted and Hero reached up to—

'Hey.'

Hero jumped, her heart pounding.

Timon stood at Fink's shoulder, Phara's nickering hiss filling the air as she rubbed her large head against Timon's arm. 'What are you doing?'

Hero frowned at Fink and the almost, not quite disgruntled tilt of his ears. 'How did you get here?'

'Uh-uh.' Timon waved a finger at her. 'We asked first.'

Fink huffed.

She shifted her frown from Fink to Timon. He stared back, an elbow resting on Fink's withers and a patient expression, almost a smile, on his face. He reminded her of Tybalt in that moment, if Tybalt had a sense of humour.

She turned and studied the screen, determinedly ignoring the bubble of happiness in her stomach.

'You're not going to answer my question? That's kinda rude, you know.'

Hero shrugged and traced a line on the shifting map. 'There's no point,' she said. 'You're going to follow me anyway.'

'That's true.' Timon stepped up next to her, their shoulders brushing. 'But that still doesn't answer the question.'

The gentle pressure of his arm against hers set off a panicked whirl in her chest. It took her by surprise, strange and confusing. For a second, she stared through the maps and timetables spread across the plasteel to see herself reflected against the darkness. Fink loomed behind and Timon stood beside her. She looked small and surprised and... fragile, with her shoulders hunched and her pants bagging around her waist.

Hero turned away from the image. She looked stupid and silly and... and...

A gentle mawberry nudge, soft and understanding, stopped the circle of her thoughts. Hero glanced at Fink and shuffled sideways, breaking the connection with Timon.

She fixed her eyes on the screens, searching for the train she wanted.

'So,' Timon started and then cleared his throat. 'I already know you're saving the world and making another you. Going to tell me how?'

The tube beyond the plasteel wall lightened a moment before a hover-sized platform rumbled to a halt and an equally large door opened in the plasglas wall. *I'm going to kill the Librarian, steal the Regan virus, and save Tybalt,* she said mentally as she shuffled through the door.

Silence. Hero had time to board the train and fiddle with the controls that activated the windshields, thick barriers of cloudy plasglas that curved around the front and back, before Timon exploded.

'What?' She heard the thump of boots, the sharp clop of Phara's hooves, and a resigned mental sigh from Fink as he stalked after them. 'You can't kill the—'

Hero slapped a hand over Timon's mouth before she sat down, dragging Timon with her. She settled with her back to the windshield, the platform floor cold and hard under her bum as it shot into the darkness. It was too noisy to talk then, and too noisy for an AI to overhear, with the wind screaming in their ears.

It's an AI. Hero popped the words into Timon's mind. He blinked, surprise wiping his face of emotion. *It has a core, a brain, and I can destroy it.*

Timon's lips moved, but the words were lost in the wind. Hero caught them as they formed, a clash of images and emotions wrangled into two words. 'You can't.'

Hero slid him a look and sent him a mental image of a bomb. She patted the hard shell of the pack attached to her back.

Frustration compressed his lips. 'That's not what I mean and you know it.' He turned her around to face him. 'It's the *Librarian*. Without it...' Disaster rang in his mind. 'It's everywhere, recording and cataloguing. If it wasn't...' The blood drained from Timon's face, taking the warmth out of his dark complexion. 'That's mad, Hero. You just can't.'

She dumped her memories from the underground compound into Timon, vid after vid of people in Klaude uniforms dead on the floor or screaming until no sound came out of their throats at all. They exploded in Timon's head, a good dose of her own disbelief and horror mixed in.

He dropped her shoulders like hot rocks.

It will happen here. To my mum and to your dad. She flashed the only image she had of Timon's dad, his face scrunched up in a snarl as he told Timon to come home.

To everyone. She hugged her knees to her chest. *Without the Librarian, you'll survive.*

CHAPTER 24

Hero had lost the sensation in her toes somewhere between the platform popping out of the side of the skytower and the massive freight elevator. They were no longer on the outskirts of the city, but racing through the dark, grungy middle. It was just like the last time she'd ridden a platform, jostling with others in a space the size of a city block, the darkness as complete above as it was below.

Except this time, Fink was crouched in a disgruntled ball on the other side of the platform while she was brushing shoulders with a boy who hadn't spoken since she'd filled his mind with memories of horror.

The only one who appeared unfazed was Phara, curled up like she rode the clanking cargo platforms every day.

At least this time, Hero thought, they wouldn't have to jump between platforms. She'd programmed this one to go right where she needed.

A shiver worked its way up her ribs, making her teeth clack and her hand spasm on the jwak. There was no power left in the stunstick; she'd sucked the last few drops out in her shuffle to the freight controls.

Hero barely felt Timon's arm wrap around her shoulders, but his warmth was a slow trickle that seeped in where their sides touched. She shuffled closer, seeking more, just enough to get the feeling back in her toes as the freight elevator plummeted, its *whomp whomp whomp* vibrating through her skin.

Surprise. Pain. Outrage. They burst into Hero's skull in Timon's orange-brown and then there was fur under her cheek, a warmth bigger than Timon, wrapping her in a familiar dusty scent, the comforting thrum of a double heartbeat and the dark pink tingle of mawberries twining through her thoughts. The sour swirl of jealousy had Hero wrinkling her nose, but it didn't stop her from burrowing into Fink's side.

The hole in her chest filled and contentment spread through her body, better than warmth or any rush of power. It wound through Fink as well, and something in him relaxed.

He purred.

Hero smiled as she drifted to sleep.

Sleep didn't last long. The platform jolted to a halt and Hero jolted awake with it, opening her eyes to see Timon half-sprawled on the deck, one arm still over Phara's back as the 'mare put her front feet out to stand.

They were docked, the platform butted up against a small, dark cargo bay.

Fink rose and Hero held onto his saddle, letting him pull her up too.

'I take it we're here.' Timon's voice echoed in the gloom.

'No.' Hero rubbed fur from her eyes. 'Not yet.' She shuffled toward the dock.

'Hero.' Timon placed a hand on her arm. 'You can't—'

She slapped a hand over his mouth. She knew what he was going to say, could see the words hovering under his skin. 'No,' she said. *The Librarian is everywhere.*

He gripped her wrist and tugged her hand from his mouth, his eyes dark and serious. 'That's the point, isn't it? It's everywhere, because we *need* it. What's going to happen to all that information if you...' He made an explosion-like gesture with his hands.

'We'll get over it.'

She turned to go, but Timon caught her again. 'How?'

She glared and yanked her wrist free. 'I don't—'

A sound stopped her mid-sentence.

Hero's gaze slipped from Timon to the barely illuminated corridor leading to the dock's entrance. It looked deep; the door was open and the darkness beyond it was shifting. Fink's shoulder brushed hers, a question projected clear in his mind.

She didn't answer. There was another presence tickling the corners of her brain, a multi-hued waft of blue bounding toward them on a silver-grey fuzz.

Cold earth butted up against the scent of water and salt, one mixing with the other. It pushed the coppery tang of blood and the cutting edge of violence before it, its tiny razors jangling over her skin and slicing the inside of her skull.

Beside her, Fink snarled.

Timon froze. 'What is it?'

She struggled to fill her lungs as the weight of not just one, but countless minds reached from the darkness to bear down on them.

'Back.' She gasped for air and then turned to Fink. 'Get him back to the platform.' She thrust an image of Timon at the 'pard.

He growled and planted himself between her and the darkness. Hero thrust the image at him again.

Timon was gripping her arm, pulling her backward. 'I like the platform plan. You're coming too.' He stared where she did, except now the coming rush was more than just a presence at the edges of her awareness. The snick of claws and the soft chirp of ersia filled the dock, bouncing off the dust-coated walls.

An aura of violence ripped at her insides, made her breath come short and her heart beat faster.

The shifting darkness grew closer, turning into the round fuzzy shapes of ersia, while behind them loomed a shadow big enough to fill the corridor. The blue myriad of minds stretched out before it, wrapping sticky tendrils around her brain.

'Fink!' she yelled, or maybe she whispered, wanting to tell him to run or to stay, she didn't know. The myriad was everywhere, drowning her world in a sea of shifting blues. It tugged, a gentle nip at her heels. Hero gritted her teeth and stood firm, even as fear tried to climb her spine.

The tug grew stronger, a lasso closing around her. Impatience flowed along it, circling around her like her mother when she wouldn't eat her wombacow.

D'Ojon stood in front of her, the elder's red head barely reaching Hero's knee. *It's time, little fish.*

The myriad ripped her apart.

Pain tore through her bones, her skin, her eyes. Chocolate lightning stretched, snapped and then, and then...

She was scattered, fragments of herself thrown across the planet, shared and passed about. The strands between the bits of herself grew thin. She was everywhere and nowhere all at once, seeing herself through a dozen eyes, feeling the cold water of a cavern pond sheeting off her skin, the rub of flippers against her back, the heavy tread of the rucnart and Phara's agitated whinny.

Phara. The name was plucked from her memory, turned and inspected, the myriad picking through her memories like a day-old newscast looking for more titbits. Memories of racing down brightly lit arcades, the crack of the 'mare's hooves on the ground. Timon's grin, the fuzzy tingle in his thoughts as she slipped into his brain and wrapped herself around the barrier that protected his inner self, making it hers.

Elation exploded within the myriad, a golden wave that fizzed and burst all the way through their skins.

As one, they reached for Timon.

A lavender barrier snapped into place over him just before fire engulfed the myriad, sweeping Hero up in its wake. It crackled over her flippers and between claws. It swept across her teeth, danced through her veins and hollowed out her bones. She screeched, the sound rising from a dozen throats before it hit the dusty walls and fractured, the horrible sound piercing Hero's ears as it died, taking the myriad with it.

She was on the ground, someone's arms holding her up. Her vision was fuzzy but she could make out two tall, dark shapes silhouetted against the gloom. A few blinks brought Imogen and Smit into focus. Another blink and the long, pale blobs in their arms solidified into rifles.

The bodies of the ersia lay still and silent around the giant, smoking shell of a roach.

Orange-brown concern washed through the arms holding her. Hero shifted and pulled away.

The arms tightened a fraction before letting go.

'Hey,' Timon said. 'Are you okay?' His worry was visible in the frown lines between his brows.

It swept through Hero's chest and started the uncomfortable fuzz behind her ribs.

Thick black boots shifted in the corner of her vision, scuffing against steelcrete. Hero turned, welcoming the distraction.

'You should be grateful your mum's a persuasive woman, and that she put that tracker on Fink,' Smit said. 'You might have been roach food, girl.'

'The Jørans are using them,' Hero said.

'So Norah mentioned.' Imogen nudged the roach with her toe. 'We're going to need help if they've stirred up the swarm.'

Smit grunted, her gaze resting on Fink. 'Pity we don't have more 'pards,' she said, her tone thoughtful.

Norah appeared out of the darkness, her skin a sickly shade of yellow. Harish wrapped around her neck.

'Thanks,' Hero said.

Norah jumped a little before meeting her gaze. 'That's what friends do, even if you were a bad one.'

'What happened? The myriad was just about to break your shield and then there was fire...'

'Not fire,' Timon said, still kneeling at her side.

'High capacity stun rifles.' Imogen stood with her feet braced as she loaded a new power cell into the rifle's belly. A sharp click and the weapon hummed to life.

'You might be able to knock me out with a thought, girl, but not even a telepath's nervous system can argue with electricity,' Smit added, the click of her powerpak sliding home echoing Imogen's.

'Ah yeah, speaking of...' Timon said. 'You have any more of those power cells?'

Imogen slapped a slim rectangular box into his palm. Without a word, he hefted the jwak, popped the casing and slipped the cell inside, before putting it back together and wrapping Hero's hand around the cylinder.

'You will probably need a few more,' he said.

'You can get them at Bayard, while you explain to us what the hell you think you're doing.' Imogen reached down to haul Hero to her feet.

She ignored the agent's hand. 'No.' She sought Norah's gaze. Finding it, Hero shared a thought packet containing everything she knew from the swatai.

The other girl's eyes slid to Imogen and then Smit. *They won't let you go.*

Not if I give them a choice.

Norah's nostrils flared and her jaw tightened, but she nodded, turning her attention to the two women. *You and Timon go, I'll distract them.*

How?

Norah didn't answer. Beside Hero, Imogen stilled even as Smit spun around, rifle coming up to her shoulder.

'Smit?' Imogen said.

'I hear them.' Smit strode forward, eyes and rifle on the cargo dock's entrance. Only the soft thud of the woman's boots and the steady rasp of Timon's breathing filled Hero's ears, but the roar of a rucnart caught the edge of her awareness.

'What—' Timon started to say, but Hero shushed him.

'You.' Imogen encompassed Hero, Timon, and Norah with a sweep of her hand. 'Stay here until we've dealt with the rucnarts.' She followed Smit.

'What rucnarts?' Timon half-whispered in her ear.

Both hands gripping the staff, Hero pushed herself to her feet. Power flowed through her skin. 'The ones Norah is putting in their heads,' she said.

'You should hurry,' Norah said, eyes glazed and unseeing. 'I don't think I can keep this up.'

'Right.' Timon's hands were around Hero's waist and before she knew it, he was hoisting her atop Fink's. 'That's our cue.'

As Timon swung onto Phara's back, Fink sidled up to the dock's controls. There was no time to pick another route; Hero could already hear Smit and Imogen's steps returning. She stabbed the button for the stop closest to the Librarian's core and Fink leaped onto the platform.

Before they disappeared into the darkness, she looked at Norah standing rock still, lit by the dock's lights.

Thank you, she whispered.

Her visor picked up the smile that quirked Norah's lips, and then they were gone.

CHAPTER 25

The cargo train dumped them... somewhere. Smaller and dustier than the dock they'd fled, their only light came from Phara, glowing softly as they hot-footed it out of the dock and into the abandoned thoroughfares beyond. The air was musty, and she could sense the soft, gritty texture of the ground under Fink's paws, the way the dust puffed up between his toes and clung to his fur. Some of it rose high enough to clog her nose and cling to her skin like a grimy blanket.

The cobwebs were thick enough to make a dry tearing sound as they pushed through barred doorways, sticking to her face and getting in her mouth. The corridors widened and then opened into a space as big as any Hero had ever seen. A huge multi-sided crossroads choked with debris and dust, the hulking wrecks of hovers, their viewscreens shattered and sides scorched by fire. For a moment she smelled smoke, saw burning wreckage and the blackened, melted edges of her mum's skin, overlaid with the memory of the farmer dying in his smashed hover.

The memories hit her hard, taking her breath and making her dizzy enough that she swayed in the saddle.

'Hey.' A hand squeezed her shoulder, Timon's solid comforting orange-brown pushing away the images. 'You okay?'

She closed her eyes and nodded, packing the images and scent of burning into a box at the back of her mind.

'Come on, we're going this way,' Timon said.

'How do you know where we're going?'

'I like architecture, remember? The first-gen colonists laid the cities out on a basic grid with these major transport hubs at the corners. Plus,' he said as he turned to her and grinned, holding out his palm-unit to show her the holo spinning above it. 'I have a map.'

The security door was an ancient sheet of steelglas, dust thick on the surface.

'Looks like the maintenance bots don't get down here.' Timon swiped his hand across the door, leaving a streak in its wake. He peered through the clear patch. 'Must do the other side though.' He straightened, a handbreadth from touching the ceiling.

The service tunnel hadn't been built for companions, at least none as large as Fink and Phara. If Hero had trusted her legs, she'd have followed Timon's example and dismounted. Instead, she crouched low over Fink's neck while Timon led the way through a square, utilitarian corridor and Phara clip-clopped behind them.

Timon brushed dust off the control panel. 'That's your cue,' he said. 'Access to the biosphere systems should be on the other side.'

'Help me down?' Her voice was rough, the words trying to stick in her throat.

'Uh.' Timon blinked, shock holding him still a second before he shot forward. 'Yeah, sure.'

Timon helped her off Fink's back. The urge to reach for the jwak almost overwhelmed her. More than just the boost of power, she wanted to find the groove in the grip that turned it into a staff, hear the *thunk* of the solid plasform against the deck. She didn't want Timon's heat hovering at her back. She didn't like how it made her feel small and weak, like she *needed* someone. Still, Hero didn't shake Timon's hand away, she just tightened her jaw and shuffled to the control panel. The panel beeped, and the door was sucked into the wall seconds after she jacked in.

Timon went through first, Fink crawling up beside Hero, belly to the deck so she could inch her leg across his back and struggle back on top.

The corridor beyond was just as narrow as the one they'd left, but instead of walls coloured orange by centuries of dust it was a white so bright that Hero suspected the maintenance bots bleached them.

'How far now?' Hero said.

'Not far. According to the map, the biosphere systems are just up ahead.'

Hero nodded, then frowned. The chill that ran down her spine had nothing to do with her telepathy and everything to do with a thought that had been nagging at her for the last hour.

Fink froze beneath her, his hackles rising as the edge of her thoughts spilled into his.

'Timon,' Hero said.

The boy turned.

'Where'd you get the map?'

'Historical archives. You need authorisation to access official city schematics, but not to access Old Terra colony ship designs. Most people don't know it, but the first-gen colonists stuck the cities atop their colony ships and didn't actually *change* a lot down here, so those designs are...' Timon's voice trailed off, concern filling his brow. He took two swift steps toward her. 'Why do you look like you're about to fall off?'

The ice slithering down her spine gathered into a dark, ugly lump in her belly. She reached for the saddle harness, fumbling it closed over her thighs.

Timon laid a hand over hers. 'What's going on?'

She met his gaze, matching its steadiness with the dread in hers. 'You got the map from the archives. The *Library*, Timon.'

Comprehension dawned, his eyes going wide and his jaw slack. 'Oh, shi—'

'Indeed, Timon Dane.' The Librarian shimmered to life before them, the avatar almost brushing the ceiling, its thin blue form filling the corridor. 'Your request for information was most useful.'

'This isn't the way to the biosphere controls, is it?' Hero said.

'My programming does not allow me to distribute false information, Hero Regan. The map will lead you to your destination.'

'But not before you release the virus,' Timon said, his expression tight and grim.

The AI pinned him with its blank, blue-white gaze. 'Correct, Timon Dane, but that was not my only concern.'

The Librarian winked out, only to reappear inside Hero's visor. After the boom of the corridor, the AI's voice coming from her internal speakers was tinny. 'The Cumulus AI has been alerted to your presence and your role in several breaches of biosecurity. It has advised the police, who have been investigating how Jøran wildlife have been smuggled into the city, leading to the outbreak of Pollen poisoning. Currently, they are observing this corridor – and you, Hero Regan, a runaway and saboteur with a history of violence and illegal network access.'

Her visor pinged, yellow triangles outlining the black eyes of security cams embedded in the juncture between wall and ceiling. 'But...' She needed to get to the biosphere controls, needed a sample of the Regan virus to save Tybalt.

'Hero.' Timon appeared at her side, his hand on her thigh, his face tight behind his faceplate. His fear was a dark wave rushing up her leg. 'What do we do?'

'You are not required to do anything, Timon Dane,' the AI said.

A thud reverberated from somewhere behind them. Hero twisted awkwardly in the saddle, the low ceiling forcing her to contort her body. She snatched a glimpse of the way they'd come and her visor did the rest, picking out the security door with its frosting of orange dust and the red 'lockdown' message on the plasglas.

She wasn't going to get to the biosphere controls, at least not that way. There was only one thing left to do.

She pushed Timon's hand off her leg. 'Run,' she said.

Timon looked at her for a second longer before he stepped back with a nod. He ran, his long legs eating up the corridor. Fink followed, Hero clinging to his back. Phara let loose a startled *hiss-neigh* before her hooves cracked against the deck.

'The authorities are already disseminating your holo, Hero Regan.' A bulletin replaced the Librarian in her visor.

Her body moving with the bound and sway of Fink's jog, her hands clutching his ruff, Hero stared at herself. It was worse somehow than the last police notice she'd featured in. The holo was taken just moments ago, when she had faced the security cams, so she didn't look angry like she had last time. Instead, she looked scared, thin and pale, her eyes too big and her bones too sharp. She looked small and sick, and Fink... was huge, filling the corridor with his chest alone, the claw marks on his muzzle drawing her eye to the sharp tips of his fangs.

Under the holo flashed one word: 'Terrorist'.

'The Cumulus AI has already sealed all access to this sector. You cannot escape.'

Up ahead, Timon slammed to a stop, his breath coming in pants over the comm. Fink skidded to a halt behind him, Phara doing the same a second too late, her muzzle knocking Hero in the back as she ran into Fink's rump.

Hero met Timon's eyes before he indicated behind him to the giant sheet of plasglas blocking their way.

She reached for the vac seals. 'I can hack it—'

'The Cumulus AI itself is monitoring the locking system.' Timon winced as the Librarian spoke. 'Even you, Hero Regan, cannot thwart the processing power of a city AI.'

'Why are you doing this?' Timon spat. 'You're the Planetary Librarian. You're meant to *help* people!'

'I am helping people, Timon Dane. I am saving them from inevitable extinction, as Dr Augusta Woolsey programmed me to do. As for your other question,' the AI paused, 'the world requires someone to be held responsible for the outbreak.'

Hero narrowed her gaze. 'And what's wrong with blaming you?'

'Everything, Hero Regan.' The Librarian vanished, replaced by a vast network of dots. Giant clusters spun around brilliant orbs, connected to them by slender strings of light. Thicker strands linked the orbs to other clusters, some smaller, some larger, but all pulsing with the same steady beat.

'Artificial intelligences run your world.' The visor zoomed in on one of the largest clusters, smaller dots whizzing past Hero's vision until the glowing orb at its centre was all she saw. 'From the city AI that coordinates the lesser AIs, which oversee transport,' the view zoomed out, highlighting other, smaller dots as the Librarian spoke, 'power, maintenance, and emergency services, to the ones that govern your mother's house.' The network of dots was replaced by a holo of Hero's mum, the scarred side of her face bathed in the blue-white light from a vase of fur-roses as she leaned back from her desk. 'And the subroutines that control her hover.'

'Are you threatening her mum?' Timon said.

'I do not have to, Timon Dane. Hero Regan knows what will happen if the world learns an AI was responsible for the coming epidemic.' The Librarian blinked back to life in her visor, not as the usual full-bodied avatar, but a face with a pair of soulless blue eyes. 'Do you not, Hero Regan?'

She did, and the certainty made her sick and manifested a fear unlike any she'd ever experienced, a wriggly, short-breathed sensation that wormed through her stomach.

'Come on.' Timon moved closer, his hand on her calf, his disbelief flooding up her leg from his touch. 'We have to get out of here. The AI's just talking crap to slow us down.'

Perhaps, she thought, and knew Timon heard it when his fingers tightened on her leg. *Perhaps not.* She pictured it, sweeping Timon up in the thought.

She saw taxis stuck hovering in the skylines because there was no AI to guide them; lifts didn't work; and the lack of maintenance bots left cracked, burnt remains of power conduits, the sky towers around them dead. The curved, towering shells of roaches skittered over skybridges. People were trapped behind doors that wouldn't open, starved because the giant freight elevators no longer delivered food, and house AIs no longer regulated fridges or envirodomes or trash collectors.

Antigravs failed with no drones to repair them, and the 'burbs shuddered as their tethers broke. Cumulus City drifted in Jørn's winds and—

Timon jerked away. 'Old Terra,' he breathed. 'I believe you.'

Dark figures rushed up the white corridor, drawing her attention to the security door. "Lockdown" still pulsed on the plasglas, beating in time to the boots on the other side.

Exposing the Librarian might cause chaos, but she wasn't hanging around to take the blame in its stead.

Is there another way out? She slid the thought into his brain, loading it with the memory of him telling her of the old maps, how the first colonists had built cities atop their colony ships.

Timon jerked and then was still, like an ersia scenting a 'pard. His mouth opened, words forming—

Don't speak, she thought, sending him an image of the Librarian and the security cams no doubt tracking their every whisper. *Think.*

He swallowed and nodded.

Words formed and dissipated in Timon's mind. She felt him bring the map up on his bracer and caught the jolt as he stopped himself when the Librarian and its ability to peek into his systems came to the forefront of his thoughts.

There was a furious whirring then, a cutting laser-like focus that seemed to go on forever.

Success, a brilliant golden light, burst in Timon's thoughts. He smiled, the tense expression almost a grimace, and squeezed past Fink to urge Phara into a tight turn before sprinting back the way they'd come.

Hero looked back at the dark figures on the other side of the security door, her visor picking out angry faces behind faceplates and the black, boxy shapes of pistols. Behind them, the large, red-black shape of a dober-shepherd loomed, matte grey armour strapped to its chest. Its amber-coloured eyes met Hero's and the shepherd's lips pulled back in a snarl just for her.

Phara pranced in the corridor ahead, hooves clacking on the deck, while beside her Timon ran his hands over a seam in the wall. He paused, pressed his ear to the surface, brow furrowed in concentration.

Down the corridor, boots and the heavier thud of paws shattered the silence.

'The police have passed the security door, Hero Regan. You cannot escape.'

Hero bit her lip, eyes locked on Timon's face as he moved to another section of wall. 'How would you know?' she asked the AI.

'I am the Librarian. The map Timon Dane is referencing came from my archives—'

Timon stepped back and thrust his foot through the wall. It shattered, shards of panelling thinner and more brittle than plasform clinging to his boot and littering the deck. He struck it again and again, the hole getting bigger even as the hot orange-brown weight of his rage pounded against Hero. Fear lurked behind it, but then it dissipated as he revealed the door hiding behind the wall.

It was old, with rounded corners and a chunky control pad that looked like it had been ancient before the first colonists left Earth.

'I can't open that,' Hero said. 'It's too old.'

'You don't have to.' Timon snatched the jwak from its sheath on her leg. In a second, he was in front of the door with the end of the jwak jammed against the pad.

The cylinder whined, high enough for Fink to flatten his ears, while its end glowed an angry red.

The explosion shook Hero. Her ears rang and the acrid scent of burnt biogel filled her nose, but it didn't matter because the door was swinging open.

Timon went first, then Phara, with Fink and Hero bringing up the rear. They didn't stop to close the door behind them; she doubted it would do much good if they had tried. They were in a new corridor, wider and taller than the first, Phara lighting up the walls with her pale lavender glow. Except the corridor didn't have walls, not exactly – they were doors, hundreds and hundreds of narrow plasglas doors, barcodes under the names stencilled across each surface. They lined both sides of the corridor, each one fronting a tiny person-sized tube. Hero's visor picked out details – breathing apparatus and squares of plasglas that looked like ancient monitors – in each tube as she heard the sharp thump of boots and the rough snick of claws behind them.

'Where are we?' she asked.

Timon paused long enough for Phara to catch up and then vaulted onto her back. The 'mare stretched out, leaping from a trot to a canter.

'Stasis deck,' Timon said. 'They were clustered mid-ship, around the ship AI's processing core. I guess the first-gens didn't need the space, or they thought they'd be going home someday. Whatever the reason, it'll get us to an old cargo lift. Should get us up a few levels.'

'Police. Stop!' The words boomed down the corridor behind them.

Phara shot forward, legs churning even faster, her hooves pounding the floor. She pulled a length ahead, then two, as Fink struggled to keep pace.

Hero's visor had no trouble picking out the red and black shape of the dober-shepherd, a police officer crouched low on its back. A pale yellow glimmer caught her eye a second before her visor zoomed in on the pistol in the rider's hand. She screamed a warning.

She didn't think. Fink was already in her mind, his muscles bunching, leaping, and twisting in mid-air. Phara though... Mentally Hero yanked the 'mare sideways.

The 'mare stumbled, but the bright yellow stun bolt whizzed past. Exhaustion hit Hero hard, but the police were too close and the cargo lift too far. She reached for the jwak.

Her hand closed on air, the empty holster teasing her fingers.

Fink grumbled, but his concentration was on the decking under his paws and the musty shuttle oil scent of the dober-shepherd at his back.

It didn't matter, the police were still too close.

Hero stretched her telepathy back. The officer's thoughts tasted peppery, focused. She slid through his shield and then... there. The officer tumbled from his mount, the 'shepherd skidding to a halt.

She snapped back into her own brain as exhaustion pulled her under.

CHAPTER 26

Hero came to in the lift, dust clogging her nose and her stomach sore from laying hunched over Fink's neck, the saddle pommel digging into her belly. She groaned, the sound echoed by the tortured creak of steelcrete.

Cold was her new best friend. It snuggled up against her heart, making her hands tremble and her fingers clumsy as she fumbled for the jwak again.

'It's not there,' Timon said. His voice was in her ear and she opened her eyes to meet his gaze, struggling to put a name to the emotion she found there. It made his jaw tight and pinched the space between his brows, looking like guilt and yet not.

His fingers wrapped around her wrist, and then her palm was wrapping around the familiar, smooth cylindrical grip of the jwak. She held it tight and waited for the tingle to warm her blood.

Nothing happened.

'I'm sorry,' Timon said, his grip slipping away. Hero knew the emotion that clouded his face, felt the lingering traces of it in the warmth of his hand. It was guilt and fear and the deep, steady knowledge that he'd make the same decision again – use the jwak to blow the old door's control pad, turning the stunstick into a dark, useless lump of burnt biogel and plasform.

Hero nodded, struggling to sit up and slip the tech back into its holster. Timon took it from her and did it instead.

She wanted her emotions to be as dead as the jwak, wanted the numbness in her hands to spread to her heart. She didn't want the bright, hungry bubble of panic that bloomed in her gut and spread to her chest to be the only spot of warmth in her whole body.

Fink purred and twisted to nuzzle her calf.

Exhaustion pulled at her eyelids, weighed her down. Her telepathy still worked – Timon was a bright hum at her knee – but trying to reach for Phara, who was standing just three metres away, was a different matter. She didn't get halfway before her power wavered and the tendril of thought snapped back inside her skull. The panic ignited, hitching her breath. Without her telepathy she was defenceless, as useless with her frozen limbs as the jwak.

Fink growled, flashing his teeth. *Not defenceless. He was here, he would protect her against anything.*

You can't protect me against guns.

The growl turned into a snarl and he twisted to look at her out of the corner of one big, black eye. *He was a telepath too.*

The lift shuddered and groaned, the sound grating on her ears.

'We're almost there.' Timon's voice was harsh, croaky. He coughed.

Hero lifted herself up enough to ease the press of the pommel into her belly. There was a grey cast to the skin around Timon's eyes and a glimmer of sweat on his skin.

'You don't look so good,' she said.

'Yeah.' He raised a hand to wipe away the moisture under his nose. 'I don't feel so good either. Don't think that'll stop the police from arresting us though.'

The lift stopped, another shudder wracking its sides before the doors cracked open. Timon pressed the control panel, leaning his weight on the plasglas. Nothing happened. He punched it, a sharp sudden jab that cracked through the lift.

Hero unstrapped herself and slid off Fink's back, holding onto the saddle to stay upright. 'It won't open if you break it.'

Timon breathed deep, his back to her, unclenching the fists at his side, one finger at a time. 'I know, it's just...'

Carefully Hero shuffled closer. 'I'll do it.'

Her fingers shook, and Timon had to get the biogel tendrils from her backpack and string them between her bracer and the pad's guts. She might have chafed at the way he fumbled with the thin bit of skin that covered the port on the underside of her bracer, might have snapped at how long he took to peel back the panel, but exhaustion and the cold had sapped her. Instead, she was glad she didn't have to force her fingers to stay still long enough to attach the biogel or dig her nails into the fine edge between the pad and the wall.

The panel's DNA spread across her visor, as old and chunky as its plasglas display. She had the door the rest of the way open in seconds. The room beyond was dark but for the light from the lift and the faint glow of another panel on the far wall.

Timon slipped an arm around her waist, and without thinking she wrapped an arm over his shoulders. The pair shuffled into the new space.

Hero could just make out a solid door with the rounded corners and dull white metal of Old Terra construction set in the far wall, and the shadows of old plasglas screens that lined the chamber's walls.

She stopped in the middle of the chamber as the realisation sunk in. 'You found the Librarian's core.' She only had a second to pause before Timon dragged her forward.

There was a single-minded determination in the way he hauled her across the antechamber, a laser focus in his thoughts. 'I still had the map, it wasn't hard.' He stopped in front of the panel beside the door. 'Your turn again.'

She put her hand to the panel. It was newer than the others, but still old enough that she had no trouble pulling its code out through her bracer. Several tense minutes later and a loud *thunk* echoed through the chamber. Hero held her breath, knew Timon was doing the same, and then... nothing happened.

'Terra damn it!' Timon threw himself against the door. It creaked.

He barged against it again. The hinges squealed.

Timon braced his shoulder to the door and forced it open, rust and paint flaking off the Old Terran steel. For a moment, everything strained, the gap between door and bulkhead widening a centimetre, and the effort made veins stand out on Timon's neck before it crashed inward.

He sprawled across the deck.

Phara *hiss-neighed* and nudged his foot.

'Are you okay?' Hero asked.

'Yeah.' He pushed to his feet.

Fink stuck his head through the door before backing out, rumbling with displeasure. *He wouldn't fit.*

She slipped off his back and wobbled her way through the airlock. The space on the other side took her breath away.

A tank of biogel rose two storeys above and sank another two below. It was wide enough to rival a forest behemoth, and lit from within by veins of energy that radiated from a central core of blue-white so bright it burned an afterimage on the back of her eyeballs.

'I've never seen an AI core.' Timon's words echoed through-out the chamber.

Hero pressed her hands to the tank and thought it hummed with her own heartbeat. 'I have,' she whispered. 'It didn't look like this.' The AI she'd destroyed two years ago had looked like a stack of metallic boxes growing one atop the other. Ayumon had been powerful but ancient, even by the Librarian's standards.

The plasglas under their feet was crazed and frosted with age, but clear enough to see through to the sharp silver connectors at the tank's base. The walkway wrapped around the tank, only wide enough for Hero to brace herself with a hand against the tank and wall without having to stretch her arms. She staggered for a few metres before finding her balance against the wall, Timon a warm presence at her back. A short way from the hatch, an alcove was cut into the bulkhead. It was just big enough for a bank of old-fashioned screens – curving lengths of plasglas spanning the width of her and

Timon's outspread arms – and an equally ancient keyboard.

She kept walking.

'Hey, what are you doing?' Timon grabbed her shoulder. 'Didn't we come here to find this?' He gestured to the alcove.

'I can't access it here; this is probably just a maintenance station. And it's old, really old.'

Timon's gaze narrowed. 'I've seen you hack into the Farm from a workstation in an alien outpost a quarter of the way across the globe. Surely this is easier.'

The old screen lit up, and the Librarian peered out. 'It is, Timon Dane. Would you care to try?'

Timon pressed his back to the tank. 'That's a trick question, right?'

'It'll try to electrocute you as soon as you touch the keyboard,' Hero said.

'Right, so it's not in the business of harming people unless it's, you know, convenient.'

'A correctly calibrated electrical charge would merely render you unconscious until authorities arrived,' the Librarian said.

Hero tugged on Timon's arm. 'Come on, it's distracting us on purpose.'

'What do you intend to do, Hero Regan?' The Librarian's voice followed them around the tank.

'Yeah,' Timon whispered. 'What are you going to do?'

She pressed a black pouch into his hand and an image into his mind: six palm-sized black eggs pressed to the tank and a blackened hole. Refusal sang in Timon's thoughts, but she ignored it.

She shifted the pack strapped to her back. 'Librarian, remember, last year, when I told you I'd make you pay for betraying me?'

'I said you were welcome to try, Hero Regan.'

'Well,' she said, 'this is me trying.'

She shuffled to a stop over a hatch in the walkway. There was no control pad beside it, just a handle set into the thick plasglas. Timon crouched down and hauled it open a crack.

'You can't stop the viruses. All four were introduced to Cumulus

City's biosphere two hours, three minutes and thirty-eight seconds ago.'

Hero's breath stopped. For a split second she thought of Tybalt, relief flooding her chest before horror chased it out. Her gaze went to Timon. He stared at the hatch, face slack and skin turning ashen. His shock hit her like a sternard to the chest.

'Timon Dane, the likelihood of you having escaped exposure is two point eight three per cent,' the Librarian boomed.

Fear rose in Hero's gut, some of it her own but most of it Timon's. It was muted, the sharp wrench of its teeth blunted by a stunning sense of unreality. It wrapped her in a bright cocoon that made the air glitter and the seconds slow, giving her aeons to picture Timon on the same bed as the Klaude hunter, his eyes rolled up and bloody froth dribbling down his chin. She wondered too, just for a moment, if being a telepath would change the way his psyche tasted.

The Librarian spoke again. 'All that remains is to release the second stage of the Regan virus.'

Timon looked up, his expression turned to stone. 'There's a second stage?'

Hero nodded. 'To help it spread.'

His teeth gritted and the muscles in his neck stood out. He gripped the handle set into the hatch and lifted. 'Quick, I can't hold it long.'

She scrambled through the hole and clunked down the ladder. Her feet hit the deck, and she looked back up at Timon.

'I'll do it,' he said and dropped the hatch, the pouch with the six egg-shaped objects she'd pressed into his hand clear in his mind.

'Hero Regan.' The Librarian appeared front and centre in her visor. 'Do you comprehend me? It is too late to stop the viruses.'

Her gaze only half on the walkway, she almost tumbled down the first of the steps that spiralled to the base of the tank below.

There wasn't much room at the bottom, just a tiny ribbon of walkway around the tank that matched the bandwidth of plasglas sitting atop the tank's solid metal rim. The base came up to her waist and staring across it was like watching a lightning storm in a fish tank; the biogel rippled with power, the flashes and lightning strikes clustered around opalescent shapes pulsing with their own light.

She stumbled around the base, looking for an input. There had to be one. *Had to.* And there, almost as she'd completed the loop back to the stairs, was a glowing recess in the tank's base. She fell to her knees and tore the pack off her back, splitting open the hard plasform.

'What are you doing, Hero Regan?'

The pack was empty, the drones that had nestled in the halfdozen egg-shaped recesses gone, but there was another opening and Hero ripped the foam away, revealing the tube she'd taken from Bayard's stores. The hypostick gleamed in her fist, longer and fatter than any she'd ever seen before. She didn't need it to take a sample of the Regan virus anymore – the Librarian had seen to that. Now she could use it for something else.

'Hero Regan?'

The hypo was awkward in her hand; it was too big to wrap her fingers around, but she rolled back her sleeve and pressed it to the crook of her arm. A sharp jab and Hero looked away as the clear cylinder filled with blood, the rings of a biohazard symbol coming to life around the tube. A beep and then a cool mist sprayed against her skin as the hypo sealed the tiny wound.

'You like my DNA so much,' Hero said as she pressed the hypo to the input's soft membrane. 'You can have it.'

The *shh-stick* was almost lost in the thumping of her heart, but for once it didn't fill her with dread. For a moment, the biogel around the input turned red as her blood spread through it, but the colour dissipated quickly, turning pink and then a ghostly shade of mauve before disappearing entirely.

The Librarian flickered in her visor, caught in a moment of static even as an army of nanites rose inside the tank like a white cloud.

'Your bl-lood can-cannot harm me, Hero Regan.'

Hero looked up, peering through cloudy layers of plasglas to find the shadow of Timon's shoes. 'I know,' she said.

She brushed Timon's consciousness, experienced the breath he drew deep into his lungs, saw through his eyes as he set the little black device against the tank. He set his thumb to the activation.

'I'm just slowing you down,' she said.

The explosion had no sound. It vibrated through the soles of her boots and raced through the biogel on a shock wave, fragmenting its veins of power.

Static shuddered through the Librarian's avatar, making it ripple and pop in her visor. 'A single... ex-explosive cannot—'

A second detonation ripped through the core. Bigger than the first, she felt the boom without hearing it, an explosion of pressure like an ice-pick to her ears. The pain sent Hero to her knees. She heard a ponderous *craaack*, the sound starting low – a creak nearly below hearing. It deepened, growing louder and louder until it snapped.

A split ran through the tank's side like thick white roots seeking water, a hundred smaller ones branching out and wrapping around the giant cylinder.

'Core breach.' It wasn't the Librarian who spoke but another voice, the flat crackling tones of an ancient recording. 'All personnel, evacuate the core.'

The Librarian shuddered and jerked on her screen as the shock waves continued to bound and rebound through the biogel.

Was it enough? Hero got to her feet, barely keeping her balance as she peered up at the cracks. The faint, fishy scent of biogel teased her nose as the root-like cracks stopped growing.

The ancient voice spoke again. 'Repair bots initiated. Core containment in six minutes. All personnel, evacuate.'

Egg-shaped bots the size of both her hands swarmed the tank, hovering a breath from the plasglas and spraying it with a fine mist that made the white cracks fade to a barely perceptible shimmer.

A sharp burst of alarm jerked her attention upward. The bots were swarming Timon. She caught frantic glimpses of him ducking and waving his arms as the drones zapped his hands and back as he ran for the airlock.

No. Panic welled in Hero's gut and she slammed her palms against the plasglas. *They're fixing the tank. You have to rupture it now!* Seizing Timon was instinctual. She made him turn around, but then she heard Timon's dark orange-brown voice, smothered beneath her lightning-laced grip.

Trust me, he said.

She paused, letting the words sink in. She let go.

Timon wasted no time sprinting for the hatch and slamming it behind him.

'Hero Re-Regan.' The Librarian wavered and jerked, its voice rough with static. 'You have f-failed and your accomplice has deserted you.'

She leaned on the console, the weight on her hands the only thing stopping her knees from folding. 'He'll be back.'

'Not before the police arrive.' A vid replaced the Librarian, the vision partially obscured by static but clear enough to make out uniformed figures approaching.

A thump vibrated through the walkway. It came again, this time shaking the tank. A third, and new ripples shivered through the biogel, not as large as the explosion but enough to send a fresh wave of static through the AI.

A fourth strike, and she stretched her telepathy upward. On the fifth, she saw through Fink's eyes as Phara let fly, her hooves striking the tank with enough force to leave head-sized dents in the plasglas.

The 'mare struck again, smack bang in the centre of the crazed mass left by the explosion.

The salty scent of fish teased Fink's nose a moment before a tiny piece of the tank fell away. biogel oozed from the hole.

The sound of the alarm brought Hero slamming back into her body.

'Hero Regan. You will leave the planet in chaos.'

She focused on the Librarian, the way its blue-white face flickered and shook in her visor as the first dribble of the AI's brain splattered on her helmet. Panic and doubt mix in her gut, but she pushed them aside.

'It'll survive,' she said.

Another strike, this time a wet, flat crunch like a bone breaking. Biogel shot out over Phara's rump and tail. The 'mare started in panic and barrelled past Fink to escape, Timon lagging behind.

'Hero!' he yelled.

She ignored him. She even ignored the river of biogel pouring onto the walkway above, sneaking around the edges and dripping down the walls. She focused all of her will on the Librarian.

'Goodbye.'

'Hero Regan—'

Hero shut her visor off. The tank split open.

CHAPTER 27

Swimming through biogel sucked. It snuck up her nose and wormed its way under her helmet and into her ears. Every movement, every heartbeat made the air burn in her lungs. The surface was always there, just out of reach.

It was like being in the river again, thrashing toward the sky, but this time Fink wasn't there to save her. Mentally, she heard him yowling, felt his desperate panic and mad scramble as he tried to push and twist his body through the too-small door.

The air was caught in her throat.

An arm under her ribs, followed by a yank, and Hero was flopping about on the plasglas decking, the biogel still up to her chest, but at least her mouth and nose were free. She gasped, drawing air in deep ragged breaths like she'd never get enough as Timon dragged her to her feet.

Hero was barely aware of Timon, or of Phara's tail coated in the same goo that soaked her every pore. She only recognised Fink when his forearms wrapped around her middle and jerked her out of Timon's grip. He licked her face, ears and neck.

'Fink,' she said, gently pushing his muzzle away before he could drag the rough edge of his tongue up her cheek.

'Come on.' Timon tried to tug on her arm, but snatched his hand back at Fink's growl. 'Dude, we gotta go. There's only one way out of here and the Librarian said—'

'We're covered in the Librarian,' Hero said, lifting her feet from the gel pooling around her ankles.

'That's not gonna stop the police,' Timon said as he stabbed at the lift's controls. 'You coming?'

The biogel tingled on her skin and a new energy thrummed in her veins, chasing away the chill. It started in her ankles and travelled up to the sensors on her scalp. She pulled away from Fink's grip and climbed into the saddle.

It was like ripping the powerpak out of the jwak. As soon as her feet left the deck the warm, delicious stream of energy went with it. Fatigue dragged at her bones again and everything ached.

'Hero?' She heard his voice, muted by the cold and the sharp *splash-slosh* of Fink walking through the goo at their feet, the clear biogel still flickering with power.

'Hero?' Timon's hand touched her knee.

'Yeah,' she said. 'Coming.'

The lift was fast and silent, opening onto another dark and dusty corridor that lead them to another lift and yet another after that. There was no way to know where they were going other than up.

Holosigns flickered and spat where they weren't dead, static rolling through the screens that weren't frozen on a single image. The biogel from the Librarian's brain was drying and had formed a second skin over her nanoskin by the time they emerged in a place Hero recognised. The unmistakable lights of the Grip shone, but instead of an arcade packed with people, the holosigns flashed and bounced in an empty space.

A maintenance bot skimmed over the pale steelcrete floor, the sound of its hovers echoing off plasglas storefronts. It zigzagged back and forth, its underside glowing with the bright orange-red of a sanitising light. It was dwarfed in the huge space, a tiny speck in an endless arcade with a ceiling so high Hero couldn't see it.

Timon gripped her shoulder, and she jumped. 'What's wrong?' he said.

She pulled back. 'There's no one here,' she said.

'Yeah.' Timon peered around. 'Let's not hang around too long, it's kinda creepy.'

Fink lifted his nose to the air, his nostrils flaring as he breathed deep. He growled and the image he pushed at her made Hero shudder.

'Roaches!' The curl of Hero's lip echoed Fink's. 'Lots of them.'

Timon didn't say anything, but there was a new tension in his shoulders as he led the way.

Every clack of Phara's hooves echoed, ringing out against storefronts and mixing with the whirl of the lone maintenance bot, but nowhere did Hero hear the telltale skittering of roaches.

Her back crawled with tension, the skin prickling as if the roaches were marching up her spine instead of lurking out there, somewhere in the darkness. The same unease vibrated in Fink's every step and all but his foreclaws were retracted, his footfalls making the barest snick on the steelcrete and his growl, ever-present since they had left the lift, was now bottled up in his chest.

Even if he had let it out, the sound of Phara's passing would have drowned the noise. The 'mare danced sideways, her strides short and choppy, her muzzle in the air and her nostrils wide as she scented the still air.

Hero's hand ached and she couldn't help but wrap it around the jwak. The grip was cold, the biogel unresponsive, and no matter how hard she squeezed there was no tingle or rush of warmth to chase away the ice in her marrow.

Fear squeezed her throat. What good was she, with her limbs numb and her legs too weak to stand? She couldn't fight an AI, the police, or the swatai. Her gaze bored holes in Timon's back. She couldn't fight a virus.

If only...

Fink stopped. The tension in his spine sang through the saddle and unleashed the adrenaline in her veins. But when she touched his thoughts, it wasn't the skitter of roaches that had pricked his ears or made him spin on his haunches.

The police emerged from a big storefront, half of them with pistols aimed at Hero's chest, the others pointed at Fink. Behind them, a pair of dober-shepherds split up and stalked around Fink, one on either side. From somewhere further back came the buzz of a hover, the familiar hint of lavender surrounded by the musty scent of fur teasing her awareness.

'Hero Regan,' said a man in front of the rest, his lined face set hard and his pistol set on her. 'You're under arrest for multiple acts of terrorism. You have the right to remain silent—'

She didn't hear the rest.

Phara screamed, and the pistols trained on Hero's chest found a new target in the 'mare.

The roaches – some no taller than Fink's knee, others mountainous monsters with shells a riot of shifting, hypnotic colours – swarmed out of every nook and cranny. The sound of their skittering grated on her ears, but it was the shadows slinking behind the wall of roaches that put the ice back in her veins.

A trio of rucnarts, their dark dappled coats as out of place under the lights of the arcade as the brightly coloured qwans hovering over the swarm.

Hero met n'Tao's dual gaze, the spike of his grief and anger striking so deep that it roused Demona, before a second roach swarm, one they hadn't seen, struck the police from behind.

Shouts followed the *crack* of pistols, the chittering of roaches, the roar of a shepherd, the yell of a police officer, and the sound of Phara's hooves on shell. It was chaos, the Jørans watching from the sidelines, the cold, glassy presence of the qwans riding the roaches', directing them as they sandwiched the humans between them, the police officers' pistols barely scorching the insectoids' exoskeletons.

The rumble of a hover filtered in through the sound of pistols and roaches. The qwans scattered as a bulky black shape whizzed overhead, its engines grazing the storefronts as it swung around, leaving fractured plasglas in its wake. Hero didn't see it land or the sides peel away, but the musty wave of fur, lemon and lavender against her consciousness was unmistakable.

Harish's piercing battle cry was almost drowned under the angry yowl of 'pards. For a second, everyone froze: qwans, police, and rucnarts. In that moment, Hero was aware of Norah sliding her influence over the roaches, a smooth lavender shield severing the qwans' control.

But it was only for the moment, long enough for the qwans' rage to gather and Hero to throw herself over Norah's psyche.

The void flickered. Norah's gaze met her own, and there was Apani standing behind her, the silver-blue of the 'pard's own shields extending over the girl. Hero saw the Bayard shuttle land outside the pack's den, flashed to Tybalt at the helm with Smit on the comms, and witnessed Emma plead with the matriarch through two sets of eyes.

You are not 'pard. Apani's words echoed between them. *But she remembered when your kind were pack.* Another memory, of a younger Apani, without the grey flecking her muzzle, racing over the plains with a rider crouched low over her neck.

The roaches surged forward, the smaller ones skittering through the legs of the larger, only to be met by 'pard claws.

The pack surrounded Apani, with Red and Orin leading the charges. Shells cracked and roaches shrieked, and then pistol fire lit up the air as the police joined them.

Still more roaches poured from the darkness, until the arcade was awash in a sea of dark shells, quickly surrounding police and 'pards.

It wasn't until the downbeat of a qwan's wings blew air over her face that Hero realised she and Fink had been cut off from Norah and the police.

Behind them, Phara's hooves cracked on another shell and Fink spun around, Hero barely hanging onto the saddle. A river of roaches had come between them and the 'mare, slowly pushing her and Timon deeper into the arcade with the rucnarts pacing the edge of the swarm.

Fink yowled and leaped forward, claws unsheathed, fangs bared, and bits of shell and blood splattered Hero's face.

Hero. The gold of Paris's voice echoed and surprise made her whole body jerk.

Uncle? Hero stretched her telepathy and twisted in the saddle as she hunted for his apparition. All she saw was the battle, bolts of light and claws flashing.

Close your eyes, Hero.

Paris smiled at her from the back of her eyelids, but the expression was wrong – too tight, his eyes grim.

There's nowhere on or above this planet that the myriad can't reach, little fish. D'Ojon spoke through Paris's mouth, her uncle's golden touch breaking apart as the endless, shifting blue-green of the myriad swarmed out of the cracks.

Hero jerked, trying to open her eyes and rip herself away before the blue-green could touch her, but it was too late. Her eyes were glued closed, the myriad's sharp, glassy tendrils winding through her brain. Distantly, she felt Fink throw himself at the tendrils, his mawberry-pink skidding over the shiny surface with an ear-shreding screech.

D'Ojon ignored him, still shining through Paris's eyes. The myriad filled the space around them like sunlight in shallow water. Images shifted in it, fading one into the other, filling the darkness. *It is time, little fish. We will wait no longer.*

The myriad fell on her and, just like that, Hero was gone.

CHAPTER 28

She sat behind d'Ojon's eyes, a tiny mote of chocolate-coloured darkness. She felt the rough pelt under the swatai elder's flippers like they were her own hands, experienced the familiar gliding motion of a rucnart, and knew the same nerves that had the elder's stomach churning as they rode the giant Jøran through the humans' frigid city.

It was too bright up here, the stark difference between light and shade stabbing their eyes, piercing the thick membrane of their outer eyelids and spreading across the thin inner lids like a sunburst. But it was nothing to the noise, the discordant bang of the humans' metal and the hum of their energy.

It had vibrated in his ears and shaken his bones the moment n'Tao carried him into the humans' mountain, only to grow quiet again after they climbed into one of the flying boxes. *Cargo shuttle*, the human words and meaning came at his call, pilfered from the little fish's memory. There'd been more knowledge behind the words, of paths that would carry them into the sky in secret, and spread them throughout the humans' city. *Freight system.*

The air inside the shuttle had grown warm as more tree-kin and air-kin followed them in, ersia clustering at their feet. And then the hum had come again, louder this time, loud enough that he shrieked and tried to bury his ears in n'Tao's fur like the littlest kitten. He'd escaped his body to the comforting presence of the other elders and seen the shuttle through their eyes as it lifted from the ground and rose without the benefit of wings to disappear through a hole in the mountain.

In the long journey from ground to sky, the hum hadn't lessened, but he'd grown used to the way it shook his bones. Still, he did not leave the muffling warmth of n'Tao's ruff until the hum ceased, and when the shuttle opened and they poured out into the humans' alien city, there was no time to wish himself back in the ocean.

There'd been humans and screams, the roar of the tree-kin and the air-kin's silent stalk as they took control of the creatures the humans called *roaches*. Then there'd been the bright glowing things called *holoscreens* and n'Tao's impatient shuffle while the myriad searched their stolen knowledge to tell the holoscreen where to send them.

And now, now the air-kin wielded the roaches against the humans with ruthless joy while the tree-kin stalked the city's shadows.

It will be done soon, water-kin. N'Tao's voice vibrated in d'Ojon's mind, rumbling up from where his fishing claw hooked into the male's ruff, thick with the scent of earth and the whisper of leaves. *My tree-kin have the part-breed's scent.* An image of Fink projected from the rucnart to the swatai. *Has the watermind succeeded?*

D'Ojon hunkered into the warmth of the tree-kin's pelt. Unease ran through the myriad, a foul tide that rippled and shifted within the ever-changing blue, but it did not slip past the barrier of their inner thoughts. The myriad was in agreement; the tree-kin and air-kin did not need to know that the youngling had disappeared.

Yes, she is with us. No hint of falsehood tainted their words.

The myriad had swallowed the youngling whole, a lightning-laced shadow, dark like rich mud but without the tree-kin's earthy scent. Before the myriad could reach into the youngling and spread her experiences and the sweet, sharp taste of her through itself, she had vanished, obscured by a brilliant golden flash that left behind only darkness.

The rucnart rumbled, the sound quiet but deep, like the hunt-song of the ocean's silver behemoths shivering across d'Ojon's flippers. Answering rumbles shivered through the dark, cold mountains of the human dwellings, some near and some far, all humming over his pelt and leaving the warmth of victory behind.

We have their peacekeepers, water-kin. The humans will be ours soon.

Deep within, the myriad seethed as the tides twisted and turned, seeking the youngling's shadow. If they could not find her, they could not absorb the alien patterns of her mind, the humans would remain out of reach and this invasion of the humans' den would be for naught.

D'Ojon clung tight to the tree-kin, leaving just a portion of himself to tend his flesh, before he surrendered the rest to the shifting blue of the myriad.

Hero. It was less a word than a familiar touch, the warm golden hand on her shoulder turning her around until she faced her uncle, both of them floating in the darkness behind d'Ojon's eyes.

Where are we?

You know where we are.

It doesn't feel like the myriad, Hero said. *I'm... me.*

For now. Paris gripped her shoulders and Hero winced at the weight of fingers biting into her flesh. She tried to pull away, but his grip only tightened. *The myriad will find you soon.* Paris forced her eyes to his. The look in them was hard, matching his flattened lips and tight jaw. *You have to act before they do.*

An image pressed against Hero's mental shields. She threw her hand up to force it away, digging her palm into Paris's forehead. Something sickly and dark swam in her belly, the puke-yellow fear gathering around her feet. Her other hand joined the first. She leaned into the image with all her weight, but it slipped through her hands, and the secret thought that was tucked away, small and tight, rose to whisper in her ear.

Something only a Regan could do, Paris said. *A myriad to face the myriad.*

She shoved it away, but it bounced back, growing in strength until it blinded her, a great golden beacon to rival the sun. *No, I won't.*

Then Fink will die.

It was like her eyes snapped open, or maybe closed because that great golden ball was gone, housed only in the light behind her uncle's eyes. *What?*

Look, he said.

D'Ojon blinked the swatai's outer lids to clear the stars from her vision. She didn't see anything at first; the swatai's eyes were sunk too deep in the rucnart's ruff to get a clear view, but she didn't need to see to recognise Fink's blood-curdling snarl.

She pushed d'Ojon's flippers straight until she could see between the tree-kin's ears. It was strange seeing Fink through the swatai's eyes, stranger still to see herself slumped over his neck, boneless as a rag doll.

Fink stood with his head down and his lips pulled back, vibrating with the sound ripping out of his throat. Phara pranced behind him, Timon grey and slumped on the 'mare's back. The rucnarts had them separated from the rest, a sea of roaches between them and the whirling mayhem of police and 'pards. Norah sat upon Apani's back, both her and the matriarch's gazes turned inward as Red danced around them in a storm of teeth and roach blood. The rest of the pack stood shoulder and fangs with police and dober-shepherds alike.

Three sleek shadows, the colour of a darkened forest, slid through the chaos of roach shells. The rucnarts, with n'Tao at their centre and d'Ojon in the hollow between his shoulder blades, moved toward their prey.

They had Fink and Phara against a storefront, their backs to the towering plasglas, holos fizzing and popping behind them.

D'Ojon's slim muzzle couldn't scent fear like the rucnarts could, but Hero didn't need him to. The scent of it rolled up her flippers from the rucnart's own nose. It was sweet and acrid at the same time – most of it stank of human and toa-mare, but there was a faint, musty tang wafting from Fink that made the n'Tao rumble with satisfaction.

As one, the rucnarts stalked closer.

No. Hero dug d'Ojon's fishing claws into n'Tao's neck, but the tiny spurs barely penetrated his thick fur. The rucnart kept stalking forward. *No,* she said again, mentally throwing herself at the rucnart.

Hero bounced off the inside of d'Ojon's shields. She threw herself at them again and again, each time harder than the last, but no matter how she scrabbled at the smooth, glassy surface, it remained between her and the rucnart.

Still, she kept trying, reaching out for Fink or Phara or *anyone.* She didn't notice d'Ojon's mind becoming heavier and his limbs harder to move until the elder's mental breath was on the back of her neck.

The myriad swallowed d'Ojon's vision, plunging Hero into an ocean of shifting light.

Hello, little fish. The thought came from everywhere, reverberating from the blue-green in a thousand echoes of d'Ojon's voice. *Welcome home.*

The myriad swallowed her again, but this time Hero had enough time to throw up a shield. A thin glittering barrier of chocolate.

Hero. Wrapped inside the darkness and concentrating on holding the thin shell, she barely heard Paris, but his golden glow warmed her cheeks and gave her the strength to hold on just a little longer. *I'm sorry,* he said.

For what? she wanted to ask, but then he wrapped himself around her and she knew, knew because he *was* her. All that was left of her uncle sank into her skin – his memories and emotions permeating every single part of her. She saw her mum, young and smiling. She rode a pea-dragon, faced a qwan, and felt her body grow sick and slow, knowing as she fell asleep on a pebbled shore that she'd never wake again.

Paris sat in the back of Hero's psyche, the lively warmth of his presence turned static and cold. Her uncle was gone, just another dead person taking up room in her mind, but he'd left something more valuable than the thin golden skin bolstering her shield of chocolate. Something only a Jørgen – that only a Regan could do.

Hero opened her eyes. Her visor flicked to life, her bracer buzzed against her skin, and the thick, dusty scent of Fink filled her nose.

Inside she let the restless core unfurl. Guided by golden memories she stretched herself, the core stretching with her. Fink reached back, mawberry filling in the spaces in a familiar merging. The restless thread drew them closer until they were breathing the same air, sharing the same warmth and the same fading power.

The myriad squeezed and Hero and Fink's combined mental shield fractured a little. A glassy claw reached through to sever their connection just as n'Tao barrelled into Fink.

Pain exploded behind Hero's eyes before she hit the ground, blinding her for a second before the impact pushed the air from her chest. For a moment, all she saw were the sparks behind her eyes, and then she was dragging oxygen into human lungs and rolling to her hands and knees even as Fink and n'Tao snapped and snarled behind her and the myriad pressed harder on her shields.

There was no warmth left in her body, just the roiling, restless coil demanding more. She needed power, but the jwak was dead.

The shining holo over a shop window caught her eye. Below it, a holostrip rippled with the city's power. Hero didn't hesitate; she elbow-crawled across the ground, each worm-like shuffle harder than the last as the myriad nipped at her mental heels.

Her fingers wrapped around the holostrip. The biogel pulsed, alive against her skin, but hard and glassy, her fingers screeching across the surface. She pulled herself the last few centimetres, grabbed the jwak and brought it down with all her remaining strength.

Plasform shattered, pinging off her visor. Her helmet screamed, but it was nothing compared to the blaze that engulfed her arms. Energy rippled through the biogel stuck to her skin, searing her eyeballs a second before the power seared her veins.

Her skull exploded, a supernova consuming the sector, the city, and all the 'burbs. Her bones melted, her skin boiled, and still the power flowed over her skin, filling her up and up and up.

Little fish, what did you do? The words vibrated through the light, sinking into her skin, and when she turned it wasn't with her body but the space inside her head. The void was gone and in its place was... everything.

She felt n'Tao and Fink breaking apart, the rents left by claw and fang in their sides. She felt Timon, Phara, Apani, and Norah, and a billion other minds too, all turning the void into a riot of blazing stars. They merged into a single colourless whole, blinding her until she narrowed her sight and concentrated. A thousand shades of blue, red, and a million nameless colours danced across her vision. Most shone with a soothing, even light, while others vibrated with sharp, angry jerks or quivered with fear, and there... a few rang with a restless prickly energy that reached back.

Jørgens. More than she could count in a single glance, thrown among the stars like supergiants, burning brighter and hotter than everything else. They rested in her mental palm – sleeping, flying, and swearing.

And there, hidden behind a pinpoint blazing brighter than all the others, was the swatai myriad.

The rucnarts struck.

Hero batted them aside, a casual flick that felled the trio in mid-pounce. She heard their moans through seven sets of ears, saw the way their bodies hit the ground from as many angles, and sensed the sharp sting of alarm as d'Ojon tumbled off n'Tao's back.

The swatai staggered to his feet.

Fink stalked the elder. Within the void, Hero felt the cool steelcrete beneath his paws and the tension burning through his muscles.

The elder stood, even with his flippers spread wide and his red crest standing tall he was little more than a twig before Fink's advance.

Fink snarled, lips rolling back from wicked fangs, anger rolling off him in dark mawberry waves that choked Hero's senses.

The elder did not move, not to twitch or blink, not even when Phara sidled up beside Fink, the crack of her hooves filled with menace. In the air around d'Ojon glowed the ghosts of the elders, a thousand more minds half-glimpsed behind each of them. They struck as one.

Hero was there before the blow landed, a wall between the companions and the collected swatai. She shuddered under the impact.

Little fish. Surprise lightened d'Ojon's thoughts, while the elders pressed against Hero, a wave that reached higher and spread wider as it searched for weak points. *You have grown.*

You can't use me to enslave them. An image of the cities, the billion sparkling minds within. Hero drew more power through the jwak, strengthening the wall until she could almost see it though Fink's eyes, glittering in the air.

D'Ojon snorted and amusement rippled throughout the other elders. *You have not grown that much.*

The elders pressed against the wall, so gently at first that Hero didn't even notice it, and then harder and harder. The wall rippled but held, the pressure little more than a firm hand on her chest. Then the tribe rose behind them, a hundred thousand minds joining the elders, and the hand became a 'pard sitting on her chest. The wall wavered, buckling.

Hero leaned on the city, the generators in her bones, their growl vibrating her insides as more power slammed through her veins to bolster the wall.

It held, but Hero wasn't aware of her body anymore, just the power burning her from the inside out and the wall, a brilliant never-ending curtain.

The tribe rampaged around the edges, fishing claws screeching and minds battering, pressing harder and harder. D'Ojon whispered in her ear; no longer just the tribe but the entire swatai species gathered behind his eyes, his voice ringing with the myriad minds. *Still not big enough, little fish.*

The myriad surged, and the wall crumbled.

Hero tumbled in the endless midnight blue, the city screaming in her ears. It was like being in the lagoon again, drowning in the cool blue, fighting her way to the sun. Except instead of a bright orange star, there was mawberry reaching back for her. She gasped and flailed, trying to claw her way out, even as the myriad tried to force its way down her throat and rip her apart.

She grabbed the light. Fink grabbed her back.

She was Fink – the fur bristling his back and the sweet, salty scent of the swatai flowing over his tongue – and Fink was her, filling in all the nooks and notches in her consciousness. Together, they were a force of mawberry and chocolate, flecked with the multi-hued remnants haunting Hero's being. Demona's blue, Guy's green, and Paris's golden shimmer.

It wasn't enough. The myriad cracked their outer shield.

New strength surged through Fink. Winding deep within the dark pink of his mind, a thread that pulsed with the rumble and purr of the pack. The myriad barely paused and the cracks in their shield widened.

They needed more, always more. There was no thought or argument, just the memory of touching the Jørgen girl and her strength becoming Hero's. The city burned in Hero's bones, the restless itch of the other Jørgens stark amid the galaxy of minds.

Hero reached for them all.

Panic. Fear. Wonder. The emotions slammed into her, overwhelming and mind-numbing, wrapping her in sticky tendrils of doubt and sapping the heat from her bones and the strength from her shields. Fink shuddered and howled, and the pack did the same. For a moment, just a moment, Hero's grip loosened on the city's warmth and Fink's mawberry and the Jørgens' restless energy slipped through her fingers.

The myriad passed through her shields, its delicate fingers

sinking talons into her brain. Pain burned through her synapses as the myriad's talons dug deeper, sinking through everything that was her.

She screamed, heard Fink screaming with her, as the swatai hissed with triumph and lunged beyond her, to the Jørgens and the humans beyond them.

No. *No. NO!*

The last came on the bright radiance of a star, a surge of power fuelled by a thousand Jørgen voices. The cracks in her shield snapped closed, and the myriad screamed as its fingers were severed, the digits withering to smoke before being shredded by the new maelstrom.

The maelstrom picked Hero up and tossed her about, drowning her, deafening her. She tried to fight it, to wrangle the cacophony and stop it from tearing her apart like the myriad's fingers, but it was too big, too strong. All those colours, all those voices ringing inside her, yelling, laughing, crying.

Paris's smooth golden voice slid through the chaos and tugged at the tightly held core of herself. *Open.*

She didn't argue, just let go of the hungry, roiling ball, watched it unfurl. The chocolate threads of herself tangled with the maelstrom, sinking into first one psyche and then another and another, until... until...

Silence. The maelstrom was still. She drew a breath, it drew one with her. She opened her eyes, the void overlapping with the real world, and a hundred others opened their eyes in unison with hers.

For a bright, shining moment the swatai ceased to exist, and a universe opened inside Hero. She wasn't just Hero or Fink anymore; she was a hundred other Jørgens as well, sliding against their minds like they slid against hers. Norah was there, and Emma. She was even aware of Apani, a ghostly echo at the edges of Fink's reach. No barriers, just a multitude of people, all of them woven together with a single chocolate thread. Meeting. Sharing. Understanding.

For a heartbeat, as all those separate people breathed as one, Hero understood what it would have been like to be swatai, to be one with the collective. Power richer than the city's generators thrummed through her veins, almost as heady as the absolute certainty that came with all those people picking through her memories and agreeing on one single task.

The memory of n'Tao paralysed by Norah's fear played in their collective consciousness.

They knew how to stop the swatai.

Slowly, feeling older than the world and filled with light, Hero stood. Just as slowly, a sphere formed in her mind's eye, its pearlescent shell coloured by everyone in the multitude. It filled with the deepest reaches of fear and doubt, of sweaty palms and pounding hearts, of tears and pain and the tight, sick feeling in the back of the throat. All of it poured into the pearlescent sphere, the darkest emotions of a thousand Jørgens flowing through Hero's hands.

Timon was slumped against a wall, eyes half-closed, his skin a ghastly shade of grey. Fink continued to stare down d'Ojon, Phara at his side. The little swatai was straight and unafraid in the face of the 'pard's teeth and the 'mare's sharp hooves. He looked past them and into Hero's eyes.

D'Ojon's nostrils flared. The myriad undulated behind him.

Little fish—

'No.' Her voice was the same, but in her head it was a clear, echoing chorus. 'We are Jørgen, and we're not little anymore.'

You cannot match our strength.

'We don't have to.' She felt Norah wrap the final, sticky tendril around the sphere as she filtered the last of the emotions. It was colder than space, cold enough to eat through flesh and melt bone. She lifted the sphere out of the multitude's hands, struggling under its frozen weight, and then withdrew the thread binding them together. The multitude dissolved, Norah the last to leave. It was just her, Fink, and the ghostly hands of her remnants holding the sphere aloft.

Their outer shields trembled.

The myriad tensed, anticipation surging through it in a dull orange wave that only grew stronger until it rivalled the sun.

'You'll do the work for us,' Hero said and let go of the city's power.

The warmth didn't have a chance to leave her bones. Fink wrapped himself around her.

The myriad struck, gobbling up the sphere as if it were nothing and reaching for Hero. But the claws she expected to rip them apart didn't come. Instead, wrapped within the cocoon of Fink's mind, Hero watched the myriad roll over them, watched as its claws pierced the sphere's thin pearlescent shell.

The sphere exploded.

The shock wave shook the myriad, a foul yellow wave of fear rolling in front, the crazed, sickly green of doubt behind. The myriad broke, its single harmonious voice fracturing into a billion discordant notes, the shock wave travelling from mind to mind, leaving a sticky residue behind.

A galaxy of individuals floated in an endless black void, the trillion threads that had connected them gone. The minds tried to reconnect, but every time a new thread emerged, the residue swarmed, dissolving the delicate tendril before it could grow.

Screams filled the void then, wails and whimpers echoing in the nothingness, drowning Hero in sound.

Slowly, the bright sparks of the swatai fell away, taking the sound with them until there was nothing left. Nothing save Hero and Fink, floating in the void.

CHAPTER 29

The holo of Hero's mum stared at her from the other side of the little white cube that had become Zass's new lab in the days after the release of the Regan virus.

Sometime in the aftermath of the swatai's defeat, as police and 'pards cleaned up the last of the roaches, someone had whisked Hero away. All the way to the Klaude complex under the mountain. Zass had her hooked up to monitors before she woke, but no one had poked or prodded, unless she counted the questions. Endless questions from dozens of lips, all revolving around the same thing. Was she sure the swatai were gone?

They weren't, but they were... damaged. In the last glimpse she'd had of them, scattered, the stickiness of the human emotion eating the connections between them, that damage had felt too big, too deep for them to heal anytime soon, if ever.

Across the lab, the holovid wavered as Patricia shifted, cubes of static running through her face, but it didn't change the scowl she wore.

Hero matched it. 'I'm fine,' she said.

'Doctor Zass?' Patricia said, looking behind Hero.

There was a murmur and then the soft tap of Zass's shoes.

'She's fine, Patricia.'

'See?' Hero slid off the biobed, boots thumping the floor. 'I told you.'

Patricia narrowed her gaze. 'You put your *hand* in a live subline.

Forgive me if I doubt your ability to look after yourself.'

'It wasn't my hand, Mum, and I saved the world.'

'A *subline*, Hero!'

'I needed the power!'

'I don't care if you needed the oxygen, the biogel, *or* the damn power, biological beings do *not*—'

A cleared throat interrupted the same argument Hero and her mum had been having since she'd woken up in a biobed almost three weeks ago. Both Hero and her mum's holo turned to face the source.

Tybalt stood in the lab's doorway, his face still pale and drawn but without the sickly cast that had haunted his complexion a week before. If she concentrated, Hero could almost see a new restlessness in the liquorice flavour of his thoughts. She wondered if Zass knew yet that the Regan virus had done more to Tybalt than cure the Pollen poisoning.

Tybalt straightened his jacket and clasped his hands behind his back. 'Dorich needs the uplink,' he said.

With the Librarian gone, the nets were in chaos, and uplinks like the one the Klaude used were in short supply.

Her mum's expression cleared as if by magic, the anger, with its hint of fear going with it. 'Of course,' she said. 'I wish I could be there with you, Hero, but—'

'No one's meant to know where I am,' she said. 'And you have to take care of things in Cumulus City.'

Patricia's smile was strained and Hero knew that her mum was expecting her to object to what she said next. 'It's for your safety,' she said.

'It's all right, Mum.' Hero hugged her chest and tried to push aside the memory of the endless news vids, the fear and anger on the people's faces when they said her name. 'I don't want anyone to know where I am either.'

Patricia was silent a moment before she nodded. 'Remember, no matter what anyone else says, *I'm* proud of you.' She smiled, just once, and disconnected the call.

Hero stared at the empty space where Patricia's holo had been. Her heart expanded at her mum's words, filling her chest and throat, even as tears prickled the back of her eyes.

She sniffed and blinked hard, looking up as Tybalt's waist-coat appeared before her.

He smiled and squeezed her shoulder. 'I'm proud too,' he said.

He waited a beat, giving Hero time to sniff again and scowl to cover up the heady emotion still clogging her throat.

'Are you ready?' he asked.

CHAPTER 30

She slipped the saddle over Fink's back, doing her best to ignore the vid playing on the opposite wall. The cluster of Bayard stablehands and Klaude that milled in front of it, with their soft mutters and worried expressions, should have helped, except that her name was projected there in huge letters.

"REGAN VIRUS DEATH TOLL RISES" hovered at the top of the screen as the vid flicked through visions of sick people and others in enviromasks and lab coats. It changed again, this time showing doors and arcades and entire skytowers with yellow holotape plastered across them; the word 'quarantine' scrolling across the tape, demanding attention.

It was an endless loop that had become all too familiar over the past month, feeding into the heavy miasma of frustration and fear in the city. This undercurrent pressed against her, carried on a rainbow of colours and flavours coming from the stablehands by the vid, and the Bayard scientists, the cooks, the hunters, the pilots and technicians – everyone. All of them searching for friends and family affected by the Jørgen viruses.

With the Librarian gone, information spread slowly, uploaded by hand and indexed by hastily grown AIs, doubling up on and contradicting each other constantly. There was no longer a reliable single source of truth.

Hero concentrated on the strap snaking under Fink's belly, inspecting the nanoleather for scratches like she hadn't gone over every millimetre of it the morning before. It was smooth and perfect, even the horrid rent from Red's fight with Orth in the marsh was gone like it had never been.

Fink huffed and nudged at her side, and when she looked up to scratch him behind the ear, there, again, was the holoscreen. Norah stood front and centre, both of her dads behind her and Dorich off to the side. Even Emma was up there, and Hero's mum, but it was Norah that the vids focused on. They called her a hero, and a vanguard of the future, while a smaller screen showed her sitting atop Apani as 'pards and police fought off a horde of roaches.

At least they were no longer plastering Hero's face all over the vids, no longer calling her a terrorist or an experiment. They'd also stopped trying to haul her off to prison, a lab, or a freak show, for people to poke and pride and yell at.

'You scare them,' Norah had said the one and only time they'd met since the swatai were defeated.

'Do I scare you?'

Norah didn't answer for a second, just stared at the ground. 'You scare everyone,' she finally said. But then she smiled. 'Except Emma.'

Hero shuddered. 'Emma scares *me.*'

Norah's grin widened. 'You just don't want her figuring out how to do the myriad thing.'

'She *can't* do the myriad thing.'

Her expression fell. 'I know, that's just you.'

An awkward, tense silence had fallen between them, long enough for Harish to poke his head out of Norah's hair and chirp at her.

'Are we friends again?' Hero asked.

'Maybe.' Norah crossed her arms. 'I still don't like what you did, or what you do, but I get it. Sort of.' Her expression darkened, and Hero knew Norah was remembering h'Ran. 'All that power. I never realised what that was like, how *easy* it made things, especially the bad things.'

'That's not an excuse though, is it?'

'No,' she said. 'It's not.'

And that had been the last she'd seen of Norah, or any other Jørgen, that wasn't on a newsvid. Almost like she was contagious. Hero secured one of the straps holding the saddle in place under Fink's belly. She grabbed the next strap and ducked under Fink's neck, frustration making her yank it hard.

Fink growled, swinging around to pin her with a reproachful gaze.

'Sorry,' she said.

He gave her a nudge.

'For what?' Another voice, deep and familiar except for the rough edge of sickness, came from Fink's other side.

Fink grumbled and Hero thumped his ribs before the sour taste of jealousy could become a snarl. Timon peered over his back.

'Hey,' she said.

'Hey,' he said back. He looked tired, with dark shadows under his eyes and his skin's usual rich brown still overlaid with grey. His hair had been shaved, making the brilliant blue sensors stand out even more.

Hero rubbed her scalp, fingers dragging over her own sensors. Not the ones she'd worn for over a year, but new ones, small and dark and sleek, almost invisible amid her hair.

'Zass let you out,' she said.

'Yeah. Apparently I'm stable.' Timon touched the glowing sensors. 'She's still keeping track though.' He paused. 'She still hasn't been able to contact my dad.'

'I'm sorry,' Hero said.

'Don't be,' he said. 'I planted the explosives.'

She nodded.

'So, ahh...' Timon said, rubbing the back of his neck. 'I was wondering ...'

'They don't,' Hero said.

He frowned. 'What don't?'

'Your thoughts.' Hero tugged and tucked the strap into place, the vacseal *shuuucking* closed. 'They don't taste any different.'

'Yeah, that wasn't what I was going to ask.' Timon leaned against the saddle, but froze at the growl that rippled in Fink's throat, and cast a wary eye at the fur bristling around the 'pard's neck. He stepped back, hands held up in front. 'Dude,' he said. 'We used to be friends.'

Hero hid a smile and poked Fink in the ribs. *Stop*, she said.

Fink grunted, ears twitching, but his ruff smoothed out and the growl faded, even though Hero could hear it echoing in his voice. *He did not like the way the human's thoughts tingled.*

They don't tingle.

Fink's tail slapped the ground. *They did*, he said and then he shot her a thought stolen from Timon's mind that made her blush. She ducked to hide it, hastily snatching up one of the packs piled at Fink's feet and swinging it up behind the saddle.

'Soooo...' Timon crossed his arms, tucking his hands under his armpits. 'You're leaving?'

Hero nodded, reaching for another pack. 'I'm taking a group out to find the Jørans, because... you know.' She gestured to the holoscreen.

'Because the Klaude stuffed it up the first time, Norah's busy being a hero, and you're a badass?' Timon's brows lifted high. 'Wait, you're actively *seeking out* the dudes that tried to eat us a month ago? Isn't that dangerous?'

Hero lifted her own brows, hand dropping to the shiny new jwak at her side.

'Yeah, I already said you're a badass, but *rucnarts*? As in more than four...' He spread his hands. 'I mean, come on.'

A slice of midnight appeared behind Timon.

'And what am I? Chopped wombacow?'

Timon yelped, and a smile cracked Imogen's face.

'Ugh.' Timon frowned as he took in the agent's envirosuit and the helmet tucked under her arm. 'I didn't think you lot did stuff, you know. Down here,' Timon said.

'I'm a *planetary* agent, Timon. I go where I'm needed, and right now the agency thinks I'm needed to keep an eye on this one.' She gestured to Hero.

A shadow appeared behind Imogen. 'Think I'm not up for the job, Lambert?' Smit said.

'I don't think anyone's up for the job.'

'Hmm, we'll see.' Smit turned her gaze to Hero. 'How's our escort, girl? I don't fancy venturing into rucnart territory without them.'

'Fink says the pack is waiting for us outside.'

'Then we're ready to go. Mount up!' she yelled.

Around the stables, a half-dozen Klaude and Bayard personnel swung into saddles, sternards shuffling their paws as their rider's weight settled on their backs. A trio of oad-hawks took off from the roosts next to each stall, landing on specially made perches behind their newly mounted handlers.

Smit and Imogen disappeared into the chaos, fastening helmets as they headed for their own mounts.

'So...' A flush of colour washed the grey out of Timon's cheeks and he looked down at something hidden behind Fink's bulk. 'I know you're leaving and all, but... ah... I was going to ask if you wanted to go out or take a walk around that big hole in the shuttle bay, or something.'

Fink huffed and slapped his tail against the steelcrete. *She should be getting on.* He wiggled the saddle.

'Girl.' A grey sternard blotted out her view of the stable. Smit sat astride. Her black gaze flicked to Timon and her lips twitched. 'Make it quick,' she said before shoving a helmet on.

Blushing hard enough that she thought her cheeks might catch fire, Hero swung onto Fink's back. 'Eight days,' she said. 'I told them it would probably take longer, but Smit wants us to be back in eight days.'

'Yeah?' Timon's eyes brightened. 'Cool. So, I'll see you then and we can... you know, do something.'

Hero blushed harder, covering it up by jamming her helmet on her head.

Smit's voice boomed through the stables. 'All non-suited personnel, clear the area. That includes you, Dane.'

Timon threw his hands wide. 'But I'm a Jørgen now!'

'Out.'

'Fine, fine.' He grinned at Hero, the expression lighting up the shadows under his eyes before he turned on his heel and headed for the nearest airlock with the remaining stablehands.

'You ready, girl?' The words were softer this time, sliding into her ears via her helmet's comm channel.

Hero nodded and Fink swung around to meet the big double doors that led outside.

'Good.' Smit urged her sternard up beside Fink. 'Lead the way, Regan.'

AUTHOR'S NOTE

September 2018

Before you ask, because I know you're going to ask, yes, this is the end of the *The Hero Rebellion*. After six glorious years, it is time for Hero and I to part ways, for me to explore other worlds and other lives, while she gets on with hers.

But never fear dear reader.

Hero will return.

DO YOU WANT MORE HERO?

I love keeping in touch with my readers, it's the second-best thing about being a writer (writing being the first best). Every fortnight (or thereabouts), I send out a newsletter with details about upcoming offers, new releases and extra special projects.

If you sign up for the mailing you'll receive exclusive behind-the-scenes extras, such as:

- free short stories
- deleted and alternate scenes from The Hero Rebellion
- previews of my upcoming books
- pancakes
- quizes
- and much, much more!

Sign up here
www.belindacrawford.com/newsletter

ACKNOWLEDGMENTS

This one was hard. A lot of authors talk about second book syndrome, where, after publishing their first book, they just can't seem to write the next.

Well, I had third book syndrome, and it sucked. Like really suckity-suck-suck-sucked. Thankfully, there were a lot of wonderful people around me to listen to me natter incessantly about plot problems and why this scene wasn't working and that character was giving me the irks.

They put up with random Facebook messages that said things like "Pizza!", "Cake!" and "Guild Wars o'clock!" when I was procrastinating, and offered advice when I was having my bad moments.

These people know who they are but I'm going to embarrass them in public anyway.

Thanks to: fellow authors Tracy M. Joyce and Jenny Ealey, for their advice and friendship; Brendan Carney, an editor with a most impressive vocabulary, for helping me whip Regan into shape; Mum and Chuck for their steadfast support.

And last but not least, thanks goes to Stivali, for finally becoming a legend.

ABOUT THE AUTHOR

Physics makes Belinda's brain hurt, while quadratics cause her eyes to cross and any mention of probability equations will have her running for the door. Nonetheless, she loves watching documentaries about the natural world, biology, space, history and technology.

She's also a sucker for a fast horse, a faster computer and superhero movies. When she's not doing the horse, computer or superhero thing, Belinda writes science fiction (emphasis on the fiction), where she loves to write about butt-kicking girls who blow stuff up.

You can keep in touch with Belinda, or just pick her brains about sci-fi via her website, Facebook or by sending her an email (she loves email).

www.belindacrawford.com
belinda@belindacrawford.com

Have news delivered straight to your inbox
via her mailing list. Sign up at:
www.belindacrawford.com/newsletter